## Pra...

ARY

"Fast-paced ... introduces pol... ethereal house...

—Julie Hyzy, national bestselling author of
*Grace Under Pressure* and the White House Chef Mysteries

"Police sketch artist Rory McCain, moonlighting as an amateur detective, assisted by the ghost of an 1870s federal marshall. Sharon Pape takes this improbable premise and makes it work—and how! Rory is memorable, her sidekick intriguing. Exceptionally well-written, a standout mystery. I'm looking forward to more."

—Susan Witting Albert, national bestselling author of
*The Darling Dahlias and the Naked Ladies*

"The fun in this lighthearted frolic is figuring out who the killer is before the heroine and her poltergeist partner do. Readers will admire and adore the intrepid heroine."

—*Genre Go Round Reviews*

"This is the first in a new series, and it looks like it's going to be a fun ride."

—*CA Reviews*

"Sharon Pape's debut novel, *Sketch Me If You Can* (the first in her Portrait of Crime Mysteries), is part mystery, part paranormal and all spine-tingling suspense. This promises to be a great beginning to a dynamic ongoing series that both mystery lovers and paranormal fans will enjoy."

—*Fresh Fiction*

*Berkley Prime Crime titles by Sharon Pape*

SKETCH ME IF YOU CAN
TO SKETCH A THIEF

# To Sketch a Thief

## Sharon Pape

BERKLEY PRIME CRIME, NEW YORK

**THE BERKLEY PUBLISHING GROUP**
**Published by the Penguin Group**
**Penguin Group (USA) Inc.**
**375 Hudson Street, New York, New York 10014, USA**
Penguin Group (Canada), 90 Eglinton Avenue East, Suite 700, Toronto, Ontario M4P 2Y3, Canada
(a division of Pearson Penguin Canada Inc.)
Penguin Books Ltd., 80 Strand, London WC2R 0RL, England
Penguin Group Ireland, 25 St. Stephen's Green, Dublin 2, Ireland (a division of Penguin Books Ltd.)
Penguin Group (Australia), 250 Camberwell Road, Camberwell, Victoria 3124, Australia
(a division of Pearson Australia Group Pty. Ltd.)
Penguin Books India Pvt. Ltd., 11 Community Centre, Panchsheel Park, New Delhi—110 017, India
Penguin Group (NZ), 67 Apollo Drive, Rosedale, Auckland 0632, New Zealand
(a division of Pearson New Zealand Ltd.)
Penguin Books (South Africa) (Pty.) Ltd., 24 Sturdee Avenue, Rosebank, Johannesburg 2196,
South Africa

Penguin Books Ltd., Registered Offices: 80 Strand, London WC2R 0RL, England

This is a work of fiction. Names, characters, places, and incidents either are the product of the author's imagination or are used fictitiously, and any resemblance to actual persons, living or dead, business establishments, events, or locales is entirely coincidental. The publisher does not have any control over and does not assume any responsibility for author or third-party websites or their content.

TO SKETCH A THIEF

A Berkley Prime Crime Book / published by arrangement with the author

PRINTING HISTORY
Berkley Prime Crime mass-market edition / June 2011

Copyright © 2011 by Sharon Pape.
Cover illustration by Dan Craig.
Interior text design by Laura K. Corless.

ISBN: 978-0-425-24192-9

BERKLEY® PRIME CRIME
Berkley Prime Crime Books are published by The Berkley Publishing Group,
a division of Penguin Group (USA) Inc.,
375 Hudson Street, New York, New York 10014.
BERKLEY® PRIME CRIME and the PRIME CRIME logo are trademarks of Penguin Group
(USA) Inc.

PRINTED IN THE UNITED STATES OF AMERICA

10  9  8  7  6  5  4  3  2  1

With love and gratitude to all the
four-legged members of our family,
past and present—Apollo, Buck, Kodi, Jesse,
Lyla and NikNak—who've enriched our lives
beyond mere human expectation.

# Acknowledgments

I'd like to thank:

Michelle Vega, for seeing the forest as well as the trees. I couldn't ask for a finer editorial eye.

Mike Farris, for helping me navigate the publishing world. I'm fortunate to have him in my corner.

Dr. Doreen Acuff, for the skilled and gentle care she's given the canine members of our family. If not for her, we would have missed those wonderful last years with our amazing Jesse.

Dr. Alexander Mauskop and Lynda J. Krasenbaum, for giving me back my "eyes."

My husband, Dennis, the first to read each chapter, for picking up on inconsistencies and flaws in logic, since logic and I have only a nodding acquaintance.

All the readers who were kind enough to write and let me know how much they enjoyed *Sketch Me If You Can*, the first book in this series.

And as always, my family and friends for their loving support.

I invite everyone to visit my website at www.sharon pape.com.

Any liberties I've taken with regard to veterinary care were solely for the purposes of the story.

**The Long Islander**

EST. 1839

September 7, 1878
Published in Huntington, New York

## ARIZONA MARSHAL
## MURDERED IN HUNTINGTON

Ezekiel Drummond, federal marshal for the Arizona Territory, was discovered dead of gunshot wounds to his back
yesterday in the house belonging to Winston Samuels. Mr.
Samuels has stated that upon returning from a trip into
town to purchase feed for his horses, he found his thirteen-
year-old daughter lying unconscious in the parlor with
a gash to her head and bruises on her arms. The body of
Marshal Drummond was lying nearby. Samuels further
stated that the room was in disarray, as if there had been a
scuffle, and that his hired hand, John Corbin, was missing
along with one of his horses. A trail of blood led from the
parlor through the kitchen and out to the barn, leading
authorities to conjecture that Corbin had been wounded.
The only weapon recovered at the scene was a Colt Single
Action .45, favored by lawmen in the western part of the
country. The Colt, which had not been fired, is believed to
have been the property of the marshal.

When the young Miss Samuels regained her senses, she
told a chilling tale of being overpowered by Corbin, who
was determined to have his way with her. She remembers
struggling to break free of his clutches, but claims to have
no recollection of the events beyond that point. After a
complete and careful examination of the young woman,

Dr. Edmond Stuart has pronounced her quite fit, given the horrific nature of her experience. He has additionally stated that a bout of amnesia is not uncommon in a victim of such a tender age and sensibilities.

Upon contacting the office of the territorial governor in Arizona, it was learned that Marshal Drummond had left his post without notice two months earlier. It was believed that he was on the trail of a fugitive by the name of John Trask, who had raped and murdered several young girls, but this could not be corroborated. The authorities in Arizona are convinced that the hired hand, John Corbin, is in fact an alias of the above-mentioned Trask. Should anyone have additional information regarding this case, they are asked to present themselves at the office of the Suffolk County sheriff.

As Marshal Drummond was not known to have any kin, he will be laid to rest at The Burying Ground Cemetery tomorrow morning at eight o'clock with all rites and respects due any brave member of the United States Marshals Service.

# Chapter 1

Ghosts don't make the best business partners. The thought scrolled through Rory's head like the news crawl on CNN. It was an old loop of news that found its way to the forefront of her mind at least once a day. Some days a lot more often. What had cued it up this time was the latest e-mail to pop into her in-box: "You fixin' to live out there?" The note was signed "Zeke," as if she might have received similar questions from any number of people.

"I'll be in soon," she wrote back, stopping herself before she could add, "You need a hobby." The problem was that *she* was his hobby—she and the investigative firm she'd started that bore both their names. Whenever her patience with him was wearing thin, she reminded herself that Mac believed without reservation that the success of *his* PI firm had been due in large measure to the experience and canniness of Ezekiel Drummond. And to be fair, she had to admit that the marshal had been helpful, maybe even pivotal, in breaking the double murder case that had launched their strange partnership.

The trouble with Zeke sharing her business life was that he also shared her domestic life in the old Victorian home Mac had left her. She could hardly blame him, since he seemed to be pretty much stuck in that haunting ground. Yet whenever she'd suggested he look for the light that might lead him out of his limbo, he'd become enraged and would say only that he wasn't going anywhere until he knew for sure who'd shot him in the back more than a hundred years earlier. Rory had given up trying to convince him that having such information would be worthless, given that whoever the player or players might have been, they were all long dead themselves. Since Zeke was not without common sense, she was sure that there had to be another, more profound reason why he was hanging around. A reason he hadn't as yet felt inclined to share with her.

She brushed her hair back. It was definitely past due for a cut. The short, low-maintenance style that had framed her face and accentuated her wide hazel eyes was now often concealing those eyes. Somehow since she'd opened her own business, there simply weren't enough hours in the day to take care of everything.

She stretched her arms up over her head to ease the knot that was tightening in the small of her back. She'd spent the better part of the afternoon hunched over the keyboard, writing progress reports for the two cases she was presently working on, paying her bills online and trying to balance her checking account, which seemed determined to stymie her efforts. Sometimes it felt as if the microprocessors in the computer secretly had it in for her. Zeke would have loved to hear her say that, she thought wryly. Although he'd developed a measure of interest in the Internet after she'd shown him how to navigate it, he still complained regularly about how much time she spent at work on it. Rory chalked his attitude up to a case of sour grapes. According to the marshal, her only source on the subject, it took a lot of energy for a ghost to manifest in the third dimension. Even if he were to remain invisible and just use his energy to work the keyboard, there was a limit to how much time he could spend at it before needing to rest and recuperate. Ever since she'd nearly become the third victim of the killer she was investigating, the marshal hadn't allowed himself to become too depleted in case she needed his help again. There was no convincing him that she'd had the situation under control before he'd popped in to save the day. They'd argued the subject up one side and down the other, until she'd decided to let him have the hero status he seemed to need so desperately. Apparently you could take the lawman away from the tin star, but you couldn't take the tin star away from the lawman.

Rory glanced out the window over her desk. The mid-September sun hung low in the sky, playing limbo with a band of stratus clouds. She might still have enough daylight to tackle the weeds in the flower beds that ran like a scalloped hem around the front of the house. She hadn't intended to leave the impatiens, pansies and petunias to fend for themselves, but the summer had been nonstop busy, what with leaving her job as a sketch artist for the Suffolk County Police Department and setting up her own firm.

Fortunately, the concerns she'd harbored about attracting business had proven baseless. Once the local newspaper ran the story of how she'd solved two murders the police had failed to solve, one of them sadly that of her beloved uncle Mac, she'd been inundated with requests for interviews from the major networks as well as from most of the cable news channels. After a good deal of consideration, she'd agreed to appear on just one of them. She politely but firmly turned down the others, not eager for her life to become a three-ring circus. As long as she was making headlines, it was hard to put Vincent Conti behind her. She still couldn't

believe she'd been naïve enough to fall for the drug dealer
who'd had her uncle murdered. But in spite of her efforts to
downplay the story, it seemed to have more legs than a cen-
tipede. Print journalists across the country rehashed tasty
sound bites plucked from her interview and managed to
keep it alive for the better part of a week, until Rory found
herself wishing for some kind of world crisis that would
knock her off the stage. Just when the hoopla finally seemed
to be winding down, a zealous young reporter, posing as
Vincent Conti's terminally ill brother, emoted his way into
a jailhouse visit. Although the subterfuge was immediately
evident to the suspect, who didn't have a brother, let alone
a brother on the brink of death, he decided to use the visit
to his own advantage. And when the reporter begged for a
headline, Conti gave him a whopper.

The story appeared in dozens of newspapers, the headlines all variations on one theme: "Murder Suspect Cap-
tured by Wyatt Earp." Quick as a wink the case was again
story one. Conti's attorney ran with the ball his client had
thrown him and sprinted for the goalposts of an insanity
defense.

The district attorney lambasted the sheriff's department
for having allowed the reporter access; the sheriff's department barred the reporter from the courthouse, the trial and
anything else they could think of for the rest of his professional life. By the end of the day, everyone on Long Island
had an opinion on the subject. When Rory was asked to
comment, she demurred, saying that she didn't want to
taint the case. Although she was horrified by the prospect
of Conti being sentenced to a mental institution from which
he might one day be deemed healthy enough to return to
society, she had no wish to join him there by corroborating
his ravings about his ghostly encounter. On the other hand,
if she'd denied his ghost story, she might still be promot-
ing the case for his insanity. It was a lose-lose situation, so
she kept her mouth shut. In New York, multiple homicides

entitled a murderer to an untimely death of his own at the state's expense. Although the appeal process could take years, Rory looked forward to the day when Conti would draw his last breath.

She logged off the computer and turned off the light in the small office she'd had built in the detached garage behind the house. The garage had started life in 1870 as a carriage house and stable for the original owner and was large enough to accommodate three cars, several ladders and assorted gardening equipment. Even after it had been partitioned for the office, there was ample room for one car. Since Rory had sold her Honda in favor of the red Volvo convertible she'd inherited from her uncle, that was all the space she needed. Even so, she only parked the car inside when snow was in the forecast, preferring to leave it on the driveway where it was closer to the front door.

She went from the office into the garage through the connecting door and found her gardening gloves, a sturdy weeder and a small plastic bucket she'd bought specifically for that chore, so that she wouldn't have to drag a large garbage can around with her. Then she let herself out through the office door and locked it behind her.

The temperature had dropped off while she'd been working, and her shoulders immediately hunched against the unexpected chill. The lengthening shadows of autumn had swallowed the day's warmth whole, like an old-timer knocking back a shot of whiskey. Even after twenty-eight years on Long Island, the turning of the seasons always managed to surprise her. She'd have to detour through the house to grab a jacket for her gardening.

As Rory hurried across the backyard, she gave herself a mental thumbs-up for having had the office built. It was a great commute and far and away the smartest money she'd ever spent. Of course Zeke had tried to talk her out of it.

"It's been fine with you workin' right here in the house," he'd said. "Why do you want to go changin' things now?"

Rory had been prepared for his reaction. Since she couldn't very well admit that she needed time away from him, she focused on other, more politic reasons for wanting a separate office. She talked about how the living room looked like a furniture store with her desk, filing cabinet and fax and copy machines all crammed along one wall. And how it wasn't very professional to have clients traipsing through her house, especially if she'd forgotten to take the laundry basket upstairs or had left her slippers beside the couch the night before. She thought she'd presented a reasonable case, grateful that mind reading wasn't one of Zeke's otherworldly talents.

"You know I can't be out there when you're talkin' to clients," he'd grumbled.

*Precisely,* Rory thought, trying not to look as pleased as she felt.

"What if you need protectin'?"

"Well, I'm not exactly without abilities, you know. I'm damned good with a gun. I bet I could even outshoot you. Plus I've had all sorts of martial arts training."

"Marshal arts . . . what's paintin' got to do with it?"

Rory choked back the bubble of laughter rising in her throat. She knew better than to laugh at him. For a lawman from the old Wild West, Zeke had proven to be surprisingly thin-skinned, especially when he thought she was being condescending.

When she finally opened her mouth to reply a little hiccup of laughter escaped, so she faked a coughing spasm to cover it. "Martial arts are just forms of self-defense," she said with a shrug, trying to gloss over his mistake.

"Since I don't have the hang of leavin' this place whenever I want to," Zeke said, so focused on his own agenda that he didn't even seem to have heard her, "there's a right good chance I couldn't help you out if you was to need me."

The only time he'd managed to leave the house had been when Rory's life was threatened. Somehow fearing for her safety had enabled him to break through the forces that kept him imprisoned where he'd died. He and Rory had tried to re-create the situation, without success. Either his concern for her had to be real, or that day had been a one-time-only anomaly. They'd both been disappointed when the experiment failed, but Rory had realized almost immediately that it was a blessing in disguise. While it would have been handy to have an invisible partner, a proverbial fly on the wall, privy to all sorts of information she could not otherwise obtain, there would also have been the downside of having a ghost tagging along wherever she went.

In any case, she was more than willing to trade the possibility of Zeke's aid for the reality of some time alone. In spite of what he thought, she was perfectly capable of taking care of herself.

She opened the back door and walked into the kitchen, nearly plowing right through the marshal, who had chosen that moment to materialize a few feet from the doorway. She slammed to a stop, the bucket, weeder and gardening gloves flying out of her hands. She teetered there on her toes for several moments, doing an impression of an awkward ballerina, before regaining her balance enough to back away. She'd come close to touching him a dozen times before. Sooner or later her luck would run out. She didn't let herself dwell on what the encounter might be like, although she supposed it could range anywhere from a yawner to a *Ghostbuster*-like sliming. She'd find out when it happened and she wasn't in any hurry to rush that moment.

Zeke, on the other hand, having no doubt experienced the mixing of mortal flesh and spiritual ether at some point during his long tenure there, had stood his ground, obviously enjoying her discomfort. His lips were canted up in a sly smile, his mustache twitching with suppressed laughter. Above the sharp planes of his cheeks, his dark eyes twinkled with mischief.

More than once she'd thought of asking him what it felt

like, but each time she'd decided against it, since it was likely to be a very different experience depending upon which side of the veil one was on.

"What happened to making the lights flicker before you appear?"she demanded instead, hoping to wipe the grin off his face.

"There wasn't exactly time for that. First you weren't here, then suddenly you were. I'm a ghost, not one of those sidekicks, you know."

"Psychics," Rory muttered, sidestepping around him to retrieve her gardening things. She usually found his trouble with modern vocabulary endearing, but she wasn't feeling very charitable after being the target of his amusement. "Yeah, too bad about that. A psychic would be more useful and less inclined to startle me."

Zeke's smile only widened. "I'm pretty sure I would still be inclined to startle you. It just wouldn't be as easy."

Rory slipped her hands into the thick gloves as she walked out of the kitchen. "I'd love to stay and trade barbs with you, but I have a date with some weeds."

"You surely do know how to hurt a fella," he said, following her down the hall to the front door. With practice over the summer his hitching gait had improved so that he no longer resembled an actor in a flickering silent film. Although his stride wasn't completely fluid yet, it was good enough that the casual observer might think he suffered from a touch of arthritis or the lingering effects of a sports injury.

Before meeting Zeke, Rory would never have guessed that a ghost might have problems approximating the walk of a mortal. For that matter, before she met Zeke she would never have guessed that ghosts actually existed. She still hadn't confided in anyone that she lived with a departed soul who hadn't completely departed, let alone that she had a business relationship with him. Her mother was a worrier who didn't need the additional concern that her daughter had bought a one-way ticket to a room with padded walls and bars on the windows.

Her father, who generally left the worrying to his wife, would have reached for the remote in much the same way that a toddler might reach for the comfort of a pacifier. Of all Rory's relatives, Aunt Helene was the only one who might be counted upon to take the mention of a ghost seriously. Her eyes might bulge out of her eyelids, and she might stumble over all the questions that sprang into her mind, but she would treat Rory's claim with respect and an eager desire to meet her ghost.

There were times when Rory so longed to have someone, anyone, in whom she could confide about Zeke that she nearly called Helene. What invariably kept her from reaching for the phone was the fact that Helene was notorious for not being able to keep a secret.

The only other person Rory had considered telling was Leah Russell, her mentor and colleague when she'd worked for the police department and still her dearest friend. They confided in each other about every aspect of their lives. Zeke was Rory's one holdout on her and she actually felt guilty about it, as if she were hiding some dirty little secret. Yet she couldn't quite bring herself to say the words out loud. Leah would surely want to believe her, try to believe her, but Rory was afraid that their relationship might never be the same.

Of course the easy solution would have been to invite Leah and her family over for a meet and greet. It would be hard . . . no, it would be downright impossible to deny the existence of Zeke if the rugged, six-foot-one lawman were to materialize in front of them. But the marshal had wanted no part of it.

"I'm not some damned ol' rodeo nag you can trot out to entertain folks," he'd said harshly.

"I don't see what the problem is. You certainly didn't waste any time trotting yourself out to meet *me*."

"That's different. You're sharin' this place with me, same as Mac." His face had been set hard, his jaw clamped down in a way that let her know it would be futile to pursue the issue any further.

"You gonna be long?" Zeke asked once they reached the front door.

"I doubt it. It's hard to garden in the dark."

"That may be true, darlin', but when you make up that mind of yours, there's precious little that can change it."

Look who's talking, Rory thought, struggling not to say it aloud. It was sometimes just easier to let him have the last word. She paused at the coat closet to pluck her denim jacket from its hanger, then she unlocked the front door and went outside.

After depositing the gardening tools beside the farthest flower bed, she pulled on her jacket and got down to work. She'd been tugging away at the weeds for no more than fifteen minutes when something unpleasantly cold and wet slid across the back of her neck. She whirled around and came face-to-face with a huge dog, gray and white and shaggy as a yak. She could barely make out its eyes through the cascade of hair on its face. The dog seemed delighted to see her. His plumed tail wagging madly, he wriggled closer to lick her face, miscalculated the distance and sent her sprawling into the flowers.

She sat up, laughing and brushing off the loose soil that was clinging to her. The dog seized that moment to slather her face with his wide, raspy tongue. When she reached out to hold him off, her hand hit the metal tag hanging from the collar in the thicket of fur around his neck. Leaning closer to read what it said, she bought herself another bath in doggie saliva.

According to the tag, his name was Hobo and he lived at 9 Cooper Street, a mile or so away. His name fit him well. He looked like a dog without a nationality or a pedigree. He had the coat and bulk of a bearded collie, but he was also clearly part Samoyed or husky or one of a dozen other breeds, because his ears stood up straight, just the tips folded over as if caught in genetic indecision. Rory doubted there'd been a pureblood of any kind in his family tree for many generations.

"Hobo," she said, "what are you doing all the way over here?" He cocked his large head to one side and then to the other as if that would help him to better understand what she was saying. The tips of his ears flapped up and down with each movement, adding to his quizzical expression.

"Are you lost, boy?"

Rory braved another look at Hobo's tag, hoping there was a phone number. She found it on the reverse side, and since Hobo had paused for a snack of pansies, she managed to avoid any additional moisturizing.

She reached into the pocket of her pants, pulled out her cell phone and dialed the number. The phone rang five times before it went to voice mail. It was possible that Hobo's owner was even now out looking for him. She left a message along with her number and weighed her options. If she lived alone, specifically without a ghost who had developed an aversion to dogs, she would have invited Hobo inside while she waited to hear back from his people. As it was, she decided to drive him back to his home and wait there for someone to return. The flowers would have to wait another day to be rescued. Of course, a good third of the pansies were no longer an issue, since they were already making their way down Hobo's digestive tract. It was a good thing she'd planted edible flowers.

She stood up, grabbed the dog's collar and headed toward her car in the driveway. Apparently Hobo enjoyed car rides. As soon as he saw where they were going, he took the lead and Rory had to run to keep up with him. She opened the door and the dog bounded in, taking up most of the backseat.

"Be a good boy. I'll be back in a second," she promised,

shutting the door. She went into the house, slowing down just enough to maneuver around Zeke.

"What's goin' on with that dog out there?" he asked with a sour look on his face.

"He must have gotten out of his yard," she said, grabbing her keys from the bench near the stairs. "He has a tag with his address, so I'm just going to take him back."

"You oughta just let him be," Zeke grumbled. "He'll find his way home sooner or later."

"He could run into the street and be hit by a car or something," Rory said, surprised by his reaction. "What do you have against dogs anyway?"

"Dogs and I don't get along well since I cashed in my flesh and bones."

"It's not like I'm asking *you* to drive him home," she said with some attitude of her own. She pulled the door closed behind her and ran back to the car.

Hobo had smeared the side window with drool in the two minutes she'd been gone. She turned on the engine and opened the window enough for him to stick his muzzle out, but not enough for him to think about jumping ship. And off they went.

She found Cooper Street without a problem. The houses, all brick and clapboard Cape Cods, were set closer to one another and to the street than in the area where she lived. But they were well maintained and inviting, lawns mowed, bushes trimmed, woodwork freshly painted. She turned into the driveway at number 9 and parked behind a Honda Civic. "I think we're in luck," she said to Hobo. "Looks like someone's home now."

She opened the car door and was immediately trampled by Hobo, who'd jumped into the front seat in his zeal to get out first. He made a beeline for the front door. Rory ran after him, hoping he wouldn't be distracted by a squirrel and take off on another jaunt. As she rang the bell, she noticed that the door had been left ajar. Hobo didn't waste a moment. He trotted right inside.

Rory waited on the cement stoop for the owner to respond to the bell. A minute passed. She called out, "Hello, anyone home?" No answer. She stepped inside and found herself in a small, neat living room. She called out again, but the only sound was the clicking of Hobo's claws on a floor somewhere in the rear of the house. Having decided she'd done all that social protocol demanded, Rory followed the noise through the living room and dining room to the kitchen. There she found Hobo whimpering and licking the ashen cheek of the middle-aged woman who lay sprawled on the floor in a dark pool of blood.

# Chapter 2

Rory hunkered down beside the woman, being careful not to disturb the puddled blood that formed a grim outline around her. She put her finger on the carotid artery. No pulse. Not that Rory had expected to find one. The kitchen knife that had killed her was still embedded deep in the left side of her chest. She'd never stood a chance.

Rory rose and made her way around the body to where Hobo was now lying. He'd stopped licking the woman's face as if he'd accepted that she was beyond awakening. His head lolled on the floor between his paws and he was whimpering. His sense of loss was so keen that Rory felt her eyes filling in empathy. It had been only a few months since her uncle Mac had died. Losing him was a unique pain, quite unlike any she'd known before in her twenty-eight years. Even when the ache in her heart seemed to have played itself out, it never actually left. It crouched in silence beneath the placid surface of her emotions. Sometimes it was reawakened by a simple memory, like

Mac laughing as she raced to finish her ice cream cone before the sun melted it, or holding Mac's hand and ice skating to Christmas music until their noses were as red as Rudolph's. And sometimes all it took to reanimate the pain was the mirrored sorrow of another's loss.

Rory shook her head and blinked away the tears. There were procedures to be followed, people to be notified, a crime scene to be protected. Grateful for the demands of life, she reached for Hobo's collar. With a gentle voice and soft words to console him, she tried to coax him away from the woman who'd been the center of his universe. Hobo wasn't moving. He lifted his big head and howled at the heavens. Rory tugged harder. She had to get him out of the kitchen. He'd already stepped in the blood and possibly even licked away a hair that belonged to the assailant or a microscopic bit of fabric from his clothing, evidence that would be crucial in bringing the killer to justice.

She tried a stronger voice, a more demanding tone. Hobo dragged himself to his feet, his shoulders slumped with despair, and allowed himself to be led to the kitchen door. Rory stepped outside alone first to do a quick recon of the backyard. It was all fenced in and the gate at the side of the property was latched. The killer had apparently come and gone through the front door. Either it was someone the victim had known or a stranger who had strong-armed his way in when she'd answered the doorbell. Hobo had no doubt escaped that way as well.

He was standing at the kitchen door where she'd left him, watching her dully. She had to go back inside and put both hands on his rump to shoo him out. Even then he looked over his withers at her as if to ask her why he was being banished.

Since Rory didn't have an answer that he was likely to understand, she forced herself to move away from the door and the distraction of his misery. She pulled the cell phone out of her pocket and dialed the local precinct to report the murder. She was immediately put through to a Detective Cirello. Having put in five years with the Suffolk Police Department, she knew a lot of detectives in the county, but she'd never met Cirello. She identified herself as a private investigator and retired detective and gave him a brief assessment of what she'd discovered, along with the victim's address. When he asked for the deceased's name, she couldn't supply it. It hadn't been on Hobo's tag and she hadn't wanted to waste additional time looking around the house for mail or other papers that might have provided that information. Rory heard the cold edge of suspicion in the detective's tone when he ordered her to stay put and wait for the police. She'd had no intention of leaving, but it occurred to her that she would be in a better position if she'd bothered to bring her purse along with her ID. Too bad she couldn't just give Zeke a call and ask him to drop it off.

After she'd finished with Cirello, she called headquarters in Yaphank, which housed the homicide division for the county. Cirello would have to contact them anyway, but Rory wanted to speak to Leah directly.

"Can't stay out of trouble, can you, McCain?" Leah said, once Rory had brought her up to speed.

"Not guilty. This time trouble came looking for me in a fur suit."

"I'm not even going to ask."

"Doesn't originality count for anything these days?"

"Lord knows it should. Hang out till I get there?"

"It's not like I have a choice. Besides, I'd never miss an opportunity to be questioned by the best."

"You know you don't get points for sucking up."

"Hey, it was worth a shot."

Rory pocketed her phone, feeling a little lighter of heart. Leah had that effect on her. Like the vent on a pressure cooker. She looked at her watch. She had a few minutes before the police showed up. She would have liked to look around the rest of the house to see what she could turn up, but that was out of the question. There was always the possibility that she might leave a stray hair or another bit of DNA behind and further confuse the case for the crime scene investigators. But since she'd had to walk through the living room and dining room to reach the kitchen, a fact that the police would have to take into account anyway, she decided there was nothing wrong with browsing through those rooms as long as she didn't touch anything.

She retraced her steps to the front of the house, passing first through the dining room, where a large oak table and six bulky chairs dominated the space, leaving no room for anything else. No need for further scrutiny there.

The living room had far more potential. Rory made a careful circuit around it, really looking at everything for the first time. The furniture was old, but not yet shabby. The couch and two armchairs were done in cocoa-colored imitation suede, liberally decorated with Hobo's fur. They were grouped around a rectangular oak cocktail table that was dust free, but marred by numerous fine scratches and a few deeper gouges. Half a dozen magazines were stacked on one end of the table, the top one a copy of *Newsweek*. Rory stepped closer to read the mailing label. The subscriber was Brenda Hartley, and since the address on the label matched the address of the house, Brenda was also likely to be the home owner. But there was still no way to be sure that she was the woman whose life had drained away on the kitchen floor. The victim could be another member of the family, or even a friend who'd stopped in to take care of Hobo while Brenda was at work or out of town.

There was a small brick fireplace, its mantel crowded with photos in an assortment of sizes and frames. All but two of them featured Hobo and a tiny white mop of a dog with dark eyes and a topknot of fur tied up in a pink bow. Of the two remaining photos, one was a faded black-and-white of a bridal couple, the other a group shot of four women wearing summer colors and broad smiles that had probably erupted into laughter a moment after the photo was snapped. Brenda was the second one from the left. It was hard to connect this vital Brenda with the woman who was lying dead just two rooms away.

Rory was on her way back to the kitchen when a flash of movement in her peripheral vision brought her to an abrupt stop. She spun in that direction, her heart shifting into overdrive. Nothing was there. Maybe it had been a moth or a fly that had caught her attention. She looked around the room. For a moment nothing moved. Then brief snatches of color and texture flashed in front of her and one thing was certain—it wasn't an insect.

Bits of Zeke kept appearing then vanishing as if he were trapped in a transporter malfunction on the old *Star Trek* series. She couldn't imagine how he was doing it, but one thing was certain—his timing was awful.

"You have to stop this right now," Rory said urgently to the empty room. There was no way to time her remarks to coincide with his brief appearances. She just hoped he could hear her and, more important, that he would listen.

"The police will be here any minute. We'll talk when I get home." She held her breath and waited. To her relief, the room remained empty. If Zeke started popping in and out like a jack-in-the-box wherever she went, life was going to get a lot more complicated, but she didn't have the time to dwell on the problem just then. She glanced at her watch. She might still have a few minutes before the police arrived.

She made it back into the kitchen without further interruption. Since the room was small and already crowded with a breakfast table and four molded plastic chairs, as well as Brenda, Rory took up a position by the back door. From there she could see the entire room as well as the yard. She peered outside to check on Hobo. He was at the fence line, watering an arborvitae whose lower branches were already brown from his past attentions.

She turned back to inspect the room. The counters were clean and uncluttered, with only an electric coffeemaker and a dish rack that contained a cup, several utensils and a pair of hot pink rubber gloves. But the kitchen table held some items of interest. There was a checkbook, a pen and a haphazard pile of papers that looked like bills. Brenda had probably been sitting at the table about to tackle those bills when she was interrupted by her assailant. One moment paying the mortgage was the most important issue of her day, the next it didn't matter at all. It was dizzying how swiftly the currents of life could change.

Rory debated the ethics of looking through the papers for the better part of a minute before she reached for one of the paper napkins that sat in a dog-shaped holder on the table. Draping the napkin over her thumb and index finger as a buffer, she managed to sift through the papers without actually touching them. There were bills from the electric company, the phone company and a place called Boomer's Groomers, along with one from a Dr. Stanley Holbrook, who was most likely a veterinarian, since a cartoon dog and cat decorated his letterhead. It seemed Brenda had taken good care of her animals.

Rory stuffed the napkin into the pocket of her jeans. She'd reached the limits of her investigation. She'd ask Leah to keep her posted as the case went forward. She felt strangely invested in it, maybe because she'd been the one to find Brenda or maybe because of poor, bereft Hobo. She was lost in these thoughts when a horrified scream jolted her nervous system with the power of a lightning strike.

# Chapter 3

A heavyset woman in her forties, with pepper-and-salt hair as short as a man's and a deep shelf of a bosom, stood frozen in the kitchen entryway. She'd run out of voice, but her mouth was still wide open. She clamped her plump hands over it as if she were afraid of what else might jump out.

Rory saw the color drain out of her cheeks as she started to rock back on the heels of her flip-flops. For a woman of her girth, she had surprisingly slender legs and delicate ankles. Rory noted this as she was rushing toward her. She grabbed hold of the woman's substantial forearm before she could rock backward again and overbalance. It was like playing tug-of-war with the law of gravity, and for a few hectic moments it seemed that gravity might win.

Fortunately the pressure of Rory's hand seemed to focus the woman, bringing her around like someone being awakened from a trance. Once she was in control of her faculties, she was able to help keep herself upright. Rory waited a few moments to make sure that her charge was no longer in danger of keeling over, before she maneuvered her out of the doorway and down the hall toward the front door. The woman rocked from side to side as she walked, as if she were trying to navigate the deck of a ship in heavy seas.

"What happened to Brenda?" she asked breathlessly. "Where are you taking me?"

"This is a crime scene, ma'am," Rory said, "so we're going to have to leave the premises and wait outside for the police."

The woman nodded, her double chin waggling, the leather tote on her arm swinging back and forth with each step like the pendulum on a grandfather clock.

When they were outside, Rory helped steady her as she sat down on the top step.

"Can I get you some water?" she asked, remembering the unopened bottle in her car.

The question didn't seem to register with the woman, who was busy riding her own train of thought.

Rory repeated the question.

"No—yes—I mean . . . oh dear," she said, struggling to regroup from the grisly scene in the kitchen. "No, no water. I don't need water."

Rory had yet to meet anyone in this situation who actually needed water. Some of them would say yes to the offer, but after an initial sip would just hold on to the glass or bottle until someone else relieved them of it.

"What happened to Brenda?" the woman asked, her cheeks beginning to pink up. "Is she . . . dead?" She whispered the word "dead" as if saying it aloud would give it too much power, make it more irrevocable than it already was.

"Yes, I'm afraid she was gone when I got here," Rory said. "I'm so sorry."

"Right." The woman bobbed her head, then looked up at Rory as if she were seeing her for the first time. "Who are you?"

"Rory McCain." She held out her hand and the woman grasped it more as a lifeline than a handshake. Rory could feel her trembling, vibrating as if her whole body were a tuning fork. "How did you know Brenda, Mrs. . . . ?"

"Sugarman . . . Marti Sugarman. Brenda's one of my closest friends . . . oh dear." Her hand went to her mouth again. "I guess I should have said *was*. For more than ten years. In fact she called me just this morning and asked me to come over. Were you a friend of hers too?"

"No, I never actually met her," Rory said, gently withdrawing her hand since it was becoming awkward to stand there, leaning over and holding hands with Marti. "I found Hobo wandering around near my house. When I saw the address on his ID tag I figured I'd bring him back."

"That was very nice of you," Marti said, social conditioning kicking in on autopilot. "Hobo can be a handful, but . . . wait a minute, where's Tootsie?"

"Who's Tootsie?"

"Brenda's Maltese." Marti looked around the small front yard as if perhaps Tootsie might have been there all along and just escaped her notice.

"I haven't seen another dog since I've been here," Rory said, flashing back to the photos on the mantel. So the little white dog with Hobo was a Maltese who presumably answered to the name of Tootsie.

Marti's eyes were filled with a new horror. "Do you think this was a dog abduction gone wrong?"

"I think Tootsie probably just ran off like Hobo when the intruder left the door open," Rory said. Why look for zebras when there were perfectly good horses around?

Marti didn't seem convinced; worry worked at the lines between her eyebrows. "I have a bad feeling about all this," she murmured as the first police car turned onto the street, followed closely by an unmarked unit, both with sirens wailing.

Rory wondered how it would have been possible to have a *good* feeling about her friend's violent death, let alone her missing dog, but she chalked the remark up to shock. Surely Marti hadn't meant it the way it sounded.

The police cruiser pulled up to the curb and two uniformed cops jumped out, one of them holding a reel of yellow crime scene tape. The unmarked car swung into the driveway, coming to an abrupt stop inches from Rory's Volvo, the rear half sticking out into the street. Two detectives emerged and conferred briefly with the patrolmen, who then began to set up a perimeter to protect the crime scene and keep the curious away.

Rory met the detectives halfway down the walk. The older one was in the lead. Rory pegged him for maybe fifty, a hard fifty. He was tall and reedy, with hollowed cheeks that looked like he'd sucked a few too many lemons dry.

"McCain?" he said, coming to a stop in front of her.

"Rory McCain." She nodded. "Detective Cirello?"

"Can you show me some ID?" he asked, ignoring her question.

Given the circumstances, Rory decided to let the snub go. After all, without ID she could claim to be anyone. For all he knew, she could be the killer. It wouldn't be the first time that kind of thing had happened. And if the proverbial shoe were on the other foot, she might be just as wary.

"I'm afraid I left it home," she said, adding the short version of why she was at the crime scene.

"Harvey, she's the one headquarters vouched for," the younger detective said. He had a thatch of red hair and the fullness of youth about his face. "She was with Homicide till a few months ago."

"Yeah, now I remember hearing about you on the news." Harvey scowled at her. "Gave the department a bit of a black eye closing those cases by your lonesome."

"I just got lucky." Rory shrugged, wondering what expression they'd wear if she told them she hadn't done it alone, that she'd had help from a certain U.S. marshal who'd been dead for a century or so. "Besides, I was on the job at the time. My win was a win for all of us."

Harvey refused to be jollied. He turned his attention to Marti, who actually seemed to shrink under his scrutiny. "Who are *you*?"

Marti heaved herself up and tottered down the steps to stand beside Rory. "I'm Martha Sugarman," she said respectfully. "I was a friend of Brenda's."

"Did Brenda have a last name?"

"Well, yes; yes, of course she did," Marti said, flustered by his sarcasm.

"And what would that be?"

"Hartley. Brenda Hartley."

"She was the single owner of the residence," the young detective said. "I checked it out."

"Don't know what I'd do without Danny Boy the computer geek," Harvey said dryly.

To Rory there was nothing good-natured in the ribbing. She'd had enough. She was about to tell Harvey what she thought of his social skills, but Danny caught her eye and, with the barest of head movements, made it clear that he didn't want her to say anything.

"Where's the deceased?" Harvey went on, oblivious to the undercurrent swirling around him.

"In the kitchen," Rory said tightly, "exactly as I found her." She'd be damned if she was going to be pleasant to this boor. She took less than a minute to tell him where she and Marti had been in the house and that she'd secured Hobo in the backyard.

Harvey wagged his head as if he were tired of suffering the fools of the world and made his way up to the front door. "Hang around," he threw over his shoulder as he walked inside. "Homicide's gonna be here soon."

"Thanks for your help, ladies," Danny murmured before following his partner into the house. He said it with the easy grace of one who's had a lot of practice smoothing ruffled feathers.

"I have to wait here for some other detectives?" A peevish tone had crept into Marti's voice, and she was starting to sound more put out than saddened by her friend's death.

Rory nodded. "The detectives from Homicide will need to speak to us. If you have another appointment, you should cancel it A murder investigation takes precedence over pretty much everything else, short of a stroke or a heart attack."

Marti made a noise somewhere between a grunt and a sigh and went back to her seat on the front stoop. Too restless to sit down, Rory walked around the side of the house to check on Hobo. He met her at the gate, tail wagging, butt wiggling with pleasure at seeing her. She was surprised by the enthusiasm of his greeting, until she realized that on this sad day she was the most familiar face around. Well, Marti was there of course, but either his nose hadn't told him she was nearby or she wasn't on his list of favorite humans.

She hung out with him there, the chain-link fence between them making her feel like she was visiting a prisoner at a work camp. Ten minutes later she saw Leah's unmarked car arrive, her partner Jeff riding shotgun. In spite of how much Rory enjoyed being self-employed, she sorely missed her closest friend. When she'd left the police department, they'd vowed to see each other regularly. But life had a habit of getting in the way, especially for Leah, who had a husband and three kids. So they did their best to enjoy whatever time they spent together, even if it was during the course of work.

Leah walked across the lawn to Rory. She was wearing her business face, her wild curls pulled back in a sturdy clip. Off duty, Leah left her hair unfettered so that it framed her face and softened her angular features. She'd recently complained to Rory that the few gray hairs she'd had at thirty were well on their way to claiming dominion over the brown hair of her youth. Any day now she'd be joining the ranks of the dye dependent.

The two women hugged and Rory provided her with what little information she had. By the time they'd walked back to the stoop, Jeff was done questioning Marti. He handed her his card in case she thought of anything else that might be helpful.

"Why don't you go on inside?" Leah said to him. "I'll be right there."

"So that's it?" Marti asked, glancing longingly at her green Highlander parked across the street.

"Wait a minute," Rory said. "What about Hobo? Do you think you could take him home for the night?"

"Hobo?" she repeated, as if it were the strangest request she'd ever heard. "I don't think that's a good idea. No, no, that's not a good idea at all."

"But he knows you and it doesn't have to be a permanent thing. Just to get him over this rough spot. I'd hate to have to turn him over to Animal Control after what he's been through today."

"He doesn't get along with my dog," Marti said, her mouth setting in a stubborn line.

"But surely you could manage for one night, considering the circumstances and all. I'm sure it's what Brenda would have wanted," Rory added, playing what she thought was her trump card.

Marti wasn't budging. "I'm afraid it's out of the question," she said, her words snapping like a flag in a high wind. "Am I allowed to go now?"

Leah looked at Rory, who just shrugged. They couldn't very well detain her until she broke down and agreed to take Hobo, even if the idea was somewhat appealing.

"Yeah, you can go," Leah told her.

"Wouldn't your dog like a playmate?" Rory asked her as they watched Marti toddle off in her flip-flops.

"Not a chance, my friend. You had a better shot with Marti."

The CSI van arrived as Marti was pulling out. Other cars crawled by, the drivers trying to figure out what was going on in their neighborhood. A crowd of people had gathered on the lawn across the street, courtesy of the local gossip mill. Dinner and homework were forgotten. Kids threw Frisbees they could barely see in the waning light or ran after the last lightning bugs of the season. TV crews and reporters were suddenly swarming everywhere, like cicadas that had sprung straight from the ground. The police called in reinforcements. Brenda's death had become an event.

Cirello and his partner emerged from the house and headed back to their car.

"I'd better get in there," Leah said. "Why don't you take the dog, Rory? He'd be good company for you."

Good idea, Rory wanted to say, except I live with a ghost who's got dog issues.

Cirello paused beside her. "Did you call the pound to come for the mutt?" He said it in much the same way he might have said, "Did you take out the trash?"

"Don't worry," Rory said tightly, "I'm on it."

Danny heard the disgust in her voice and lagged back long enough to commiserate. "I sure wish I could take him. He looks like a great dog. But my wife's allergic."

Everyone seemed to have an excuse, but since Rory couldn't bring herself to abandon poor Hobo at the pound on the night that he was orphaned, she found herself driving home with him once again in the backseat of her car, along with a leash and a twenty-pound bag of kibble.

# Chapter 4

Rory pulled into her driveway, turned off the engine and sat there trying to figure out the best way to introduce Zeke to their new boarder. Fifteen minutes passed without a single epiphany. Hobo whimpered and snuffled the back of her neck, confused as to why they were still sitting in a car that wasn't moving. Rory reached up and scratched his head to comfort him, wishing someone would do the same for her. She was tired and in no mood to do battle with an irascible ghost.

To make matters worse, the house looked far from inviting. She hadn't left any lights on, since she'd expected to be back in twenty minutes. So much for expectations. The closest street lamp cast only a dim puddle of light that barely reached her property line. In front of her, the house loomed dark and somehow larger than it should have been, as if it had lost its familiar contours and was merging with the night.

"Stop it! Just stop it!" she scolded herself out loud, causing Hobo to immediately stop nuzzling her neck.

"Oh, not you, you silly boy," she said, her voice dropping into the soft, cooing tone she generally reserved for babies. "Not you."

What was happening to her? She'd never been one of the delicate, faint-of-heart types. This was her house and it was dark simply because it was nighttime. There was nothing sinister or otherworldly about it. Well, except for Zeke of course. And she had no intentions of letting him wield this much power over her. If she wanted to have a dog, she was damn well going to have a dog!

She stepped out of the car as if she were setting foot on Omaha Beach. There would be no withdrawing in disgrace. She opened the rear door and Hobo jumped out. She grabbed hold of his leash as he started up the walkway ahead of her. No ambivalence there.

When they reached the front door, Hobo stopped suddenly and Rory rammed full tilt into him. As she was trying to keep herself from flying headfirst into the door, she wondered what had caused the dog's sudden loss of initiative. Had he smelled, heard or intuited in his canine bones that all was not as it should be in this house? That someone who had shuffled off his mortal coil still somehow resided here? At that moment, while she was still partially draped over Hobo's back, the house lit up like an elaborate birthday cake. Every light inside went on simultaneously, as if someone had hit a master switch. Or a certain ghost was trying to make a point. Hobo yelped and danced backward several feet, dislodging Rory in the process. She picked herself up and snagged a handful of his fur before he could flee any farther. On any other night she might have enjoyed the light show, but given the current circumstances a less dramatic homecoming would have suited her just fine.

It took all of her strength to drag the trembling Hobo

indoors, and once there he stuck to her side as if he'd been sewn on to it, his tail tucked securely between his legs. Zeke was standing near the staircase, arms folded, glowering at them.

"I thought you were taking the dog back where it belonged."

"So did I," Rory said, "but as you might have learned some years back, and in this very house, things don't always work out the way you'd like them to." With Hobo matching her step for step, she gave Zeke a wide berth, dropped her jacket and keys on the bench beside the stairs and headed for the kitchen. She unhooked Hobo's leash and filled a bowl with water for him. He wasn't interested. His food was still in the car, but she doubted that he was any more hungry than he was thirsty. He was locked into full survival mode, which for the moment seemed to mean cowering under her protection. There was a pretty good chance that the marshal was his first ghost. She could empathize completely.

Zeke appeared beside the center island, causing Hobo to give a high-pitched yelp of surprise and ratchet his shaking up to something measurable on the Richter scale.

"I assume there's more to the story," Zeke said, his tone reminding Rory of an unpleasant trip to the principal's office in junior high. "Seein' as how you were gone for hours."

"Only if you consider murder worth mentioning," she said tightly. "And I'd drop the attitude if I were you." She pulled a half-full bottle of pinot noir out of the refrigerator and poured herself a glass. She needed a drink even if Hobo didn't.

She could tell by the way Zeke's eyebrows had inched upward that she'd piqued his curiosity. But his jaw was still set hard. He wasn't going to be bought out of his anger all that easily.

Fine with her. If he was determined to be in a black mood, she had no obligation to coax him out of it. She took her glass to the table and sank into one of the chairs, her back to him. Now that she had a lap, Hobo wanted to be in it. She tried a variety of commands to dissuade him, before succeeding with "off." Even then it took a firm voice and a lot of pushing to keep him on the floor. Denied that comfort, he burrowed his way under her legs like a self-guided hassock.

Zeke was silent. Either he was still standing where she'd left him or he'd gone back to whatever dimension he inhabited when he wasn't co-opting her life. She didn't even bother turning around to check. She was finally starting to relax from the tensions of the last few hours, a sweet lassitude hitching a ride on the wine that was spilling through her body. She could almost have convinced herself that she lived in an ordinary house where the paranormal was trapped safely within the pages of books by Dean Koontz and Stephen King.

A moment later Zeke popped into the seat across the table from her, shattering the lovely fantasy and causing Hobo to renew his campaign to launch himself into her lap. It took her another five minutes to calm the dog from panicked to merely frightened again.

She thought of asking the marshal to confine his movements to the more traditional kind for poor Hobo's sake, but he was probably trying to prove that he could make her life miserable too. Of course, in the end she and Zeke both knew that she held the wild card in their little game. That card was the house, Mac's house, with its precious cache of memories tucked away in every corner. It would be almost like losing him again if she had to sell it, but she would, if living there with Zeke became untenable. Mac would understand. And as hard as it would be for her, it would be even harder for Zeke. He'd once again be subjected to a parade of owners who would pack up and run at the first hint of ghostly goings-on. How long might it take before she found another sympathetic, open-minded buyer who would not only hang around and put up with his antics, but also try to help him solve the mystery of who had murdered him? Rory doubted there was a matchmaking website for lonely ghosts.

"I'm guessin' the deceased was the mutt's owner," Zeke said casually, as if they'd been having a polite conversation all along.

In the name of tranquility, Rory decided to accept the scrawny olive branch he was extending. "Brenda Hartley," she said, between sips of wine. "And the dog's name is Hobo."

"Hobo, right. So, for some strange reason you're feelin' obligated to give Hobo here a home?"

"I haven't decided yet. For now I'm just boarding him overnight."

"Don't I get a vote?"

"It wouldn't matter, since I have veto power," she said, realizing a moment too late that she probably could have chosen a more diplomatic way to put it. Still, the truth was the truth no matter how you disguised it.

Zeke's face clamped down again. "So do I," he growled under his breath.

So much for détente. Rory was quickly running out of patience and the virtue that came with it. She tried another tactic. "Do you want to hear about the case or not?"

Zeke took a moment to assess the playing field. "Yes, ma'am," he said, "I surely do."

Rory swore she heard a note of mockery in his voice, but she let it go. She had no interest in spending the rest of the night in a pitched battle with him. Instead, she gave him a quick recap of what had happened at the Hartley home. Having already briefed Cirello and Leah she had the story pared down to its essentials.

"Any valuables missin'?" Zeke asked, following her lead into neutral territory. "Place torn up at all?"

"Nothing looked out of order, but I never went upstairs."

"It's a damn shame I don't know how to get outta this

place when I want. I could've scouted out the rest of that house for you and no one would ever have been the wiser."

Rory almost groaned out loud. With all that had happened, she'd forgotten about his attempt to materialize in Brenda's house. The last thing she wanted to do at that moment was dig up another bone of contention for them to argue over. Unfortunately the subject needed to be addressed and there was no point in postponing it now that he had brought it up.

"I'm sure that'll be a help one day," she said wearily, "but not until you've gotten it down pat and we've worked out a way to be sure no one else is around to catch your little 'beam me up, Scotty' routine."

Zeke's brows bunched together over his eyes. "I'm not sure I get your drift. Sometimes you make less sense than a hat without a brim."

"Sorry, it's an expression from an old TV series. Just about anyone alive today would understand the reference."

"Right there's your first problem," he said, doing a slow fade out then in again to underscore his point.

"There's a second?"

"Folks these days spend entirely too much time starin' at one kind of screen or another."

Rory could hardly argue with that nugget of wisdom, nor did she want to. All she really wanted at that moment was to eat the leftover slice of pizza that was waiting on the bottom shelf of the refrigerator and crawl into bed. But she had to make sure that she and Zeke were on the same page with regard to his future travel plans.

"Remember the media frenzy after Conti said he was caught by Wyatt Earp? That'll seem like a flea circus once a few well-respected detectives and solid citizens witness one of your entrances or exits."

"I suppose as how that might be so," he conceded in the reluctant tone of one who's been outflanked by the truth.

"Okay then, we're agreed that you won't try to follow

me anywhere unless I've determined that you won't have an audience?"

Zeke ran his long, calloused fingers through his hair as he contemplated her request. "Just so long as it's not an emergency," he said solemnly, holding out his hand as if to shake on it.

Rory's heart danced a little bebop up into her throat. She was about to find out what ghosts were made of or risk offending the marshal. She pasted a smile on her mouth and put out her hand, determined to keep it steady. She was inches away from touching him when he pulled his hand back.

"That's okay, darlin'," he said, laughing, "I'll consider the effort done for the deed."

Rory shrugged as if it didn't matter to her one way or the other, but relief surged through her as her heart settled back into place. She'd let him enjoy this little triumph at her expense. She was satisfied that she'd won the other rounds of the bout.

"You have yourself a good night there with Hobo the lionhearted," Zeke said and he was gone while his words still hung in the air.

Hobo waited a minute, snuffled the air and decided that it was safe enough to leave his hidey-hole beneath Rory's legs. But he wouldn't venture far from her side. Together they took the slice of pizza out of the refrigerator and heated it back to crispness in a pan on the stove—a little trick she'd learned from a chef on TV. While it cooked, Hobo rediscovered his appetite and was rewarded with a good portion of the crust.

After dinner, Rory brought in the bag of kibble and scooped some into a bowl that she left beside his water dish. If she was going to keep Hobo she'd have to buy him proper dog bowls as well as some toys and maybe a bed of his own. But that wasn't a decision she wanted to make until she'd had a good night's sleep.

# Chapter 5

When the telephone rang it awakened Rory from a deep, exhausted sleep to the sound of someone snoring. Who on earth was in her bed? As her eyes snapped open, she burst into laughter, waking the snorer, who yawned and thumped his tail lazily against the quilt.

She grabbed for the phone on the third ring, before it went to voice mail. The stranger on the other end introduced herself as Tina Kovack and launched right into the reason for her call, chattering so rapidly that each word was partially swallowed by the next. To Rory's sleep-fogged brain she might just as well have been speaking Swahili as English.

"Excuse me, Ms. Kovack," she interrupted, "would you please repeat that a bit more slowly?"

"Sorry I'm sorry I was a friend of poor Brenda Hartley's and I just found out that she's dead not just dead dead would be bad enough but she was murdered."

Although Tina was making an effort to speak more

distinctly, she'd completely abandoned punctuation, as if she were too agitated to concentrate on more than one speech issue at a time.

"I know, Ms. Kovack, my condolences," Rory said, sliding out of bed and pulling a cotton robe on over her nightgown. Hobo groaned and stretched out, claiming the vacated pillow.

"How can I be of help?" She headed for the kitchen. She needed a strong cup of coffee and fast.

"I know you're a private investigator you solved those murders a few months back and I need to hire you."

Rory filled the coffeemaker and turned it on. "Okay, if you'll hold for a minute I'll get to my computer and we'll set up an appointment." She made a point of speaking slowly in the hope that Tina would follow her example.

"Oh, okay." Tina sighed, as if she were disappointed about having to wait the requested minute.

Rory started to have second thoughts about a client who wanted instant results. She hoped it was just the unexpected tragedy of Brenda's death that had spiked the woman's anxiety level and dealt her common sense a nasty blow.

She trooped back upstairs to the room that had once been Mac's study. When she'd moved her office into its new venue in the garage, she'd equipped it with a new computer and transferred the older one out of the living room and into the study again. She sat down at that desk now, pulled up her appointment calendar and took Tina off hold.

It came as no surprise that Tina was ready to get in her car and drive over right then and there. Rory supposed she should be grateful that the woman had at least waited until dawn to call her. After a bit of negotiating they settled on two o'clock that afternoon and Rory supplied her with directions.

When she returned to the kitchen, the recessed lights were flashing and Zeke was filtering into the chair he'd occupied the night before, much like sand filling an hourglass. Rory headed straight to the coffeemaker, with barely a glance in his direction. It wasn't quite done brewing, but she pulled the carafe out and filled the mug she'd left in the dish rack the day before. Without the carafe there, the dripping coffee splashed onto the metal heating element and sizzled as if scolding her. She'd have to clean it up later, but not having to wait for the coffee was worth it. She stuck the carafe back in place and took her mug to the table. No milk this morning. She needed it black.

"We have a new client?" Zeke asked casually, as if the argument of the previous night had never happened.

Rory took a bolstering sip of coffee before answering him. It bothered her that the marshal could listen in on any conversation she had in the house, even if it was only her side of a phone call. For that matter, she had no way of knowing if he was watching her at any given moment either. As a precondition of their strange living arrangement, she'd exacted his promise to respect her privacy in the bedroom and bathroom. But she really had no way of monitoring how well he kept his word. It occurred to her that a dog might be able to do just that. If Hobo continued to react to Zeke as strongly as he had at their first meeting, he would make an excellent sentry to guard her privacy. Her very own canary in the coal mine. Of course the downside would be putting up with Zeke's foul moods.

"You out gatherin' wool somewhere?" Zeke prodded. "Do we have ourselves a new client or not?"

"Could be," she said, focusing on him. "That phone call was from Tina Kovack, another friend of the late Brenda Hartley's."

"I was wonderin' if we'd get a chance to work that case." Zeke sounded pleased at the prospect.

"Don't get too excited. I have a feeling Tina isn't going to be the best kind of client."

"I thought the best kind was the payin' kind." He smiled. "Success has gone and made you a trifle picky, Aurora."

"Cut the Aurora crap, you know I can't stand it."

"Probably why I'm so partial to it." His mouth stretched into a full-out grin.

During the few months Rory had known Zeke, she'd learned that he could be charming when he wanted to be, a rough, frontiersman kind of charming. But at that moment she wasn't interested in being charmed or won over, especially with the question of Hobo still hanging in the balance.

"Where's the mutt?" he asked, as if he'd read her mind.

Rory pushed back from the table, thankful that that wasn't one of the abilities he'd picked up in exchange for his mortal body.

"He's sleeping," she said, going to the counter to top off her coffee. She didn't bother reminding him that the dog actually had a name. If he wanted to refer to him as "the mutt," she would let him. Dealing with Zeke she'd learned to pick her battles, and that one simply wasn't worth fighting.

"Yesterday must have been awful for him," she said instead. "I wish there was some way to explain it all so that he could understand."

"Animals get death better than you think," Zeke said. "Whys and hows don't matter to them 'cause they can't change what is. People are the ones who need to dress it all up with rules and ceremonies."

"Look who's the pet psychologist," Rory said, leaning back against the counter.

"That there's just one of those newfangled words you like so much. Say what you like, but I've owned my share of dogs and horses and I know what I know," Zeke said. "Animals adapt fine to just about anything."

Hobo chose that moment to come racing down the stairs, his nails clicking like an old typewriter on the hardwood. Zeke's experience notwithstanding, Rory was pretty sure the dog had panicked when he awoke and didn't see her there. It was perfectly reasonable to assume that he was afraid of losing a second master and caretaker in less than twenty-four hours.

A moment later Hobo careened into the kitchen, lost traction on the ceramic tile and wound up running in place like a cartoon character. Coffee sloshed out of Rory's cup and onto her bathrobe as she flattened herself against the counter to get out of his way. Zeke burst into a hearty laugh that spooked Hobo into losing his balance and executing a belly flop. All four legs splayed, he slid across the room and crashed into the back door.

Rory set her mug on the counter and went over to try to help him to his feet. But at ninety pounds he was pretty much on his own. After a few abortive attempts, he managed to pull himself upright. He gave Rory's face an appreciative lick, while keeping a wary eye on his nemesis at the table.

When the marshal made no threatening moves in his direction, Hobo risked turning his back on him. He looked pointedly at the door and woofed. He couldn't have been any clearer if he'd actually spoken his request, and it occurred to Rory that it was easier to communicate with the dog than with the marshal. She unlocked the door and let Hobo outside, glad that Mac had had the backyard fenced for the Labrador retriever he'd intended to buy before death changed all of his plans.

She watched Hobo make a spirited but clumsy dash for a squirrel, who scampered up an oak tree to safety. Pleased to have secured the yard from trespassers, he went on about the business of spreading his scent and asserting his claim to the property.

"You can't be serious about keepin' that dog," Zeke grumbled, the amusement gone from his voice.

Rory turned away from the door. "I haven't decided yet," she said. When she was growing up her mother would tell her to sleep on a difficult decision, as if the right answer would be magically apparent by morning. But somehow Rory had never developed the knack. Last night had been no different. She'd fallen asleep as soon as she'd crawled into bed and if she had reached a decision while she slept, it had vanished along with her dreams when the phone rang.

She went to the sink, wet a paper towel and wiped ineffectively at the coffee stains on her robe while she thought about what to say next.

"I think a trial period, maybe a month or so, would be the fair thing to do," she said finally and with as much authority as she could muster, given that the idea had just occurred to her. She wasn't even sure if it qualified as a decision or just procrastination. She balled up the paper towel and tossed it into the garbage can under the sink.

"Fair to who?" Zeke asked sourly. "Did you ever think that maybe being around me is traumatic to old Hobo there? Maybe you're not being fair to *him*."

Rory didn't have an immediate answer for that. She'd been so focused on Zeke's objections that she hadn't thought much about what Hobo's objections might be.

"Fair to everyone," she said, although with less conviction.

Zeke shook his head. "Okay, let's not talk about what's fair, let's talk about the truth. The truth is that you've been trying to decide if *you* want to keep the dog, not what's best for him or me. You probably don't even realize it. Hell, I suspect you've even got yourself bamboozled into believing that you're bein' evenhanded."

"Oh, right, and you're the very model of being honest with yourself," Rory said tightly. "After more than a hundred years, you still haven't made peace with yourself so that you can move on." Even as she said the words she realized she'd crossed some invisible line, but she couldn't bring herself to apologize or back down. When she was being pushed into a corner, she couldn't help but push back harder.

Zeke's jaw clenched, causing the bones and veins of his

face to stand out. His eyes narrowed like a sniper homing in on a target. "You have no idea what you're talking about," he shot back at her. "And you're a fool if you think you know me."

"Know you? How can I know you, if you refuse to tell me anything?" Frustrated, Rory almost threw her coffee mug at him, but she stopped herself in time. He wouldn't have felt it anyway and she would have been stuck cleaning up the mess. Instead she thumped it down sharply in the sink.

"You want to know something about me?" Zeke snapped. "Then start by keepin' your word and figure out who killed me!"

"I've tried and you know it." She'd found articles about his death in the archives of the local newspapers, but they'd provided little useful information and led to more questions than answers, none of which Zeke had been willing to discuss with her.

"You found out I was shot to death in this house. Why, thank you kindly, ma'am, but I was already in possession of that information."

"Who was John Corbin?" Rory demanded, locking eyes with him to make it clear she had no intention of backing down. If she was going to have an angry ghost on her hands, she might as well try to harvest some information from the ordeal. "Was John Trask using the alias John Corbin when he was on Long Island?"

"How are you gonna hone those detecting skills of yours if I just provide you with all the answers?" he asked wryly, some of the venom gone from his tone.

Rory kept her guard up. She'd never known him to capitulate so easily. "If you actually *had* all the answers, you wouldn't need me to figure out who shot you," she pointed out. "And I seriously doubt I'm going to have many cases in which everyone involved is dead and gone, along with their entire generation."

"I daresay you never expected to have this case either and yet here you are."

She took a deep breath and gave herself a time-out for a silent count of ten. "If you really want me to make any progress," she went on evenly, "you're going to have to give me something more to go on."

"Corbin was Trask," Zeke said, his tone heavy with exasperation. "Does that suit you?"

Rory ignored the question since it was only meant to goad her. "Then it seems pretty cut-and-dried. Trask knew you were after him, so he killed you before you had the chance to arrest him."

"There you go jumpin' to the wrong conclusion."

"Meaning?"

"Meanin' I know for a fact that he didn't do it."

"Really? And how can you be so sure of that?"

"I had him square in my gun sights—right there in front of me—when I was shot in the back."

"I see," Rory murmured, trying to wedge this new piece into the puzzle. Someone else had been in the room that day. She couldn't see any reason for Zeke to have been hoarding this information, except as a means of controlling her and what she ultimately discovered about his death. And that made no sense, unless there was a part of him that wasn't all that keen to learn the truth after all. Since she wasn't equipped to psychoanalyze him, she focused on containing the rage that was frothing up inside her like magma in a volcano. Easier said than done.

"I cannot believe you didn't tell me this before!" Her words rose in an angry crescendo in spite of her efforts.

"You think this is easy for me? This isn't easy!" he responded, shouting her down. "To you it's just history. But it was my life. It was my damn life!" He vanished before she had a chance to respond.

Rory was momentarily stunned by the emotion she'd ignited in him. She'd had glimpses of his dark side before, but she'd never heard the pure, sharp anguish that riddled his anger now. Still, one thing was certain, he wasn't the only injured party and she was getting pretty tired of losing every battle simply because he up and left the arena.

"Maybe I should keep Hobo and send you off to the pound," she yelled to the empty room.

# Chapter 6

At one forty-five Rory stopped in the bathroom to run a comb through her hair and apply a bit of lip gloss. She lingered for a minute, somehow still surprised by the adult woman who was staring back at her from the mirror. In the family, it was generally agreed that she had her mother's sculpted cheekbones and her father's straight nose and determined chin. But no one could figure out where she'd gotten the wide hazel eyes, with their black-ringed irises, that her aunt Helene swore she'd pay good money to have herself. Rory had grown up imagining that one day a stranger with the same eyes would come to their door and introduce herself as a long-lost cousin. Smiling at the memory, she turned out the light. It was time to meet Tina Kovack.

She walked out the kitchen door with Hobo at her side. Leaving him alone in the house where Zeke might pop up at any moment seemed too much like animal cruelty. Besides, Tina Kovack had been a friend of the deceased, so the odds were that she already knew Hobo and probably wouldn't object to having him there for the duration of their meeting.

As they crossed the backyard to her office, she wasn't at all surprised to find Tina already pacing up and down the driveway. Rory had no intention of asking her how long she'd been waiting, nor was she going to apologize for that wait. It was still well before the time of their appointment and Tina was going to have to respect certain boundaries if Rory was going to take her case.

When she'd first considered having the office built on her property, rather than renting space in town, she'd written out a list of the pros and cons of each option. The only major con on the list was the fact that clients would know where she lived and might feel they had the right to intrude upon her private life. Based on their conversation that morning, Tina Kovack might well be the poster child for exactly that sort of problem.

Tina's face lit up when she saw Rory and Hobo coming. She hurried back up the driveway to meet them at the office door. Rory immediately recognized her as one of the women in the group photo on Brenda Hartley's mantel. She looked to be in her late forties, and she was tall, close to six feet at least, with the body of a one-time athlete that was just starting to go to seed. Her spandex tank top showcased a small potbelly and a bulge of excess fat beneath her bra line in the back.

Tina dropped to her knees in the grass beside Hobo and threw her arms around him. "Hobo, sweetie boy!" She kissed him loudly on the snout. "I had no idea you were here!" Hobo responded by happily slathering her cheek with saliva. Tina didn't seem to mind in the least.

She looked up at Rory. "One of the neighbors told me she'd seen him get into a car with some stranger. I'm so glad that he's okay. It's bad enough that Tootsie's missing. She's one of mine, you know. Oh goodness, I'm sorry, where are my manners?" She stood up and thrust out her hand. "I'm Tina."

Rory shook her hand, marveling at how much more coherent Tina sounded. She was still speaking fast, but certainly within the normal range and she was actually pausing for punctuation. There was every reason to believe that her phone call had been a simple aberration brought on by stress.

Rory unlocked the door and ushered her and Hobo inside. Apart from her desk and chair, the office was furnished with a small, brown leather love seat and matching armchair that sat at right angles to one another with a glass and chrome side table between them. The walls were painted a soft cappuccino and were bare except for her framed PI license and an eight-by-ten close-up of her with Mac at the circus when she was eight years old. She'd debated displaying something that personal in an office setting, but decided that the only criterion that mattered was that she wanted it there. Although there were still odd moments when looking at the picture made her sad, she'd mostly come to a place where it just stirred up sweet memories and buoyed her spirits.

Hobo immediately made himself at home on the love seat, curling up with a grunt. Based on the fur Rory had seen on Brenda Hartley's couch, he was clearly accustomed to the finer things in life. He was going to need some retraining if she decided to keep him, or other, less dog-friendly clients would wind up with ninety pounds of drool and fur in their laps, and she might well lose their business.

Tina passed up the armchair and folded herself into the narrow space beside the dog. "I hope you're going to keep him. You are going to, aren't you?" she asked, stroking his back as she spoke. Hobo sighed contentedly.

"I'm not sure. He's a lot of dog and even though I have an office right here, I'm not always around." Plus, Hobo and her ghost hadn't hit it off very well. But she refrained from saying that aloud.

"Maybe *you* should take him," Rory suggested, feeling an unexpected tug at the thought of losing him. That did not bode well. If she kept him much longer she'd be hopelessly bonded to him. "He seems really happy to be with you there," she pointed out with as much enthusiasm as she could muster.

"The trouble is I have twelve dogs now and there are more on the way."

Rory didn't know how to respond to that. Maybe Tina wasn't quite so sane after all.

"I'm a breeder." Tina laughed. "I'll bet you were thinking I was a nutcase. Like some old spinster lady with a hundred cats. Of course I'm not old, at least not by today's standards, and I'm not a spinster, and I don't particularly like cats, but you know what I mean."

Rory tripped over her words as she tried to assure the woman that she'd thought no such thing. If she'd been prone to blushing like her mother, she would have been beet red by now.

"Not to worry," Tina insisted, explaining that she enjoyed watching people's faces when she told them how many dogs she had. Sometimes she even fudged the number to get a better reaction.

"So you breed Maltese," Rory said, recovering her poise. It didn't take a detective to figure that out, but Tina seemed impressed anyway. "Did Brenda Hartley buy her Maltese from you?"

Tina bobbed her head. "I've bred some champions. I used to do the whole show circuit thing too. It just got to be too hectic and time-consuming. So now I mostly stick to breeding them. I still get a kick when I hear that one of my pups has won a show. The truth is," she said, lowering her voice as if she were afraid that someone might overhear her, "they always feel like they're mine, even after they have another home. It's actually a bit hard for me to part with them at all. But if I didn't, I think my husband Joe might just walk out the door and never come home again."

Rory squelched the desire to whisper back that she was pretty sure Joe wasn't hiding out in the bathroom or the garage with his ear to the door. Instead she said, "Why don't you tell me what I can do for you."

"Right, sorry, I tend to go off on tangents. Especially when I'm nervous. You probably have a lot of other appointments and important sleuthing to do. Do you call it sleuthing? Anyway, are you aware of all the dog abductions on the island, especially in Suffolk County, over the past few months?"

Rory remembered reading about the crimes, but since she didn't have a dog at the time, she hadn't paid close attention to the news coverage.

"Thirty-two puppies and dogs, all purebloods, stolen from breeders and pet stores as well as from individual owners. No, wait, what am I saying? It's thirty-three now counting Tootsie."

Rory tried to interrupt to ask why she was counting Tootsie in with those that had been stolen, but Tina was going full throttle and apparently nothing short of a brick wall was going to stop her.

"Every one of the missing dogs was reported to the police, but not one of them was ever found. Including my George and Gracie." Tears welled up in her eyes. She tried to blink them back, but one escaped and trickled down her cheek. "Well, maybe they'll take us more seriously now that Brenda's been murdered," she said, wiping her cheek dry.

"I think you need to back up a few steps there," Rory said, jumping in before Tina could get her second wind. "What makes you so sure that Brenda's death was even related to the dog thefts?"

"Tootsie's missing," she said as if that were all the proof anyone needed.

"So was Hobo, until I found him wandering around. Whoever killed Brenda left the front door open."

Tina shook her head. "I just know it had to do with Tootsie. I just know."

It occurred to Rory that Marti Sugarman had voiced the same concern. It wasn't necessarily a logical conclusion, but then the two women were so focused on dogs that they were probably inclined to see everything in dog-related terms.

"With all due respect," Rory said, "it's far more likely that her death was the result of a botched burglary or even an argument that got out of hand."

"Well, there you go—Tootsie is probably worth more than anything else in Brenda's house, Ms. McCain. A lot more. So you can call it a botched burglary or a botched dog abduction, but it's really the same thing."

"I see your point," Rory conceded, although she wasn't quite ready to abandon the theory that Tootsie saw the open door and took off to see the world. "But without more information, we can't ignore the possibility that an unrelated issue led to Brenda's death."

Although Tina shook her head firmly to indicate that she was inclined to do just that, she refrained from continuing the debate.

"Since these dogs are expensive," Rory said, moving on, "I guess it's safe to assume there's a black market for them. Although to be honest and again with all due respect, I don't really understand why anyone would pay a lot of money when there seem to be more than enough great mutts like Hobo to go around."

Tina shrugged. "It's like with anything else—people want what they want and some of them want a bargain to boot."

"Sounds like the perfect niche business for a motivated thief," Rory said, thinking out loud.

"Then you'll take the case?"

"To find the missing dogs?" she asked to be clear.

"Well *my* two, since I'm the one footing the bill. And Tootsie of course. Though I don't mind if you happen to find the others in the process. In fact, that would be terrific. They certainly all deserve to be rescued."

"I just need to be sure that you're not asking me to find out who murdered Brenda, because that's going to be an extremely active police investigation for the foreseeable future and I can't get in their way or I could be charged with obstructing justice."

"I understand. I would never expect you to do anything illegal or anything that would get you in any kind of trouble. I always steer way clear of trouble. Even though I still believe the two cases are one and the same, I'm hiring you to find my two dogs and hopefully in the process shut down this horrible dog abduction ring."

Rory took a minute to fully consider her decision. She'd never dealt with pet-related crimes or with the world of breeders and pedigreed dogs. But then she'd never had to care for a dog before either, and after one night with Hobo she was already feeling pretty confident in that arena. Besides, whatever she lacked in experience she'd make up for with hard work and some on-the-job training. "Okay," she said, "we're going to find your dogs." She spent the next few minutes explaining her fees, including the retainer she required up front before beginning any case. In return, she would keep Tina updated on her progress and provide her with a written log of all the information she acquired, as well as a line-item list of additional expenses she incurred while pursuing the investigation. Tina wrote her a check on the spot.

Over the next forty minutes Rory took down as much background on the case as Tina could supply. When Tina stood up to leave, Hobo hopped off the couch and followed her to the door as if he expected to go with her. She knelt down so that she could look him in the eye and she cupped his shaggy head in her hands.

"No, boy," she said slowly, in a tone that was both loving and firm. "You have to stay here for now. I promise I'll come see you soon. Okay?" She paused a moment as if she were actually waiting for his response. Hobo licked her nose and gave her a single wag of his tail, but his eyes looked glum. He lay down on the carpeted floor with a heavy thud, as if gravity had finally gotten the best of him.

Rory stood to say good-bye to Tina. "I think he'd rather be going with you," she said, wondering if the breeder would be as good at communicating with ghosts as she appeared to be with dogs.

"He knows me better than he knows you, that's all," Tina said, her words speeding up again now that she was talking to Rory. Apparently she had different settings for different species. Rory toyed with the idea of requesting the canine speed the next time they spoke.

"He seemed content when I saw him walking with you before," Tina went on. "His tail was up and there was a bounce to his step. He's just all muddled right now. Too many changes. Dogs need to have some constants in their lives in order to feel secure. And once they feel secure, they can be happy."

Rory nodded, since it was her turn to speak and she couldn't think of anything to say. After Tina's little speech, what could she say? And how on earth could she ever abandon Hobo at a shelter?

They'd said their good-byes, and Tina was halfway out the door when a question occurred to Rory. "Do you know Marti Sugarman?"

Tina stopped in the open doorway. "Yes, she bought her Maltese from me. Why?"

"She came by Brenda's house not long after I got there yesterday. She said she'd been a close friend of hers."

"Yeah, right," Tina said dryly. "Maybe once upon a

time, but they had a falling-out two years ago. In fact, it was because of Tootsie."

"I think I need to hear the rest of that story," Rory said, leaning over to grab the pen and paper off her desk.

"Sure. It's simple enough. Both women wanted puppies from the same litter. Brenda got her deposit in first, so she got first choice and when the time came, she took Tootsie. Of course her name wasn't Tootsie yet. Anyway, Tootsie happened to be the only show-quality pup in that litter and Brenda had made it plain that she had no intention of showing her. Marti, on the other hand, specifically wanted a dog she could show. I think you can fill in the blanks from there. I didn't even know they were on speaking terms again."

Rory thanked her and promised to be in touch as soon as she had something to report. Then she sat down at her desk to create a new computer file for Tina's case and to input her preliminary notes. To quote her former colleagues in the police department, Marti Sugarman had just become a "person of interest."

# Chapter 7

"I didn't know much about the spike in missing dogs either," Leah said to Rory as they drove the two blocks from the cleaner's to the supermarket. It was Leah's usual lunch hour: short on lunch, long on errands. They'd each downed a slice of pizza in under three minutes. Rory could still feel a lump of the cheese clinging to her throat. That was the price you paid if you wanted to "do lunch" with Leah on a workday.

"It's awfully hard to be sure a dog's been stolen unless there's an eyewitness," Leah went on. "Dogs have been escaping from fenced-in yards for as long as people have been fencing them in. If they don't jump over them or dig under them, then the gardeners or the pool boys or the oil delivery guys forget to close the gate when they leave."

"That was my thought initially," Rory said, wishing she hadn't tossed her bottle of Coke before getting back in the car. "But more than thirty purebloods in the county over a few months does sound excessive."

Leah turned into the supermarket parking lot. "I know, but as far as Tootsie's concerned, we're working under the assumption that her disappearance is unrelated to Brenda's murder."

"Which means that Crime Scene didn't find any evidence to challenge that assumption," Rory said, thinking aloud.

"I shouldn't actually be talking to you about any of this." Leah whipped into a spot and shut off the engine in one well-practiced motion. "But here I go anyway. The only blood found in the house belonged to Brenda. I made sure they tested for canine blood just to cover all bases." She grabbed her handbag and jumped out of the car.

Rory trotted around from her side and they doubletimed it into the store. "Any luck with fingerprints?"

"There was only one set on the knife and they weren't Brenda's. Unfortunately we couldn't find a match for them in the system either. Nothing else in the house seemed to have been disturbed. Oh—and Marti Sugarman was telling the truth about getting a call from Brenda that morning."

"Thanks. Of course it goes without saying that whatever you tell me I take to the grave," Rory said, her stomach getting cranky about digesting and running at the same time.

"If it goes without saying, then why are you saying it?" Leah laughed. "I've never understood that expression."

Rory helped her pick out some pears and a cantaloupe that might ripen before the end of the month and they were off to the deli counter for turkey and Swiss cheese.

"I wish I could help you out with names and numbers on those stolen dog reports," Leah said, shaking her head, "but it's not my bailiwick and there'd be too many raised eyebrows about my sudden interest, especially once it gets around that you're investigating one of the cases."

"That's why I didn't ask," Rory said. "The breeder gave me the names of the people she knows personally who believe their dogs have been stolen. It's enough for a start."

"There is one thing I can do to help narrow the field. I'll take a quick look through the reports and let you know if I find any common threads." They'd reached the checkout line. "Just remember, McCain," Leah said, lowering her voice, "you're looking for a dog thief, not Brenda's killer. If those two paths wind up intersecting along the way, you call me pronto."

When Rory arrived home she received a jubilant greeting from Hobo, who appeared to have weathered his first hour and a half without her unscathed. As she was letting him out back to tend to doggie business, the front doorbell rang.

She went to answer it, wondering who would come by in the middle of a workday. As she passed through the dining room, the silver and glass chandelier over the table flashed on, then off, and a second later the marshal fell into step beside her. Rory didn't even flinch. She supposed it bode well for the future of the species that *Homo sapiens* could adapt to pretty much anything.

"I'll bet that's your aunt Helene again," Zeke said. Since he never bothered with "hello," Rory always felt as if she'd walked in on the middle of a conversation that he'd started without her.

"What do you mean 'again'?" she asked, as they reached the entry.

"She came by while you were out and when you didn't answer the door after she'd rung the bell three times, she yelled, 'I'll be back in a little bit, Rory,' as if you were here and just didn't want to let her in. She's a mite on the strange side, ain't she?"

Rory didn't respond. Something he'd said was troubling her, but she couldn't quite put her finger on it. The bell rang again, causing her to tuck the question away for the moment. She peered through the peephole she'd recently had installed. Sure enough, there was Helene standing on the porch, smiling expectantly and wearing a low-cut sundress over a tank top, the tank being a concession to her version of propriety now that she was fifty.

As Rory unlocked the door she turned to Zeke, her eyebrows raised. "So, how do you prefer to be introduced? Ezekiel Drummond or Marshal Drummond?"

He vanished without a sound.

"Aunt Helene," Rory said, opening the door, "what a great surprise. Come on in."

Helene stepped inside and engulfed her in an enthusiastic hug. Although she was as petite as her niece, her effusive personality made her seem twice the size.

"I actually came by before, but you weren't home," Helene said, one arm still encircling Rory's waist as if to prevent her from getting away this time.

"I had no idea you were coming."

"Of course you didn't; you're not a mind reader. I was in the neighborhood, so I just stopped by to say hello. We don't get to see you very much anymore." By "we," Rory knew she meant her parents, the other two members of what her dad referred to as the geriatric musketeers. To Rory they were somewhere between the musketeers and the three stooges, but she kept that thought to herself.

"If you'd called me on my cell, I could have told you when I'd be home and you wouldn't have wasted your time."

"I didn't waste anything, my dear. I like it better when my day's not completely planned out. It was more fun not knowing if I'd find you home. Like being on a treasure hunt. And when you weren't here, I consoled myself with one of those sinful iced coffee drinks with chocolate syrup and lots of whipped cream." She sighed happily, savoring the treat all over again in her mind. "I'm sure it had tons of fat and calories, but I said to myself, 'Helene, what's the point of living if you don't indulge from time to time?' Then I swung by again to see if you were home yet. So here I am, here you are and it's been a perfectly lovely day."

"Well, I'm glad you found me," Rory said, "I've missed you too." It wasn't any secret in the family that Helene was a bit eccentric, a polar opposite to Rory's mother, who was so rooted in reality that Helene often called her a "lovable old stick-in-the-mud." From the time she was little, Rory had found that being within her aunt's sphere of influence always made her feel delightfully off center herself.

"By the way," Helene said, "there was a dog just barking his fool head off when I rang the bell before. Is there a new addition to the family I haven't been told about?"

"That's Hobo. His owner died suddenly, so I'm giving him a trial run. He's out back if you want to meet him."

"Another time, dear, I have to run." She withdrew her arm. "We start rehearsing *Oklahoma* tonight." Her eyes were sparkling like the eyes of a kid about to dig into a hot fudge sundae with extra whipped cream and two cherries on top.

So that was it. Rory was surprised she hadn't picked up on it sooner. Helene had joined the Way Off Broadway Players only a few months earlier and had been dizzy with excitement over her role in the new production. Having inherited a windfall when an old and apparently nostalgic boyfriend passed away, she'd been able to retire from her thirty-year teaching career to pursue her lifelong interest in acting. It proved to be a match made in drama queen heaven. The troupe was strictly nonequity. They performed in a converted storefront in Bay Shore, half an hour south of Huntington. Over the years they'd developed a loyal following that could be counted upon to fill their fifty-seat theater on weekends.

"I'm Aunt Eller," Helene said proudly. "It's not a big part, but one I've spent years researching," she added with a wink. She kissed Rory's cheek. "Now remember, if you need help with any of your investigations, I'm just a phone

call away. I can't tell you how much I enjoyed running
interference for you the last time. I rather think I was born
for espionage—it's not unlike the stage, you know."

Rory promised to keep her on speed dial. Helene and
her parents had in fact made it possible for her to gather
evidence that eventually led to the arrest of Vincent Conti.
As Rory closed the door behind her aunt, she was thinking that she really owed her family an invitation to dinner, or at least a Sunday brunch. She hadn't invited them
over since it had become hers. The Zeke factor had a lot
to do with that lapse. While he insisted that he didn't want
to meet her folks, there was always the chance he might
decide to amuse himself by turning lights on and off, causing objects to move around the room or any number of
other little tricks he had in his ghostly arsenal. She was
pretty sure he'd enjoy making her squirm. And what about
Hobo? Wouldn't her parents wonder why he was so skit-
tish, jumping with fright for no apparent reason or hiding
like an ostrich with his head buried under her legs? She'd
have to come up with some plausible explanations for the
inexplicable.

As if he knew she was thinking of him, Hobo let out a
plaintive bark at the back door, a bark that clearly meant
"let me in, let me in." She went to the kitchen and held the
door open for him. He stepped inside, then immediately
bolted past her with a yelp. When Rory turned around,
she wasn't at all surprised to find Zeke seated at the table.
To give him the benefit of the doubt, she'd assume he'd
blinked the lights when she was facing the door. On such
a sunny day it was entirely possible that she hadn't noticed
the additional light.

"This is goin' to be one helluva long month," he said
dryly.

"How did he act while I was out?" Rory asked, trying
not to think about what on earth she was going to do if
Hobo didn't acclimate to living with the marshal. With each

passing hour, she was growing more hopelessly attached to the dog.

"Well, I did my best to stay out of his way and for the most part he stayed out of mine. He seems partial to hidin' under things, the table here, the desk upstairs. He even tried to squeeze under your bed, which didn't go too well given his size and all."

Rory shook her head and sank onto the chair beside Zeke, wondering if they made tranquilizers for dogs. Or ghosts for that matter. Hobo poked his snout around the corner from the dining room. He took one tentative step in, then quickly shuffled two steps back, dancing the approach avoidance two-step. He wanted desperately to be near her and just as desperately to stay away from whatever was sitting beside her.

Rory read the look in his eyes and relocated to the chair across from the marshal. Hobo dipped into his reserve of courage and made a beeline for her legs, nearly upending her and her chair in the process, all of which Zeke seemed to enjoy far too much. It was all so comical that Rory couldn't help laughing along with him. But as the laughter subsided, the conversation they'd had earlier popped into her mind and demanded her full attention. What about it was bothering her? As far as she could recall, it had been brief and ordinary. He hadn't said anything news shattering, yet all sorts of worrisome alarms had started going off in her head, as if she were bearing down on a *Titanic*-sized iceberg.

"What's goin' on in that pretty head of yours?" Zeke asked, still grinning.

And then she realized what it was. "How did you know it was Helene at the door?"

Zeke's smile faded and he looked at her oddly. "Have you plumb forgotten how many times you and your family visited Mac in this house, darlin'?"

Rory hadn't forgotten. She'd just failed to connect the

dots. Of course Zeke knew what they all looked like, as well as how they sounded, and probably a hundred other things. Including things she might not have wanted him to know. It was entirely too creepy to dwell on, which was why, from the moment she'd met Zeke, she'd pushed the thought to the back of her mind and buried it under bushels of information she never intended to use again, like geometric formulas and the battles of the French and Indian War. Now that he'd forced her to drag that knowledge out into the light of day, she was having trouble accepting that Mac had been so cavalier about the family's privacy.

"Mac didn't mind you hanging around while we were here?" she asked. "He never set up any rules or anything?"

"Now, don't you go thinkin' that Mac sold you out," Zeke said, as if he was able to read her thoughts from the set of her face. "Mac and I had us a very different relationship than you and I have. We were both men, lawmen, and we respected each other's integrity. He took it on faith that I wouldn't go crossin' any boundaries of decency. When someone trusts you like that, you want to prove their trust is well placed." Zeke's face relaxed into a smile again. "Besides, it never bothered him if I floated an object now and then or provided the occasional strange noise. For my part, I generally abstained from that sort of thing around his family. But his friends were fair game, especially if they'd been drinkin'. Truth be told, he and I had us some good laughs over the reactions of some of them. And he usually managed to convince them it was all the alcohol."

In spite of Zeke's explanation, Rory felt like the unwitting star of some bizarre reality show. It bothered her to know that Mac had allowed it to continue and, by his silence, condoned it. Yet in all fairness, she had to admit that it was very Mac-like not to take such things too seriously.

"I have a question for you," Zeke said, interrupting her

thoughts. "Are you fixin' to tell everyone who comes into this house about me?"

Rory found herself momentarily speechless. "Well, I . . . I guess I would, if you'd be willing to show yourself so that they don't bundle me off to the nearest asylum."

"Well, now, you know I can't do that. In fact, you're the one who keeps warning me to keep a low profile or quick as a cottontail there'll be news people, ghost hunters and whatnot all over the damned place."

Rory realized he was right. It didn't make her feel any better about having been a bug under the marshal's microscope for all those years, but at least she understood why Mac had remained silent about his housemate. When Zeke had insisted that he didn't want to be paraded around like some dog and pony show, the truth was that he couldn't risk letting anyone else know that he existed. And now, like Mac, neither could she.

"My uncle didn't feel the need for rules," she said, trying to find her equilibrium again, "but as you know, I do." She had to try to mitigate the Big Brother aspect of having Zeke around. "I expect you to honor my guests' privacy as you do mine. That's assuming of course that you actually do honor my privacy."

Zeke's expression tightened, but he didn't rise to the bait, which told her that he was taking the matter seriously.

"You have my word," he said. "I hope that'll be enough for you."

Although there was no apparent sarcasm in his words, Rory was sure she'd find some if she dug deep enough. But she found that she had no desire to go excavating.

# Chapter 8

Hobo bounded into Rory's car, elated to be going with her wherever she was headed. She hadn't told him that he had an appointment with the vet. Determined to do right by him, she'd bought a book for first-time dog owners and had read it from cover to cover, in spite of Zeke's grousing that Hobo's trial month was far from over. Rory had shrugged off his remark as she eased on down Dog Highway to the point of no return.

In order to be sure that Hobo had no health issues of which she should be aware, she'd made an appointment with Dr. Stanley Holbrook, the veterinarian whose bill she'd seen on Brenda's kitchen table. Continuity of care was as important for canines as it was for people, according to the book that was quickly becoming her bible. All it lacked, to her way of thinking, was a chapter on the interaction between dogs and ghosts. Maybe one day she'd write a book herself on coping with the dear, and not so dear, departed.

She had one stop to make before the vet and that was at the home of Marti Sugarman. Since Tootsie might have been the most recent victim of the dognappers, and since there was no other trail worth following, Rory and Zeke had agreed that the next logical step was speaking to Marti again.

Rory didn't believe that she'd actually stolen the dog, unless she was planning to make a quick getaway to another state. If she stayed put, she'd have to keep Tootsie hidden. She certainly wouldn't be able to enter her in dog shows, which was the reason she'd coveted her to begin with.

"Not so fast," Zeke had said. "I've seen the desire for revenge cause folks to come unraveled. And logic is the first casualty of that particular emotion."

"But even if she did steal Tootsie, I doubt she was involved in stealing all the other dogs that have gone missing," Rory pointed out.

"Granted. But what if Marti killed Brenda, then let the dogs run off to make it appear like the whole thing was part of another dognapping? Could be Marti's even hopin' that when Tootsie's found, she'll be able to adopt her."

"I think if you'd met Marti, you'd agree that's a little farfetched for her."

"I may not know this Marti, but I've known me a few women capable of murder and worse," Zeke said. "Though generally over a man or a gold mine, not a dog. And oftentimes it's the ones you wouldn't expect to have the backbone for it. There was this one gal, scrawny as a toothpick, who taught school in Tucson." He shook his head as if he found his own story hard to believe. "She took a rifle nearly as big as she was and blew away the sorry fool who'd cheated on her. Didn't even seem to regret it when I hauled her off to jail. I suppose every soul has its tippin' point."

Since Rory had no basis for arguing the issue, she deferred to his experience. But she couldn't resist teasing him. "I promise to keep my eyes open for any signs of murderous tendencies on her part."

"It's not a jokin' matter, Aurora." He frowned. "I need to know that you're takin' Brenda's death seriously, even though you're not actually investigatin' it."

Rory allowed her smile to evaporate rather than endure another lecture on safety.

"Now, I don't think you should let Marti know you're comin'," he went on, willing enough to sidestep an argument. "You're bound to get more out of her if she's not expectin' you. The coyote don't telegraph his intentions to the rabbit. If he did, he'd be one mighty hungry coyote."

Rory graciously accepted the advice, although she'd already come to the same conclusion, minus the coyote. She went through the notes she'd taken down the day Tina Kovack had retained her and found the Sugarmans' address and phone number along with the information that the Sugarmans had no children, that Larry was a CPA and that Marti wasn't employed. Morning seemed like a fine time to pay her a visit.

With Hobo loaded into the car, Rory headed to Marti's house with her wish list of questions. She'd have to be careful about what she asked and how she asked it, though, since Marti could just tell her to take a hike.

Rory was stopped at a red light a quarter of a mile from Marti's house when she spotted the first flyer stapled to a telephone pole. It was a standard-size sheet of paper with a close-up of a bowless Tootsie and the promise of a thousand-dollar reward for her safe return. The phone number beneath the photo was Marti's. Rory threw the car into park, jumped out, pulled the flyer off the pole and was back in the car when the light turned green.

By the time she reached the Sugarmans' brick and vinyl–sided split-level, she'd passed a full dozen of the flyers. She folded the one she'd taken and stowed it in her purse, a secret weapon to be drawn at just the right moment.

There were no cars in the driveway, which didn't surprise her. The odds were that Larry Sugarman was busy crunching numbers at his local accounting firm and that Marti's car was still tucked into its berth in the garage. Since Marti had made it clear that Hobo wasn't welcome in her home, Rory pulled into the driveway and left the back window open enough for the dog to stick his head out and enjoy whatever smells wafted his way.

Marti answered the door as Rory was about to ring the bell for the second time. Although the temperature had dipped into the low forties overnight, Marti was wearing a brightly colored caftan that stood out from her chest like a tent that slept three, and she had green flip-flops on her feet. She was cradling a bundle of white fur in her arms that looked a lot like Tootsie, except for the smudge of black on one of his ears, no doubt the flaw that was keeping him out of the show ring.

"Ms. McCain," Marti said, looking puzzled to find Rory on her doorstep. "Was I supposed to be expecting you?" In spite of her neutral words, she sounded more annoyed than courteous.

"No, and I apologize, but I was on my way to the vet with Hobo when a question popped into my head and I thought I'd stop by to see if you could answer it for me. I would have called first, but I didn't have your number with me," she said, trying to judge by Marti's expression whether or not she was buying the routine. "I hope that's okay?" She asked timidly to cement the deal.

"I guess so," Marti said, irritation drawing her mouth into a grim line, "but I have a lot to do today."

"Shouldn't take more than a couple of minutes," Rory assured her, stepping over the threshold so that Marti had no choice but to back up and let her in. "What an adorable dog. What's her name?"

"*His* name is Falcon," Marti corrected her. "As in Maltese Falcon." Her tone dared Rory to deride the name.

"I like that," Rory said. "Very clever."

Marti's expression softened and she produced a smile.

"Thanks. My husband thinks it's silly." She closed the door behind her guest. "We can sit in the kitchen," she said, leading the way up a half flight of stairs. "Has there been any news about Tootsie?"

"I'm afraid not," Rory said. She accepted a chair at the kitchen table. "No news about Brenda's killer either," she added pointedly. If Marti caught the irony, it didn't seem to bother her.

"It's very disturbing to know that there's a killer on the loose," she muttered as if it were a personal inconvenience specifically intended to ruin her day. "I had to have our alarm system checked out and my husband had to install chains on all the doors and more security lights. It's hard to know how to protect oneself in this day and age." Winded from her little speech, she sank into the chair next to Rory and released her grip on Falcon. The dog curled into a circle in her substantial lap, his dark eyes focused on Rory as if sizing her up.

"He's adorable," Rory said, holding her hand out to him. Falcon obliged her by licking the tips of her fingers. "Look, how sweet." She knew she was laying it on a bit thick, but she needed to slide in under Marti's radar and the only easy way appeared to be through Falcon.

"Oh, he's a love with people," she said like a mother extolling the virtues of her child. "It's other male dogs he doesn't like, Hobo in particular. Like I told you. So Brenda and I just keep them . . . kept them apart." She said the last with a heavy sigh. "It still hasn't sunk in that she's gone."

Showtime. "That sort of brings me to why I'm here," Rory said. "You mentioned how close you and Brenda were, but from what I've been hearing, you two had a falling-out over Tootsie and hadn't spoken in a couple of years."

"Gossips and busybodies," Marti said, a nervous warble stitched through her words. "People should mind their own business." Her eyes left Rory for a moment and wandered to the laundry room that was just off the kitchen.

Rory followed her gaze, but all she could see there was a

washing machine and a dryer with a row of white cabinets above them. "So you're saying it's not true?"

"No, it's true," she admitted lamely, focusing her attention on Falcon. "I was just afraid if I told the police that, I'd wind up being a suspect. But Brenda *did* call here that morning, the morning of the day she was, you know . . . killed, and asked me to come over. She acted nice on the phone, like she wanted to be friends again."

"Here's what I don't get," Rory said, aiming for the casual curiosity of a friend, "if you were so angry with Brenda that you didn't speak to her for two years, why did you run right over there the minute she snapped her fingers?"

"I wasn't going to at first," Marti replied, absently petting Falcon with such a heavy hand that he issued a little growl of displeasure and readjusted his position. Marti didn't appear to notice, which Rory thought was strange given how much she doted on the dog.

"In fact, I almost hung up on her," Marti went on, "but then I thought of all the good times we'd had together and how much I missed her in my life. The worst part is that I'll never know if that's why she called."

"Well, look at the bright side," Rory said cheerfully, "with Brenda gone, if Tootsie shows up, you may be able to adopt her."

Marti bristled with indignation. "That never even occurred to me."

Rory pulled the the missing-dog flyer out of her purse and held it out to her. "Are you sure it never occurred to you?" She knew she was risking a quick dismissal from the Sugarman residence, but she couldn't forgo the opportunity to shake things up a bit.

Marti's mouth opened, closed and opened again as if her words were caught in her throat like a big wad of phlegm. "I couldn't help myself," she said finally, her broad shoulders slumping and tears welling up in her eyes. "It's bad enough if Tootsie was stolen, but I just can't sleep imagining the poor baby might be out there somewhere, hungry and frightened and alone. I thought maybe the reward would get people out looking for her."

Rory had to give her credit. She was either telling the truth or doing a damn good job of ad-libbing. "How did you happen to have a picture of Tootsie?" she pursued.

Marti shook her head. "That's really Falcon. My husband just airbrushed away his black marking in Photoshop. Other than that they're pretty much identical."

"One more thing, if you don't mind?" Rory didn't wait to see if she did. "I know you were hoping that Brenda called to put an end to your little cold war, but you couldn't be sure about that. If I'd been in your place, I would have been wracking my brain trying to figure out what else she might have wanted to talk to me about after all this time."

"Well, I did." Marti bobbed her head, clearly eager to grab on to this bit of common ground.

Rory leaned in closer to her like a sympathetic confidant and whispered, "So what else could it have been?" She realized instantly that she'd overplayed it.

Marti stiffened and squirmed in her seat, awakening Falcon, who'd started to doze off. "I really don't want to talk about it anymore," she said plaintively. Her eyes flitted to the laundry room again.

Rory started to wonder who or what might be hidden in there.

"Would you excuse me for a minute?" Marti asked, already out of her seat and flip-flopping across the tile to the adjacent room, a groggy Falcon tucked under one arm.

"Okay, sure." Without taking her eyes off Marti, Rory unzipped her purse and slid her hand inside to grab the hilt of her Walther PPK. Zeke's warning may have been more on-target than he knew.

She watched Marti open the cabinet over the dryer and pull out a bottle of detergent, another of bleach, a couple of smaller items Rory couldn't identify and finally a narrow box in a yellow wrapper. Without bothering to put anything away, she toddled back into the kitchen with the box.

Rory let go of the gun and withdrew her hand from her purse as Marti opened the box and offered her a Mallomar. "Have one," she said around a mouthful of marshmallow cookie. "They've been my favorite since I was a kid."

Stifling a laugh, Rory politely declined.

Marti plopped down in her chair again. "You won't tell anyone, will you?" she pleaded, as she withdrew another cookie from the box and tried to get it to her mouth before Falcon could snag it. "Especially my husband. We have a deal. If I lose weight, he's going to take me on a second honeymoon to Hawaii. I've always wanted to go to Hawaii."

"I'm as discreet as a priest," Rory assured her, choosing not to point out that Marti could sneak all the contraband she wanted, but unless her husband was blind, he was going to notice that she wasn't getting any thinner.

She glanced at her watch and realized that if she didn't leave soon, Hobo would miss his appointment with the vet. And since it was unlikely that Marti was going to be any more forthcoming for the present, there was no reason to stay. Rory was about to thank her for her hospitality, when a fusillade of ferocious barking erupted outside.

From where she was seated, Marti could see out the window that overlooked the driveway. The color drained out of her face, giving Rory a flashback to the moment in Brenda's kitchen when the big woman had nearly gone down for the count.

"It's Larry," Marti rasped, grabbing the box and Falcon and hurrying back into the laundry room. She threw the box into the cabinet, followed by the laundry products, and fell back into her seat as the front door opened.

"Hey, Mart, do we have company?" a voice that was presumably Larry's called out from the entryway.

"Up here," she answered him, licking telltale chocolate off her fingers.

A moment later Larry appeared at the top of the stairs, Marti's very own Jack Sprat, wearing khaki pants and a yellow dress shirt open at the neck. He had a long face that was accentuated by a receding hairline and blue eyes caught up in the fine lines of one who enjoys laughing.

"I forgot you were coming home before the Bay Shore meeting," Marti said, setting a wriggling Falcon on the floor. The dog headed toward Larry, his tail wagging so hard it was difficult for him to walk a straight line. When he was within arm's length of his master, he flipped onto his back. Larry bent down to administer the expected tummy rubs while Marti took care of the introductions.

"I see you wound up with Hobo." Larry grinned as he stood again to offer Rory a handshake. "I haven't seen him in . . . what is it, Mart . . . more than two years now?"

"Something like that," she murmured.

"I guess after all that time he didn't recognize me."

"Yeah, sorry about the greeting," Rory said, "dogs can be so territorial when they're in a car." Another bit of wisdom gleaned from the dog bible. "I was just about to get going, but it was nice to meet you."

Purse in hand, she thanked Marti for taking the time to speak to her and promised to keep her posted if there was any news about Tootsie. There was no point in burning a bridge she might need to cross again one day.

# Chapter 9

Dr. Holbrook was running late. In a medical office, there would have been irritation, grumbling and sour expressions from those languishing in the waiting room. In a veterinarian's office it was barely controlled bedlam. There were too many dogs and cats and too little space to keep them peacefully separated. And more patients were arriving by the minute. The receptionist suggested that the newcomers wait in their cars; they'd be notified when it was their turn. No one seemed to think that was a good idea. Maybe they were worried they'd be forgotten.

There was every manner of canine behavior from sniffing to snapping and playing to dominating, a general whirlwind of activity to the continuous tune of the owners' apologizing to one another. People with cats kept their carriers in their arms or tucked under the wooden benches behind the barrier of their legs. By the time Hobo's name was called, Rory's hands were red and aching from the effort of keeping him on a short leash, and she was beginning to think that a dog the size of a Maltese definitely had its advantages.

They were shown into a tiny exam room with green linoleum floors and a small counter/sink combo with cabinets below it. The centerpiece of the room was a stainless steel table that had acquired a thick patina of scratch marks over the years. Rory sat down on the one stool in the room and tried unsuccessfully to encourage Hobo to lie down beside her. He should have been exhausted from all the excitement in the waiting room, but there appeared to be too many mysterious and alluring smells that required his attention.

After another fifteen minutes Rory was as antsy as her dog. She walked around the room reading Dr. Holbrook's diplomas and examining the large diagrams of the canine and feline anatomy that constituted the only artwork on the walls. The girl who had shown her into the room had left Hobo's file on top of the counter. Rory decided that if she was going to be paying Hobo's bill, she'd earned the right to read his file. Flipping through it she could see that he'd led something of a storied life in his five years on the planet. He'd broken his leg, had his nose dive-bombed by wasps, snacked on a small lightbulb, necessitating surgery, and hosted a flea circus. Dr. Holbrook's notes showed a flair for the creative. When she went to put the file down again, she noticed that it had been sitting on top of a yellow legal pad. The top page bore a handwritten list of surnames, followed by what appeared to be pets' names, then a "T" or an "M" and a phone number. About a third of the names had check marks next to them.

Rory was looking to see if she recognized any of the people on the list when she heard the slap of leather soles approaching the room. She quickly set Hobo's file back down on top of the legal pad. A moment later the door opened and a man walked in wearing a white coat with "Stanley Holbrook, DVM" embroidered in blue on the pocket.

Holbrook was short with broad shoulders and a flat stomach that he advertised by leaving his white coat open and
wearing a polo shirt tucked snugly into his trousers. A thick
crown of brown hair fell onto his forehead, giving him a
boyish look completely at odds with his graying temples and
eyebrows. He held himself ramrod straight as if trying to
harvest every last millimeter of his height. He flashed Rory
a broad smile, his teeth so white they looked a little blue in
the fluorescent light.

"Hobo, my man," he said, bending down and holding
out his hand to the dog. "Give me five."

Hobo offered him a wary wave of his tail instead.

Holbrook rose and introduced himself to Rory, who'd
reached the point where she wouldn't have wagged her tail
even if she'd had one.

"Sorry about the delay," he said, reading her mood and
ratcheting the smile down a few degrees out of respect for
the trials and tribulations of her extended stay in the waiting room. "We've had a crazy morning. Two car accidents,
emergency surgeries, hysterical owners—but I'm glad to
report that everyone survived. Not always the case when
dog meets car." As soon as he picked up Hobo's file, he
saw the pad beneath it and flipped it upside down without
missing a beat, increasing Rory's interest in it tenfold and
then some.

"Anyone who takes in an orphaned mutt is okay in my
book," he said, leafing through Hobo's history.

Rory wondered if being "okay in his book" might buy
her less of a wait the next time she had to bring the dog in.

"It's terrible what happened to Brenda," he said. "Such
a nice woman. I took care of her dogs for more years than
I can remember." Although he was saying all the right
things, Rory had the uncomfortable sense that there was
no substance behind his words, no emotional component.
She told herself he was just maintaining a clinical distance

from his patients in order to take proper care of them and the families who loved them. Yet the best doctors she'd ever come across didn't completely shut the door to their emotions. Holbrook seemed to have bought into the old theory with every nickel to his name.

"A lot of people think she was killed by someone who came to steal her Maltese," Rory said. She'd finish analyzing him later. Right now she wanted to hear his thoughts on the dognappings. He owed her that much, after all the time she'd spent in his waiting room.

"It wouldn't surprise me," he said, closing the folder and looking up. "A number of my clients have had dogs stolen recently. It's gotten the whole dog community paranoid." He pressed what looked like an intercom button on the wall and pulled on a pair of latex gloves from a dispenser on the counter.

"Being in the dog business, do you have any theories about who might be behind it?"

Holbrook's eyebrows arched up to meet the tumble of hair on his forehead as if this was the first time anyone had put the question to him. "It's got to be some kind of 'steal to order' ring. I doubt it's just someone stocking up on dogs in case there's a sudden shortage." Pleased with his own humor, he flashed her another dazzling smile. "But you don't have to worry about old Hobo here—mutts aren't worth stealing."

Before she could object to the way he'd phrased the remark, the door to the exam room opened and a boy walked in. He was no more than eighteen, tall and reed thin with a prominent Adam's apple. His shoulders were rolled forward, making his narrow chest appear as if someone had scooped out a large portion of it.

Given his stature, Rory was amazed when he picked Hobo up as if he were a five-pound sack of potatoes and set him down on the steel table. Hobo didn't seem at all happy about his new location. His nails skittered across the slippery surface as he tried to dig in and find traction.

"Ms. McCain," Holbrook said, "this is my assistant Zach."

Zach bobbed his head in greeting, while he kept one arm securely around Hobo's middle to prevent him from taking a dive.

As the exam proceeded, it was clear that Zach knew his role. He moved from one side of Hobo to the other, keeping out of the vet's way as he checked the dog's heart, lungs, eyes, abdomen and every available orifice. It was like watching a well-rehearsed dance team.

Ten minutes later Hobo was given a clean bill of health. Then Zach plucked him up and deposited him back on the floor much like the hook that grabs a stuffed animal and sends it down the chute to a waiting child.

"Okay, boy, you're good to go." Holbrook gave him a quick scratch around the ears. "I don't have to see him again until spring," he said, handing Rory a form to take to the front desk.

Seventy-five dollars later, she opened the car door and Hobo leaped inside, as joyful as any child to be leaving the doctor's office.

Driving home, Rory couldn't stop thinking about the list under Hobo's folder and what it might represent. She came up with a host of benign possibilities, none of which explained why Holbrook didn't want her to see it.

# 1878

## The Arizona Territory

Marshal Ezekiel Drummond was up before the sun. He'd spent an uncomfortable night bedded down near the stall in which his horse was stabled. The only thing between his body and the hard-packed earth was the small pile of hay he'd gathered from the corners of the smithy. He was not unaccustomed to sleeping on the ground, but although he ached with fatigue, his thoughts refused to be stilled. Trask was out there somewhere, putting more miles between them with every passing minute.

Since he'd paid the blacksmith in advance, there was no need for Drummond to wait until the man arose to start his workday. After seeing to oats and water for his horse, he saddled the chestnut and led him outside. The horse moved with a spring to his step and a brightness to his eye that bespoke his gratitude for the sorely needed rest.

To the east the sky was pinking up, the sun peeking over the lip of the horizon like an impatient child waiting to be discovered in a game of hide-and-seek. Drummond swung into the saddle wondering where a man might find some breakfast in this town. Although his saddlebags were packed with hardtack and pemmican, along with some peaches and tomatoes in airtights, such provisions would best be saved for times when there was no other source of food.

As the chestnut picked his way down the dark, rutted street, Goose Flats' residents began to stir. Two men came out of the saloon and crossed the street to a building at the other end of town. From his position, Drummond couldn't quite make out the sign over the door, but an establishment open for business this early in the day was most likely to be a restaurant or what passed for one in these parts. He headed that way, and before he'd dismounted, he was joined by several other men who'd come by horse from the direction of the prospectors' camp and the Tombstone mine. The men gave him a nod of the head, ample greeting for a stranger in a mining town where the population changed by the hour. Drummond dipped his head in return.

As he tethered the chestnut to the hitching post, he looked up at the sign, the unexpected words bringing a smile to his lips. "Big Bertha's Buns" was a ramshackle structure with walls that seemed to be leaning into one another for support. Inside, an enthusiastic fire crackling in the hearth managed to impart a homey feel to the room. Half the tables were already filled with men forking eggs, ham and pancakes into their mouths.

The only female Drummond saw in the restaurant had to be Big Bertha herself. She was dressed in a homespun skirt that resembled a gunnysack and a blouse grayed from dozens of washings and embellished with a palette of food stains. Her brown hair was pulled back into a knot from which a thin curtain of wispy ends had pulled free to frame her full, rosy cheeks. Beads of perspiration danced across her forehead and skipped down her temples as she squeezed between the tables holding plates of steaming food aloft to clear the heads of her patrons.

"Don't be shy," she said, catching the marshal's eye. "Find yourself a seat anywhere and I'll fetch you some coffee soon as I set these down."

Drummond took a seat at a narrow, empty table near the fire in the hope that no one would join him. He preferred to eat alone, quickly and without conversation, and be on his way, although he didn't actually know which way that was. If Trask had stopped for breakfast before leaving town, maybe Bertha had seen which way he'd headed.

He was still thinking that thought when a mug of coffee was placed in front of him along with a chipped plate that contained two sourdough biscuits and a large spiral bun, redolent of sugar and cinnamon and trimmed with a loop of vanilla icing. His stomach grumbled loudly.

"New in town," Bertha said, taking stock of him. "Eggs and ham work for you?"

"Sure does, ma'am," he replied. "As for the other, I'm just traveling through."

"I'll have you back on the trail quick as a wick on a fast-burning candle."

True to her word, Bertha was back with his breakfast as he was polishing off the bun. He couldn't remember ever having tasted anything quite so fine. If he didn't have a man to catch he might have asked for another, but as it was he was feeling guilty for having enjoyed such a treat when little Betsy Jensen would never eat another meal.

Drummond wiped his mouth with the back of his hand, since Bertha hadn't supplied him with any linen for that purpose. "I'm lookin' for a man by the name of Trask," he said when she came to refill his coffee mug. "Any chance you know which way he headed when he left town?"

Bertha's brows lowered over her eyes and her mouth contracted into a tight line that cinched in her round face like a tailor's thread. "So long as he was leavin', I was right happy with the situation," she said, looking at the marshal from a grim, new perspective. "I wouldn't figure the two of you for knowin' one another."

"Well, ma'am, the truth is I intend to hunt him down and bring him to justice." He wasn't sure why he'd admitted that, why in fact he'd felt the need to be less harshly judged by this woman whom he was not likely to see again.

Bertha's face relaxed. "Then I'll be pleased to tell you I heard him jawin' with one of them prospector fellas sittin' near him. Wanted to know how many days' ride to Albuquerque. Bein' of a curious nature, I looked out the door when he left and saw him headin' in that very direction. I'll be wishin' you Godspeed on your journey."

Drummond finished his coffee, and as he pushed back from the table Bertha appeared at his side holding a bundle wrapped in an old piece of checkerboard cloth. "I daresay this won't last you for too long, but it'll sure sweeten the road for a time."

The marshal didn't have to ask what was in the parcel; the aroma gave it away, making his mouth water even though his stomach was already full to brimming.

"On the house," Bertha said when he tried to pay her for the additional food. "I make more than enough on the lard heads who eat here every day."

When Drummond emerged from Bertha's his heart lay a mite lighter in his chest now that he knew where Trask was headed. In his youth he'd explored large portions of New Mexico, and he knew that a man on horseback would do best to keep to the flatlands until he reached Las Cruces, where he could replenish his supplies before turning north to Albuquerque. The marshal reached into his vest pocket, withdrew the tin star he'd hidden there before riding into Goose Flats and pinned it back on his chest. Where he was headed it would serve him better to be known as a lawman. Then he mounted the chestnut and headed east where the sun was climbing into the sky on a ladder of clouds.

# Chapter 10

"How did it go?" Zeke asked when he found Rory in the kitchen making a cup of tea. She and Hobo had been home from the vet for less than ten minutes and the dog was already snoring under the table, exhaustion having temporarily trumped any fear of the marshal's appearance.

"Well, I'm not entirely sure," she said. "I still don't think Marti's a killer, but she is one hell of a liar." She tossed the tea bag into the garbage and sat down at the table with the steaming mug, careful not to step on Hobo's paws.

"I wouldn't be surprised if she believes her own stories at this point." She blew on the surface of the tea, took a tentative sip and then set it down again. "But I did find something interesting at the vet's office."

Zeke popped into the chair across from her. "Just as I feared, you found out that Hobo here is afflicted with a deadly streak of cowardice." He was grinning, prepared for Rory's indignation. But she wasn't biting. Instead she told him about the list of names she'd found in the exam room.

"Let's see," Zeke said, his brows drawn together as if he were pondering this bit of information. "Nope. I'm pretty sure makin' lists ain't a criminal offense yet, even in these crazy times."

"Well, of course not," she said, ignoring his attempt at humor. "But as soon as Holbrook noticed that he'd left the list out there on the counter, he flipped it over so fast you'd think it was the code to our nuclear arsenal."

"Okay, I see what you're aimin' at," Zeke said, dropping the sarcasm, since teasing wasn't really a game for one. "But unless you can match those names with the dogs that were stolen, you've got a whole lot of nothin'. Even if they did match up, that's not enough evidence for an arrest. Besides, I don't see how you'd get a hold of that list again even if you had a mind to. If it is incriminatin' I suspect Holbrook'll be keepin' a closer eye on it in the future."

Short of breaking into the veterinary office and rifling through Holbrook's papers, she had to agree that there was nothing more she could do about the list for now. But the marshal didn't need to know that she wasn't ready to toss the idea into the shredder.

"I'll tell you one thing," she said, "I've never had a dog, and before our little trip to see Dr. Holbrook, I never realized just how many dogs pass through a veterinary office on any given day. If I were a thief looking for a particular kind of dog to steal, working in a place like that would be a handy job to have."

"Damn." Zeke slammed his open palm on the table, which had minimal impact, given that it didn't make any noise. Hobo slept on undisturbed. "We got to talkin' and I plumb forgot that Leah sent you that information she'd promised from the dognapping reports."

"I don't remember giving you permission to open my e-mail," Rory said, too pleased by the news to put any teeth into the remark.

"I don't remember being told it was off-limits," he

countered. "You're not fixin' to tack on more rules, are you? You've already got more than the entire federal government."

Rory didn't bother replying. Leaving the tea on the table, she headed upstairs to the computer.

When she got there Zeke was already seated in her swivel chair, the keyboard dancing like a marionette without strings. The first time he'd attempted to work the computer by fine-tuning his energy, Rory had cringed at the thought of the machine ricocheting off the walls and shattering into a million pieces. Luckily the marshal had proven to be a quick study. It had taken Rory considerably longer to get used to seeing a lawman from the Old West wading knee-deep in modern technology.

As she watched the screen, Leah's attachment appeared. "You'll be wantin' a hard copy," he said, maneuvering the mouse as well as anyone with actual hands.

The printer spat out five pages, which Rory retrieved before he could airlift them to her. As impressed as she was with Zeke's mastery of basic computer skills, there was a small knot of resentment forming in her gut. It was almost as if he'd staged a coup while she wasn't watching, and was now planning to call the shots. On a rational level she knew that wasn't true. They were partners and he was simply putting his best effort into working the case. Unfortunately her expression had already betrayed her, because Zeke vanished from her chair and took up a position near the bookshelves, arms crossed against his chest and a testy set to his mouth. It was a good thing she wasn't trying to earn a living as a poker player.

She considered apologizing, then decided against it. Where Zeke was concerned, it was often smarter to just move on rather than reopen an issue. She busied herself searching through the papers on her desk for the notes from Tina's consultation. They should have been right on top. She'd had them in her hand that very morning. Where could she have put

them? She stepped back to check the floor beneath the desk.
She found several printed sheets there, but when she retrieved
them she saw that they pertained to another case. Apparently
her filing skills were as haphazard as Uncle Mac's. Of course,
as flaws went, it wasn't a fatal one. What was really bothering
her was the certainty that if she were to ask Zeke where the
notes were, he'd pluck them from their hiding place and float
them into her hands like a master magician.

When she looked up again Zeke was gone. Maybe she
had misjudged how irritated he was. But a moment later he
was back, a smug expression on his face and her papers in
his hand.

"These what you're lookin' for?" he asked, holding
them out to her. "You left them in the kitchen when you
were checkin' the Sugarmans' address."

Rory thanked him, hoping this little triumph of his had
restored the equilibrium to their seesaw of a relationship.
She pulled out the information on the bereaved owners
Tina had given her. Under their names were those of the
veterinarians, groomers, trainers, dog parks, doggie day care
centers, doggie motels and pet stores they frequented, to
the best of her knowledge. The e-mail from Leah contained
approximately the same type of data And even though
Leah couldn't provide her with the specific addresses from
which the dogs had been stolen, she had included the towns
where they'd lived.

Since the surface of the desk that wasn't occupied by
the computer and printer was still awash in unfiled papers,
Rory took Leah's list and Tina's and made herself as comfortable as she could on the hardwood floor.

"Okay, let's see if we can find a common denominator
here," she said, making an effort to sound inclusive.

Accepting her white flag, Zeke hunkered down beside
her so that he could see the lists as well. They spent the next
few minutes trying unsuccessfully to find a link, someone

or someplace that would tie all the missing dogs together and point the investigation in the right direction.

Rory finally threw the papers down in frustration. "There's nothing here that points to one person who knew all these dogs and where they lived. Look at this. These five dogs went to the same vet, these six to the same groomer. Another six used to go to the same dog park and pet store. A lot of the dogs competed in dog shows, but not all of them did. There are all sorts of connections here, but nothing that actually narrows the search."

"I'd take bets that there's more than one thief," Zeke offered. "Two or more working together would be a whole lot more efficient if we're talkin' about fillin' specific requests."

"Thanks." Rory sighed. "I've been doing my best to ignore that possibility. I'll still be interviewing suspects long after the victims have gone on to doggie heaven."

"I think what we need here is a map," he said, "to get a better sense of what's happenin'."

Rory jumped up and went over to the bookcase for her uncle's Hagstrom atlases of Nassau and Suffolk Counties. She took her sketch pad off another shelf, opened it to a blank page, grabbed a pen off the desk and resettled herself on the floor. Using the atlas, she drew a rough outline of Long Island, along with the border between Nassau and Suffolk counties.

"Okay," Zeke said, "now write in the names of the towns that appear on those lists."

Rory was already busy doing exactly that. She added a dot for each dog stolen from a particular town. By the time she'd worked her way through the lists she had an aching back and a map that showed her at a glance where the largest concentration of thefts had occurred. Huntington Township, which included nearly twenty towns, villages and hamlets, came up the big winner. Smaller pockets of activity were scattered across Suffolk as well as in the closest regions of Nassau County.

At that moment they heard a frantic skittering sound, followed by a thump, then more skittering accompanied by a deep, breathless chuffing and the clinking of metal on metal.

"Looks like Hobo woke up and realized you were gone." Zeke chuckled, rising to his feet.

"He's got abandonment issues," Rory chided him. "You could try showing a bit more compassion. Dogs can sense these things."

Hobo reached the top of the stairs and raced for the study, homing in on Rory. He was so relieved to have found her that he didn't immediately realize Zeke was also in the room. When he did, he swerved too sharply to avoid the marshal and his right hind paw lost contact with the floor, causing him to fishtail into the marshal's leg. With a horrible sound that was somewhere between a whimper and a scream, he launched himself into the safety of Rory's arms.

After the collision, Zeke's image wavered and began to disintegrate, bits and pieces of it flying off in all directions like a dandelion seed-head scattered by the wind. Then he vanished altogether. It was several minutes before he reappeared, looking more than a little disgruntled. "Lack of compassion, huh? And here I've been thinkin' it's my lack of a body that was makin' the poor thing uncomfortable."

"Are you okay?" Rory asked to be polite, although she couldn't imagine how anything could be too wrong considering he was already dead.

"Nothin' that some rechargin' can't fix. But never mind about that. I've been meanin' to ask you about that clinkin' noise I hear whenever this fool dog is racin' around."

"You mean the tags on his collar?" She brushed Hobo's fur aside so that Zeke could see them. "One is an ID tag you can buy in any pet store. The other one you get when you register your dog with town hall."

"Why would you want to register a dog?"

"It's the law."

"You ain't serious."

"They want to be sure that all the dogs are up-to-date on their shots, plus the yearly registration fees pump up the town coffers."

"Just in this town?"

Rory shook her head. "Pretty much everywhere."

"Then every dog in the county is registered in one town hall or another."

"I can see where you're going with this," Rory said, shaking her head, "but it would mean that clerks from several towns were involved in the scam."

"Or someone found a way to axe their computers."

"Hack their computers." She sighed. "And that's very helpful. Now you've widened the search area to the whole island, conservatively speaking."

Zeke raked his fingers through his hair. "The way I see it, whether the needle's in a haystack or someplace else, it's still the same needle and sooner or later, if you keep at it, you're bound to find it. I'd start off at the local town hall and see if anyone's *hacked* their system recently," he said, careful to use the correct word. "Unless you've got yourself a better idea."

Rory assured him that she didn't. "And after you rest up from today's little fender bender," she added, "you can make yourself useful by looking up websites that sell dogs. Especially sites that advertise lower prices, bargains, discounts, any of those buzzwords. There's a good chance that's how they're luring customers, since they don't have the overhead of breeders or stores. Maybe we'll get lucky."

" 'Fender bender,' 'buzzwords'—sometimes it don't even sound like you're speakin' English," Zeke grumbled.

Rory provided a brief definition of the phrases, for which he thanked her with a courtly dip of his head. Although the marshal hadn't chosen to let go of the world, the world itself had gone on and left him behind. She couldn't even fathom how estranged he must feel from everyone and everything he'd ever known. She vowed to be more patient with him, a tall order at the best of times, and she made a mental note to pick up a dictionary of modern idioms and slang the next time she was out.

# Chapter 11

Rory couldn't bring herself to push back the covers and leave the warmth of the bed. Although it was still early October, the temperature had taken a nosedive overnight, producing the first official frost of the season. Even so, with the comforter pulled up to her chin, she should have been warm enough. Yet if she moved an inch away from the warm depression her body had made in the mattress, a chill flashed through her. Hobo, who was sleeping curled into the space behind her bent knees, didn't seem to be bothered by the cold, but then he had the advantage of a permanent fur coat.

Rory knew she had no good options. Staying where she was and hibernating until spring would never work. Sooner or later she was going to need food and water and a trip to the bathroom. She was also pretty sure her clients were expecting some results from the retainers they'd paid her. And this particular morning she had an early appointment to meet with the Huntington town clerk, Deirdre Lopez, whose department handled dog registration among a host of other matters. There was nothing to do but leave the cozy cocoon of her bed and check the heating system. She didn't recall ever feeling this cold when she'd visited Mac in the winter, which probably meant that something wasn't functioning properly. Damn.

She gave herself a pep talk. "Your bathrobe's right inside the closet. It's only a few steps away. You can grab it and get it on in less than a minute. Less than half a minute. Ten seconds if you're really fast." After a quick countdown, she threw back the quilt and sprang out of bed. The hardwood was cold beneath her bare feet, making her wish she'd installed thick pile carpeting.

She threw the flannel robe around herself and punched her arms through the sleeves. After some rummaging among her shoes, she located her warmest slippers and slid them on. Definitely better.

Hobo had lifted his sleepy head to see what all the commotion was about. Satisfied that nothing required his attention, he wriggled into the warm spot where she had been and went right back to sleep.

Rory envied him.

She shuffled over to the baseboard heaters. In the best of all possible worlds, she would have felt lovely warm air emanating from them, but in her world they were cold to the touch. Clearly not a good sign.

With the reward of a hot mug of coffee for motivation, she trooped down the stairs to the main floor, where it was somehow even colder. She set the coffee to brewing and then made her way down the narrow wooden steps into the basement. She knew that one of the owners long before Mac had converted the system to oil heat, and she remembered having recently received an oil delivery. Beyond that, she was totally out of her element. She walked around the oil storage tank and the furnace, having no idea what she was looking for or even how they functioned. She felt as clueless as a used car buyer kicking tires.

When she returned to the kitchen, she was heartened by the aroma of coffee filling the room. She pulled her address book out of the drawer where she kept miscellaneous papers and items she didn't need but thought she might find a use for one day. The phone number for Atlas Oil was in her list of emergency numbers on the first page of the book.

After a frustrating five minutes of selecting menu options, she was told by a computerized voice that a serviceman would be at her house sometime after three o'clock. She was instructed to press 1 if that was acceptable. Rory dutifully pressed 1. She'd work her day around it. No way was she going to waste another minute listening to a computer telling her what to do. It was bad enough that she lived with a ghost who was usually trying to do the same thing.

She was sitting at the kitchen table, huddled in her bathrobe, her hands wrapped around her second cup of coffee for the warmth, when the lights flickered. She glanced around the room expecting Zeke to appear, but nothing happened. Then she noticed that the air near the center island was strangely warped, distorting objects seen through it as if it were an invisible fun house mirror.

"Marshal?" she said, a flutter of apprehension in her tone. She didn't know exactly what was happening, but this wasn't starting out like any of Zeke's normal appearances. She shook her head, amazed with herself. When had living with a ghost become so ordinary to her that she could consider the word "normal" in the same thought?

"What's goin' . . . there?" Zeke's voice skipped and crackled like a bad cell phone connection.

Rory could barely make out what he was saying.

"Some . . . not right," he persisted.

The frigid temperature in the house was the only problem she was aware of, but that was more than enough at eight o'clock in the morning. If there was anything else, she didn't want to know about it just yet.

"Heat's not working," she shouted, as if volume alone could fix their communication problem.

"That . . . it," he said, ". . . need to . . . it fixed."

"There's a guy coming later. That's the best I can do." After a moment's thought she added, "Just try not to scare him away."

Either the cold was acting like an additional barrier or he specifically needed a certain level of heat for the process to work. So, Rory thought with a little smile, every cloud does have its silver lining.

She found the office of the town clerk on the main floor of Huntington Town Hall, a three-story brick building that overlooked Main Street. She only had to wait five minutes while Deirdre Lopez finished up a meeting with one of the women who worked in her department. When her secretary let her know that Rory had arrived, she left her desk to greet Rory at the door. She was slim and stylish in a navy suit, matching pumps and elegant touches of gold jewelry. Her short blond hair was layered, each strand lacquered firmly in place. She reminded Rory of a throwback to a more formal time when women didn't wear pants to work and wouldn't dream of going without stockings. Like most elected officials she had the wide smile and glad-handing down pat.

Deirdre offered her a seat and, once she was settled in it, went back to her own well-worn leather chair. The desk between them was large, functional and nondescript, likely one of many that had been purchased in bulk by the town. It struck Rory that the top of the desk was remarkably neat for someone with such a diverse range of responsibilities and more than a dozen people working under her. Rory couldn't help but admire her organizational skills. When they were handing out the genes for that, she and Mac must have skipped out for ice cream sodas.

"So, Ms. McCain, I understand that you're investigating what may be the theft of several dogs in Huntington," Deirdre said with the perfect mixture of interest and concern.

Rory gave her a quick rundown of the situation and the reason for her visit.

Deirdre's brows lowered over her eyes as she listened. "I had nò idea the problem had become that widespread and I have to thank you for bringing it to mỳ attention, since no one else has seen fit to do so." Her words were clipped with a touch of outrage and Rory had the distinct impression that someone was going to be hearing about the omission before the day was out.

"In any case," Deirdre went on pleasantly, her anger tucked back into its cubbyhole for the moment, "I'm happy to tell you that there haven't been any attempts to hack into the computer system in this department during my tenure, which is going into its seventh year."

A little heavy on the preening. Apparently Deirdre also had the double-jointed gene essential in someone who liked to pat herself on the back. Rory managed to keep her poker face even as these thoughts were flashing through her mind. She wasn't without a few talents herself.

"If you'd like, I can certainly get in touch with my predecessor to find out if she experienced any problems of that nature."

Rory assured her that wouldn't be necessary. Data from more than seven years ago would hardly be worthwhile anymore, since the dogs in question would at best be senior citizens by now.

"I happen to maintain a casual friendship with several of the other town clerks on the island," Deirdre went on, highlighting her social status. "If you'd like, I can touch base with them, find out if they've had any computer breaches and let them know about your investigation."

"Thank you, I'd appreciate that." Rory fished a business card out of her handbag and passed it across the desk to her. Could Zeke's outlandish theory be right? Was a cabal of town clerks involved in the thefts? No, she still couldn't bring herself to buy that. But whether she accepted the offer of help or not, she had no doubt that Deirdre would soon be giving her friends a heads-up about this reopened investigation. Not that it mattered. Rory had harbored no expectations of keeping her visit a secret.

"Is there anything else I can do for you?" Deirdre edged forward in her seat, ready to spring into action the moment her visitor left.

"You seem to run a tight ship here," Rory acknowledged, rising from her chair, "so I assume you have no reservations about the integrity of anyone in your department, is that right?"

"They wouldn't last a day if I did," Deirdre said with a little toss of her head that would have been more effective if her hair had been longer and not glued in place. She stood and came around from her side of the desk to shake Rory's hand again. "And you can rest assured that I'll be keeping an even more careful eye on every one of my people from now on."

Rory thanked her and left the office feeling a bit sorry for the additional scrutiny she'd unleashed on Deirdre's unsuspecting staff.

On her way to town hall, Rory had driven past the old Burying Ground, as she had countless times before. When she was in elementary school her third grade class had even made a trip there as part of a history lesson, since the cemetery dated from 1670 and contained the graves of more than forty soldiers of the Revolutionary War. These were the only facts lodged permanently in her head from that excursion, which was hardly surprising. Old tombstones have a limited appeal for the young. However, on this day as she drove by she remembered the article she'd read about Zeke's death and she was struck by the thought that this was where he'd been laid to rest so many years ago.

When she left the meeting with Deirdre Lopez it wasn't yet ten o'clock. She didn't have to be home for the repairman for hours. There was plenty of time to stop and pay her respects to the marshal's mortal remains. She parked in the lot adjacent to the cemetery and walked around to the small museum at the entrance gate, where she asked how she would go about finding a particular grave. The woman behind the desk explained that while there were records of where family plots were located there was no easy way to find a solitary grave. She was sorry she couldn't be more helpful. Rory thanked her, determined to give it a try anyway.

The cemetery sprawled across a hill that was just steep enough to make her immediately sorry that she wasn't wearing sneakers. The leather soles of her loafers were slip-sliding on the grass and weeds as she made her way up the slope. She passed tombstones that were only inches tall, as if the earth had been slowly devouring them. Many others were clean slates, the etching on them obliterated by time and weather so that not even a single letter or number remained visible to the naked eye.

After an hour and a half of searching, Rory was ready to give up. What had she really hoped to accomplish by seeing his grave anyway? When she'd embarked on her impromptu search she'd had no particular goal beyond just finding it. A few words set in stone by people who hadn't even known the marshal would hardly be enlightening.

She'd started to pick her way back down the hill, taking care not to trip over the smaller headstones, when her foot slid out from under her. Arms flailing, she struggled to regain her balance, fully aware that she looked like a circus clown performing on a tightrope. In spite of her efforts, gravity won and she tumbled forward, her shoulder slamming into one of the larger tombstones. She got to her feet quickly and glanced around her. Well, at least no one had been there to witness her fall. She brushed the worst of the dirt and grass off her pants and was rubbing her sore shoulder when she thought she saw the word "Marshal" on the stone marker beside her. She dropped to her knees in the long grass in front of it, the pain forgotten.

The etching had grown shallow, the words fading like invisible ink from paper. But after studying it from several angles, Rory was certain that she'd found Zeke's headstone. If she'd fallen a few feet to the right, she would literally have stumbled upon it. This was one of those moments that the faithful accepted with equanimity and gratitude, and that the questioners, among whom Rory generally counted herself, tried to explain away with logic. For the moment logic abandoned her.

She rummaged through her pocketbook until she found a pen and an old grocery list she could write on and she jotted down the inscription.

MARSHAL EZEKIEL DRUMMOND
1840–1878
DIED PROTECTING ONE OF OURS

She sank back on her heels, surprised to find her vision blurred with tears. What was all this emotion about? It wasn't as if she'd just learned of his death. And yet somehow it was. Up until now the Ezekiel Drummond she lived with had just been an enigmatic and often irascible presence. But this tablet of carved stone attested to the fact that he'd once been a flesh-and-blood man. A man who'd died at too young an age, trying to save the life of a girl he'd probably never met. He was buried here, thousands of miles from his home and the only life he'd known. Chances were no one had ever come to visit his grave before today. She should be working harder to solve the mystery of his death. She was really all he had.

Rory scrubbed the tears from her cheeks and chastised herself. She could either sit there getting all maudlin over Zeke's death, which was clearly pointless, or she could go home and actually spend some time with him. How many people ever had that option?

# Chapter 12

When Rory turned onto her block she found a van with the Atlas Oil name and logo parked at the curb in front of her house. The serviceman was hours early. It was a good thing she'd come home when she did, or he might have gone on to the next customer and left her to shiver through another night without heat. At the very least, he should have called to find out if she'd be home. As soon as she pulled into the driveway the man emerged from his van and picked up a toolbox and bucket he'd left sitting outside the van's door. He had on charcoal gray coveralls that were a good match for any soot, grease and oil he worked around. Clever of the company. That way their representatives always looked clean and presentable, even at the end of a long shift mucking around in peoples' basements.

Rory stepped out of her car as he was coming abreast of it. "Hi. I hope you weren't waiting too long. Is it Joe?" she asked, reading the name sown on his pocket.

"Sure is," he said. He glanced down at the equipment

he was holding, as if trying to decide if he should put something down so that he could shake her hand. But the moment passed before he could make up his mind.

"We must have gotten our signals crossed," she said. "I was under the impression you'd be here at three."

"Yeah, some of the emergencies before you turned out to be simple fixes."

"You're so early I could easily have missed you," she said more pointedly as she led the way up to the front door.

"I tried to reach you," Joe said affably. "Left a message on your house phone, then on your cell."

Rory was about to tell him that wasn't possible, since her cell phone hadn't rung, when she realized that she'd changed it from ring to vibrate before her meeting with Deirdre Lopez and never switched it back. She shouldn't have been so quick to indict him.

"I guess it was a case of bad timing," she said in a more cheerful, "these things happen" tone of voice. "I was in town hall on business and I had to turn the ringer off on my cell. I'm really grateful that you were kind enough to wait for me."

"Not a problem," Joe assured her. "Gave me time to catch up on my paperwork."

Rory was glad he wasn't the type to hold a grudge. She unlocked the door and pushed it open, but before she could step inside, she was knocked off her feet by ninety pounds of fur and love barreling full tilt into her. Joe's broad chest saved her from crashing to the porch floor. She fell backward against him, throwing him off balance in the process. Although he wasn't prepared for the sudden onslaught, after a moment of teetering uncertainty, he managed to stay upright, saving them both from landing in a heap.

Hobo was joyful and unrepentant, bouncing around them as if he had pogo sticks for legs, lapping at whatever parts of them he could reach. Between stern but ineffective commands to sit and stay, Rory apologized to Joe for the dog's behavior. She explained that she'd recently rescued him, which was true as far as it went. She didn't bother to add that the dog was having a hard time acclimating because of the ghost in her house. Even though the cold had probably kept Zeke from making an actual appearance while she was gone this time, Hobo seemed able to sense him in the ether. For Hobo, every time Rory returned home it was as if she were once again rescuing him.

Joe was taking the dog's assault in stride, laughing and giving him a good rubdown. "Hobo and I are old friends," he said, shooing him back into the house.

Rory followed them inside, completely baffled.

"Soon as I saw the address and the name McCain on the work order I knew it had to be you," he said.

That bit of information didn't help Rory's confusion any. "We've met?"

"Not directly." Joe grinned. "But I knew Mac. Your uncle, right?"

"Yes, but I still . . ." Her voice trailed off as she tried to put the pieces together. Even if she'd forgotten that she knew him, which wasn't likely, it didn't explain how he knew Hobo.

"Okay." He laughed. "I won't keep you in the dark. We've never actually met, so your memory isn't failing you. But Hobo and I have known each other ever since Brenda got him."

While that didn't answer all of her questions, it definitely narrowed the field. Joe had known Brenda and Mac. That was fine as far as it went, but there was still some missing connection.

"My last name's Kovack."

It was Rory's turn to laugh. She never would have figured him for Tina's husband. Not that they were a particularly strange pairing. Joe was about Tina's height, though she might have had an inch or two on him. He had dark blond hair, receding at the temples like the sea at low tide, and a face that was ordinary except for wide, blue-green eyes with thick lashes that had probably wowed all the girls back in high school.

"I guess since Tina was so involved with dogs, I assumed that her husband worked in the family business too," Rory explained, hoping that he wouldn't take her laughter the wrong way.

Luckily Joe didn't seem to offend easily. "Hey"—he shrugged—"if we were together twenty-four/seven what would we talk about over dinner? Now, you oughta make yourself a cup of something hot, while I see about getting this place toasty warm for you."

Forty minutes later Joe came back up the stairs. "I've got her chugging along fine now," he said, "just needed a good cleaning and a little sweet talk." He gave her a good-natured wink that didn't hold a hint of flirtation.

Rory offered him coffee from the pot she'd brewed.

"Smells great, but I gotta get a move on," he said. "I'm real glad I got the chance to meet you, though. Tina's been so down in the dumps since the dogs were stolen and now with Brenda being killed—well, I've never seen her like this in all the years I've known her. Anyhow I gotta tell you, from the moment you agreed to take the case, she's been calmer. More like my old Tina girl, and you've got my thanks for that."

"I'll do my best," Rory assured him, thinking that she would have preferred not knowing that in addition to finding the dogs, she was also responsible for the state of Tina's mental health. No pressure there.

She walked outside with him to check the mailbox. Hobo waited anxiously behind the screen door. He'd already learned that when she left the main door open, she wasn't actually leaving. Still he watched her like a hawk sizing up a rabbit, ready to complain if she dared to deviate from her routine.

Rory waved good-bye to Joe, scooped the day's mail

out of the box and headed back inside. She was glancing through the envelopes on her way into the kitchen when the pendant lights over the table flickered and Zeke appeared. He was leaning against the counter, looking well rested and enormously pleased to be there.

"Thanks for tendin' to the heat," he said.

Rory sat down at the table, frowning at one of the envelopes. "You're welcome, but I didn't actually do it for you," she said distractedly.

"Now, why'd you want to go and shatter my illusions like that?" Zeke hung his head with a bereft sigh. "That's a hard heart you've got there, Aurora."

Rory clenched her teeth and managed not to react, which wasn't all that difficult since she was focused on the handwritten address that was shaky and distorted as if a three-year-old had penned it. She tore the envelope open and unfolded the piece of paper she found inside.

"How's the mutt holding up?" Zeke asked, noting that Hobo was once again snoring under the table.

"What the hell is this?" she muttered, oblivious to the marshal's question.

He was at her side in an instant, peering over her shoulder at the paper. It was a crazy quilt of letters cut from newspapers and magazines and pieced together to form the words:

**Stop the investigation or we'll stop you.**

It was the type of threat or ransom note that had been used in so many movies over the past fifty years that it was trite, even laughable, but neither Rory nor Zeke was laughing.

"That came in today's mail?" Zeke asked, popping into the chair next to her.

"I got it today," she said, picking up the envelope that she'd dropped onto the table, "but I don't think it actually *came* through the mail." She studied the plain white envelope front and back again. "There's no canceled stamp. Someone must have driven by and stuck it in my mailbox."

Damn, she wished she'd noticed that sooner, but she'd had no reason to expect such a letter. Now she'd compromised potential evidence. She pushed back from the table and went to the cabinet where she kept rolls of tin foil, plastic wrap and storage bags. She took one of the bags, placed the letter and envelope inside and sealed it shut. With any luck Reggie, CSI extraordinare and old college chum of BB's, would once again be willing to help her out.

"You'll be takin' that over to the police, then?" Zeke asked cautiously, as if he were lifting a rock to see what was hiding beneath it.

"In a manner of speaking."

"And exactly in what manner would that be?"

"I'm going to give it to Forensics."

"In other words 'on the sly'—so Leah doesn't find out."

"If I told Leah she'd feel obligated to report it and that could mean the end of my case," Rory said with the defiant lift of her chin that meant there was no room for negotiation.

"You've been threatened—you don't think the police should know?" It was clear he didn't intend to let it go.

"Up until a few months ago I *was* the police, in case you've forgotten, and I know how to take care of myself," she said, clipping her words off with a steel-edged tone that she instantly regretted. What had happened to the grand compassion and empathy she'd felt for him at his gravesite this morning? It seemed like years since then. First Joe had been waiting for her, and then she'd found the letter. Hardly a moment to catch her breath. She made herself stop and take a long, unbiased look at Zeke, and instead of seeing him only as an obstacle blocking her way, she saw the concern etched in the tight line of his jaw and in the lines around his eyes and the furrow between his brows.

"Believe me, I know what I'm doing," she said softly, shrugging off the attitude.

"I'm sure you think you do."

"I'll take Hobo with me as protection wherever I go." She smiled, determined to steer the conversation onto a less rocky path.

Zeke's face remained grim. He wasn't going to be wheedled into a better mood.

"So, based on the letter, I guess you could say we've rocked the thief's boat." Maybe if she got him thinking about the case, he'd let go of his obsession with her safety.

"That'd be helpful if it meant the thief has to be one of the few people you've already talked to, but all it likely means is that word about our investigation is spreading through the dog community like wildfire. It could have been sent by just about anyone who knows Tina hired you, then there's the vet and the people who work for him, the rest of the dog community and anyone they've talked to."

Rory could tell from the monotone quality of his voice that he was answering her by rote, his mind still hooked into their argument.

"Then we might as well add the town clerk and everyone she tells," Rory said, taking a minute to update him on her meeting with Deirdre Lopez.

"Well, when you can't see the forest for the trees, you gotta start by choppin' down some of those trees. And you can begin right off with that repairman, Joe."

"You've got to be kidding."

"The man was sittin' out there right by your mailbox and he knew you wouldn't be home for a spell. He could have slipped that envelope right in there without fear of bein' seen."

Rory shook her head in disbelief. "You're actually telling me you think Joe stole two of his own dogs?"

"His wife's dogs."

Rory rolled her eyes. "Oh, well, that makes a whole lot more sense."

"Don't you go bein' naïve, darlin'. Folks are capable of some crazy things."

Naïve? He would never have been so condescending to Mac or dared to insult him that way. "I guess you'd know about crazy," she snapped. Her temper was hurtling head-long toward the edge of the cliff with all of her good intentions strapped to its back and she'd willingly let go of the reins.

Zeke looked genuinely surprised by her sharp response. "Why are you gettin' yourself all in a dither?"

That did it. "Listen," she said, rising from the table, "I am *not* naïve and I *don't* get into dithers, whatever the hell they are."

"That would be one right there," he pointed out.

Rory stormed out of the room before she said something she couldn't take back. Death may have conferred an aura of saintliness on Zeke, but as far as she could see, it was one that stopped at the edge of his grave and had no bearing on the reality of living with him.

# Chapter 13

Rory spent a restless night punctuated by dreams in which she searched endlessly for Hobo and a few thousand of his canine chums. Although the dreams had been unnerving in the dark landscape of her mind, daylight quickly revealed them for the silly mental antics they were. Even before she opened her eyes she felt the warm pressure of Hobo's back against her own, safe and sound, his legs twitching as he chased some bugaboo of his own.

The room was delightfully warm and inviting compared to the previous day, so Rory didn't have to talk herself into leaving the bed behind. She had a lot to do, and she was eager to get started. Before falling asleep, she'd decided she wanted to find some DNA belonging to Joe Kovack. And not because Zeke had made her doubt her instincts about the man. She was looking forward to proving Zeke wrong for once, to throwing that all knowing, superior attitude of his for a loop or two. But first she was going to have to come up with a believable excuse to visit the Kovack home, since she didn't have any real progress to report on the investigation.

She was brushing her teeth when it came to her. Aunt Helene would have a sudden interest in buying a Maltese, and Rory, being the devoted niece that she was, would take her to meet Tina and see her dogs.

Helene was more than happy to oblige, even though it meant rescheduling a yoga session. Rory collected her at eleven o'clock, after reassuring her that she didn't need time to research and prep for her part. Helene hopped into the car, aglow with the excitement of her new assignment. She'd dressed in what she considered dog aficionado chic: chinos, a Ralph Lauren polo and ankle boots. Her hair was pulled back into a French twist, from which numerous strands were making their escape.

"I didn't tell your mom and dad that you asked me to help you," Helene whispered, even though Rory was the only one in the car. "I didn't want to hurt anyone's feelings or anything."

"It's not a secret," Rory said. "And I doubt they'd be insulted. In fact, I think my dad would be thrilled to know that he was left out this time."

Satisfied that she'd done her duty with regard to family unity, Helene spent the rest of the trip chattering away about dogs in general and about the specific questions she'd thought up to buy Rory the time she needed.

Tina was waiting to show Rory and her potential new customer around. She, Joe and their two adolescent boys lived in a sprawling yellow ranch house with gleaming white shutters and trim, surrounded by a white picket fence, all in vinyl. Like Mac, Rory had always preferred the look of wood, but now that she was the home owner, she had to admit there was something to be said for no paint, easy maintenance. Obviously the Kovacks had come to the same conclusion. Keeping up appearances was important when you were trying to entice people to buy expensive dogs from you.

There was a green sign with gold letters posted at the entrance to their driveway that read "Kovack Farms," and in smaller lettering, "Breeders of Prize-Winning Maltese." Rory wondered how many prizes your dogs had to win in order to make such a claim and whether it was considered false advertising if you embellished on the truth.

Tina greeted them at the front door and introduced them to the three well-mannered Maltese who shared the house with the family. Rory and Helene knelt down to pet them a brief hello. Then Tina led the women through the beautifully appointed house into a gourmet kitchen with high-end finishes on every surface and appliances that would have dazzled any chef. As they walked, Tina babbled on about whatever popped into her mind, barely taking time to breathe. Rory wondered how Joe could stand it. Maybe it became a form of white noise that he was able to ignore. Like her father and a lot of other men he'd probably even perfected the benign "smile and nod" technique that made his wife think he was listening.

The kitchen opened into a large family room with custom bookcases built around a media center that showcased a seventy-inch flat-screen TV.

"What a beautiful room," Rory remarked, thinking that she might like to decorate her living room this way when she could afford it.

"And look at that TV," Helene gasped. "It's practically the size of a movie theater screen."

"I surprised Joe with it on his last birthday." Tina smiled. "You should have seen his face. You could have knocked him over with a feather, as my mother used to say."

"Lucky guy," Helene said, sounding sincerely as if she wished she had a Tina in her life.

"Believe me," Tina replied, "I'm just as lucky. He's a great husband."

Tina ushered them through French doors out to a large backyard that was shaded by a canopy of old maples. The

kennels were inside a yellow and white mini version of
the main house, heated, air-conditioned and populated by
another nine Maltese. She pointed out one of the dogs who
was basking in the sun. "That's Clementine—she'll be
whelping any day now."

Having heard her name, Clementine raised her head to
check out the visitors. She offered them a cheerful little
wag of her tail, but didn't bother to get up when the other
dogs went running to greet the women.

"She's carrying five pups, but only three of them are spoken
for," Tina said, "so if you decide you'd like one, Helene . . ."

"How exciting!" Helene exclaimed, sounding like a kid
on Christmas morning.

Rory hoped her aunt hadn't forgotten the real reason
they were there. In any case, it was definitely time to make
her play. She asked Tina if she could use the bathroom.

"Sure, just go in the back door and make a right through
the kitchen and you'll see it."

Helene shifted into second gear on cue. "Do you think
I could possibly go into the kennel to play with the dogs?"
she asked as Rory walked away.

"We actually have an area set up for that exact purpose,"
Tina said.

Rory made her way back across the lawn to the house.
She found the powder room to be small and tidy and completely devoid of any personal effects belonging to the family, which was what she'd expected. After a cursory look
around, she went in search of the master suite. She checked
her watch so that she didn't stay inside too long and arouse
Tina's suspicions. She was feeling guilty enough about
sneaking around behind her client's back. In fact, the only
way she'd been able to broker a truce with her conscience
was by putting the focus on proving Joe's innocence. Still,
the police detective in her was setting off alarms as she
made her way into the master bedroom.

She stopped short at the door to the master bath. Was she really going to do this? Damn, what a lousy time to have cold feet. No, she hadn't come this far to give up now. Besides, Zeke deserved his little comeuppance, and it would go a long way to elevating her in his esteem. Before she could debate it any further, she marched across the threshold into the bathroom. She found Joe's brush in one of the drawers of the vanity along with his shaving cream and razors. She pulled several hairs out of the brush and placed them in the small plastic bag she'd brought in her handbag for that purpose. She was on her way back to the kennels in less than five minutes, start to finish.

Tina and Helene were inside a large grassy area that was fenced off beyond the kennels. Helene was sitting on the ground with six white balls of fluff climbing all over her, jockeying for her attention. "Aren't they the cutest things you've ever seen?" she asked, beaming up at Rory.

"You're a real natural with them," Tina said. "Believe me, they don't act this way with everyone. You just let me know if you want one of the new pups."

Helene's smile broadened as she gently extricated herself from her little mob of fans.

"I'd better put a deposit on one now," she said, already rummaging in her purse for her checkbook.

Rory jumped in before Tina could close the deal. "I think you need to give this some more thought, Aunt Helene. You know how you're always running somewhere or other, and don't forget you just started rehearsals for the next play. You'll need to line up someone to doggie-sit."

Unexpectedly Tina took up Rory's cause. "Your niece is right, these are companion dogs. They don't like spending a lot of time alone."

Helene seemed to be the only one on an entirely different page. Nothing new there. "I'll ask your mom to help out," she said to Rory, undeterred.

"Listen, why don't you let me know?" Tina said. "I'll hold one back until I hear from you."

Before Helene could dig herself any deeper into a commitment, Rory thanked Tina, said she'd get back to her soon with an update on the case and hurried her aunt off to the car. By the time she'd dropped Helene at home, she was reasonably certain that she'd talked her out of buying the dog. To seal the deal she told Helene she could visit Hobo whenever she wanted. In the process she wound up inviting her to dinner so she could meet him. Helene was cheered by the prospect. After all, Hobo wasn't just any dog. Since Rory had adopted him, he was her great-nephew. Family had always held a lot of sway with Helene.

Rory left her with a promise to call and set a date once she knew when her parents would also be free. Unfortunately she was going to have to beg for Zeke's cooperation, which meant mending some fences she wasn't particularly eager to mend at the moment. She'd deal with all that later, though. Right now she was running late for her meeting with BB.

Barrett Browning III, medical examiner for Suffolk County, had been happy to hear from her, and happier still when she suggested they meet at the Starbucks near his office in Hauppauge. Apparently they made a buttermilk scone there that compared favorably with the ones he'd sampled in England.

Rory arrived with two minutes to spare and found BB ensconced in one of two easy chairs that had a diminutive table wedged between them. He was sipping a chai latte, which he proclaimed the perfect accompaniment to the scone that sat untouched on its napkin while he'd waited for her. As the son of a socially prominent family, he had the manners of a gentleman, if not always the refined tastes of one. And he'd be the first to admit that he was more of a gourmand than a gourmet, a fact easily verified by his substantial girth.

He insisted that Rory have a seat while he took care of placing her order. He hoisted himself out of his chair with some difficulty, disappointed that all she wanted was a simple cup of coffee. He took it upon himself to buy her a scone to taste anyway and refused to let her pay even when she protested that she'd invited him.

"Not at all, dear girl, I won't hear of it, not another word," he said, placing the coffee and scone in front of her and reclaiming his seat. "Now, how can I be of service?"

Rory explained the case to him, remarking about how difficult it was to narrow the spectrum of potential suspects. In the process she couldn't resist adding a quick mention of Hobo, who seemed to be ever present in her thoughts.

"Sounds a lot like the dog I had as a boy," BB said with a nostalgic smile. "Great big, hairy thing, also of indeterminate lineage. My parents had planned to buy a pedigreed something or other, I forget what, with papers and a family tree as impressive as theirs. But I wanted a dog no one else wanted." He paused for a moment's reflection. "I guess I was looking for a dog like me." His eyebrows arched with surprise at this sudden epiphany. "Of course I'm not referring to my relationship with my family," he hurried to explain. "They were more doting than any child could want or deserve. But I was the odd one in school— you know, good grades, but two left feet on the soccer field?"

Rory just smiled and nodded. She didn't feel she knew BB well enough to comment one way or the other on such an intimate disclosure.

Then BB's face split into an impish grin that puffed out his cheeks like a chipmunk gorging on acorns. "Sorry to go all maudlin there on you. Anyway, back to the subject at hand. I think you were about to tell me in what particular way I could help." He broke off a piece of his scone and tucked it into his mouth with a deep sigh of pleasure.

Rory was glad to leave the psychoanalysis behind. "Actually this is probably more up Reggie's alley than yours," she said, pulling the two plastic bags out of her purse and explaining what she needed done. "Of course if he doesn't want to get involved again, please let him know I understand."

"*C'est compris*, not to worry, *no hay problema*," BB assured her. "Reggie is always game for projects that are, shall we say, tangential to his job description."


"I've been meanin' to talk to you about that gun of yours," Zeke said a moment after he materialized near the fireplace.

Rory had been sitting on the couch reading the newspaper while Hobo snored away at her feet. She immediately put her finger to her lips in hopes of quieting the marshal. With any luck they might be able to hold a conversation without waking the dog and starting another round of "save me from the ghost." Of course she had no way of knowing if Zeke was in a cooperative mood or actually looking to cause some chaos.

"The Walther?" she whispered, hoping for the former.

Zeke took a seat in the closer of the two armchairs before replying. "It's not enough firepower," he said in a lower voice. "You should be carryin' a .45 or a .357. That way when you shoot a guy he goes down and stays down. The Walther is just goin' to irritate him."

"You're right," she said. "I've been thinking about it ever since I turned in my service pistol. I just haven't gotten around to buying one yet."

Zeke had opened his mouth ready to launch into a full-out rebuttal as he always did when she disagreed with him.

"Was there something else you wanted to say?" she asked sweetly.

"I swear sometimes you stay awake nights thinkin' up new ways to confound me."

Rory laughed. "It really doesn't require that much effort." She regretted the words as soon as she said them.

"Oh, you mean sorta like this?" Zeke's mouth tugged up in a mischievous grin. "Hobo," he called.

The dog's eyes popped open, still bleary with sleep, and Rory groaned.

Zeke vanished from the chair and popped up inches from the dog's nose with a playful "Boo."

When was she going to learn that it was never a good idea to bait the marshal?

# Chapter 14

Rory had been surprised to hear from Deirdre Lopez a week after her initial visit to see her at town hall. The phone call had been strangely cryptic. After the briefest of greetings, she'd asked Rory to come in to see her at one o'clock the next day if that was convenient. When Rory had inquired as to the reason for the meeting, Deirdre had simply said it was a matter that could best be attended to in person. Before Rory could follow up with another question, Deirdre thanked her and said good-bye.

As soon as Rory arrived at town hall, Deirdre Lopez's secretary showed her into the clerk's office.

"Thank you for coming in again," Deirdre said, rising to shake her hand. "Please have a seat." She was wearing a dove gray suit, perfectly tailored to her narrow curves, with burgundy heels and a strand of pearls at her neck. The woman knew how to dress.

"After you left last week I found myself wondering if perhaps I'd overlooked something that might help in your investigation," she said once they were both seated. "Since it's been my habit to keep a daily work log, I went back a couple of years and started reading through my entries. Pretty dull stuff," she said with a little laugh. "At least until I got to May tenth of 2008."

Pen and pad in hand, Rory found herself leaning forward in her chair as if she could reach the information more quickly that way.

"On that day I fired a woman in my department by the name of Anita Callaway. I'm actually surprised that I'd forgotten about it, because it was a particularly unpleasant incident. Who knows, maybe I blocked it out for that reason." She shook her head as if she were still annoyed with the lapse in her memory. "Anyway, Anita had been receiving substandard reviews from her immediate supervisor for close to a year. I won't go into the specifics, because they're not relevant to your investigation, and I believe in protecting employee confidentiality."

Rory murmured that she understood.

"So," Deirdre went on, "I had a frank talk with her myself to make it clear that she was at serious risk of losing her job. When her performance didn't improve by the next reviewing cycle, I followed through and terminated her employment here."

Rory was taking notes as quickly as she could, preferring not to interrupt Deirdre's narrative. She'd been privy to enough police investigations to know that a lot of valuable information could be lost that way.

"Anita reacted as if she'd never been warned that she was in danger of being fired," Deirdre said. "She became verbally abusive and even threatened me. She had to be escorted out of the building by two of our security guards." Deirdre's usually well-modulated voice had become tight and agitated as she retold the story, as if she were remembering those moments on a visceral level. "Now, I'm not easily intimidated, Ms. McCain, but I have to admit I was worried at the time that she might walk back in here one day armed with an assault rifle to even the score. Thankfully that never happened."

"I guess that's a normal fear given what you hear about these days," Rory said.

Deirdre squared her shoulders and lifted her chin in an effort to regain her composure.

"If you'd like we could take a break before continuing," Rory offered.

"If you could give me a minute or two."

"Of course." Rory assumed she was going to leave her office for a glass of water or a trip to the ladies' room, but Deirdre just settled back in her chair and closed her eyes. She took a long, deep breath, then slowly exhaled. She repeated the exercise several times, while Rory sat there trying not to stare at her. There was little else to look at other than the four beige walls adorned with a few uninspired paintings that looked like they'd come straight off an assembly line. Either Deirdre's flair for clothes didn't carry over to office décor or she simply didn't care much about her work space.

"There." Deirdre smiled as she opened her eyes again. "Biofeedback. It's really quite amazing. I didn't believe in it myself until I tried it."

She did sound calmer to Rory. "I don't suppose it would work on dogs?" she asked to lighten the mood. Or ghosts?

Deirdre laughed. "Your dog must be like my cat. Major issues."

"You have no idea."

"Thank you for indulging me. I'm okay if you want to go on now."

Rory glanced at the notes she'd taken to pick up the thread of her thoughts. "I'm assuming that while Anita worked here she had access to the dog registration files in the computer system, correct?"

"Yes. Dog registration was one of the areas she handled.

And it's probably safe to say that losing her job presented a financial hardship for her. But these days half the country is facing hard times and that doesn't automatically mean that someone is going to fall into a life of crime. So, although it was an upsetting incident, I wouldn't have contacted you about Anita based solely on that day. But after reading my log, I had a chat with one of the women she'd been friendly with in the office. I'll just call the woman Jane. According to Jane, Anita couldn't find work for months. In the end, she gave up and started a doggie day care business in her home. When I heard that I knew I had to call you."

If Rory had owned ears like Hobo's, they would have been standing at attention. What better way to camouflage a dognapping ring than by setting up a business in which there would be a continuously changing assortment of dogs around? Rory was having a hard time trying to put the brakes on her runaway thoughts. She was jumping to some very large, and as yet unproven, conclusions. And unless Congress had changed the law in the past couple of hours, Anita Callaway was innocent until proven guilty by a jury of her peers.

"I can't tell you how grateful I am that you've come forward with this information," Rory said. "It could be a tremendous help."

Deirdre's brow furrowed. "Please understand that I'm not accusing Anita of anything," she said quickly, anxiety creeping back into her voice. "And to the best of my knowledge she did nothing illegal while she worked here. I'm certainly not interested in hurting her reputation or her ability to find employment in the future."

Rory didn't need any clarification, the subtext was obvious: Please be discreet. I don't want any legal repercussions from sharing this information. I'm only trying to do the right thing here.

Rory knew she was seeing a vulnerable side of Deirdre Lopez most people never got to see. "Don't worry. I'll keep the information confidential," she promised. "I'll only turn it over to the authorities if and when I can prove that Anita's involved in the dognappings."

"I guess I can't ask for more than that." Deirdre sighed, clearly uneasy about entrusting her fate to someone else. "Oh, I almost forgot." She picked up a sheet of paper that had been lying in the middle of her neatly ordered desk. "I printed out Anita's home address and telephone number for you." She passed it across the desk to Rory. "According to Jane, the information is still current."

Rory rose and thanked her again.

By the time Deirdre stepped around her desk to shake Rory's hand, she was smiling brightly, all polished businesswoman and politician once again.

As Rory left town hall she checked her phone for messages and was surprised to find one from a woman who identified herself as Joanne Lester, accountant to Dr. Stanley Holbrook. Rory hadn't met the accountant when she'd taken Hobo in for his checkup, so she was more than a little curious to find out what was on her mind.

She hit the "call back" button as she opened her car door and slid behind the wheel. Joanne answered on the first ring. She thanked Rory for getting back to her so promptly, but when Rory asked how she could be of service, Joanne would only say that it concerned the dognappings and that the rest would have to wait until they had a face-to-face.

After setting up a date and time, Rory started her car and pulled her hijacked thoughts back to Anita Callaway. It took her less than a minute to weigh the pros and cons of developing a well-thought-out strategy or just dropping in on her. Immediate action won out. She was sure Zeke would have objected if he'd had a vote, which wound up being the deciding factor. Why waste time by going home and arguing the point with him? She had her Walther in her handbag along with her notepad and pen. What more did a girl need to interview a suspect?

The address the town clerk had given her was in an older section of East Northport that had started to look run-down five years earlier. Most of the houses on Anita's block were in obvious need of repair. The gutters had pulled away from the roofline on one house; another was missing a number of its clapboard slats. Brown lawns appeared to be in fashion.

Rory found Anita's house near the end of a cul-de-sac. It was a small ranch, its storm door hanging from a broken hinge like a snaggletooth and Christmas lights from a happier season sagging around the door frame. A small, hand-lettered sign on a post in the middle of the front yard announced that this was Dog Haven.

Rory pulled to a stop at the curb thinking that the name sounded more like a nursing home for elderly, incontinent dogs than a fun place for them to spend the day while their humans were away earning kibble money. She sat there for a moment, some of her fire snuffed out by Anita's sad circumstances. She had to remind herself that criminal activity might well be going on in that house. How would *she* feel if Hobo had been whisked away and sold to someone else? That did it. She locked the car and marched up the cracked cement walkway to the front door. Before she had a chance to ring the bell, she heard a chorus of dogs inside announcing her arrival. Someone pulled back the curtain on the larger of two front-facing windows to see who was there. Finally the front door shuddered inward and Rory was face-to-face with a woman in her early forties. Her square jaw and narrow eyes gave her a hard, "don't mess with me" appearance. She was flanked by a half dozen dogs of various sizes, some of whom were still grumbling their concerns about the visitor. Beyond them Rory could see a portion of the living room, including an old sofa in a faded floral print and a large flat-screen TV that seemed out of place given the general condition of the house.

"Anita Callaway?" Rory asked pleasantly. See, doggies, nothing threatening here.

The woman looked her up and down. "What can I do for you?" She sounded as wary as her charges. Rory tried not to read anything into it. These days everyone was cautious about opening their doors to strangers.

"My name is Lois Brady." She couldn't take the chance that Anita might have heard of her during her brief brush with fame over the summer. "Someone at the dog park mentioned that you run a day care for dogs."

"As a matter of fact I do." Her voice was an instrument with a single note. Behind her the dogs jockeyed for position. Not one of them tried to escape around Anita. Either they were afraid of her or they were perfectly content to be there. Rory voted for the former.

"I'm so glad to hear that," she said. "I've been trying to find someplace to leave my dog while I'm at work. Wow, I hope you don't mind my saying so, but that's a beautiful TV set you have."

"Actually I do mind." Anita frowned at her. "What's in my house is none of your business."

Rory apologized, taken aback by the venom in her response. Anita was certainly no charmer, but it seemed over the top even for her. "I've been saving up to buy one myself," Rory added, "and I was just going to ask what brand that is and whether you were happy with it."

"My brother bought it for my birthday, and as long as it works I'm happy with it. Now, how big is this dog of yours? What's the breed?"

"He's a big, lovable mutt." Rory laughed. Surely the woman had a lighter side hidden somewhere.

"I don't take pits or Rottweilers," Anita said. "Not even breeds mixed with them."

Then again, maybe not. "Not a problem," Rory assured her.

"I charge fifteen a day for dogs over fifty pounds. That's eight a.m. to six p.m. Monday through Friday, paid in advance. Doesn't matter if you pick the dog up early, the fee's the same. It's simpler that way."

"Makes sense to me. By the way, have you had any problems with dogs being stolen around here?"

"No. But with this gang I'd know the second anyone wandered onto my property." Her lips edged up just short of a smile.

Rory wondered if Anita was enjoying a little inside joke about stolen pooches alerting her to potential dog thieves. "Dog thefts are becoming a real epidemic lately and there have been so many in such a short time," she said, trying to ease into a conversational rhythm. If she could engage Anita in a dialogue, the woman might slip and say something useful.

When she didn't comment, Rory went on. "I know the police have put extra detectives on the case. They think it might even be someone with access to town records, can you imagine?" She watched Anita's face for signs of concern or interest. Nothing. "Well, anyway, I'm really glad to have found your day care. I wonder if you'd mind giving me someone to call as a reference?"

"I don't need anyone vouching for me," Anita replied tartly. "If you want to leave your dog with me, fine; if not, suit yourself." She started to close the door.

"Wait a minute, I didn't mean to imply—"

"Look, I'm busy here. Drop your dog off at eight if you want. No need to call first." Anita pushed the door closed with a reverberating thud, leaving Rory on the front stoop with a list of unanswered questions.

# Chapter 15

Rory was finally on her way to Northport to speak to Eddie Mays, proprietor of Boomer's Groomers. He was a difficult man to pin down. If he was to be believed, he was perpetually shorthanded. This week one of his groomers was away on vacation and another had left without notice. According to Eddie, most people didn't last a year there. Rory wasn't surprised; the job didn't offer much in the way of a career path. At times like this, if Eddie wanted to keep his enterprise going, he had to roll up his own sleeves and wash, clip and dry his clients himself. He'd agreed to see Rory if she didn't mind talking to him while he worked. She assured him that wasn't a problem. She didn't mention that she was desperate.

Zeke had found close to a million sites when he'd searched the Web for dog-related businesses on Long Island. Since he could only work at it when he'd stored up enough energy, he was making little progress. At this rate the case could go unsolved for another fifty years, conservatively speaking. He suggested putting his time to better use by checking the local newspapers for ads hawking pedigreed dogs at bargain prices.

Rory was game to let him try that approach. Even though nearly every town and hamlet on Long Island had more than one free local paper, the numbers were still more realistic than the number of websites. Based on the map they'd drawn, he could limit his search and concentrate on the Huntington area. Rory reminded him to look for words like "discounted," "lowest prices" and "must sell" in the ads; she tried not to focus on the fact that her own leg of the investigation was limping toward a dead end.

She'd spoken to nearly every person and followed up every lead connected with the lists she'd received from Tina Kovack and Leah. A few of them had left lingering questions in her mind, like Dr. Stanley Holbrook, the vet with his own curious list, but no one had struck her as the epitome of a dog thief, whatever that might be. In any event, Eddie was one of the few people of interest she hadn't yet interviewed. She'd reached the point where she would have offered to assist him with his work just to get in the door. As it was, he thought she was a freelance journalist coming to interview him for a magazine article on pampered pooches. Journalism was a cover that had served her well in the past. People were generally eager to talk about themselves and their interests, and believing that they were the subject of an article stroked their egos quite nicely. In Eddie's case it also doubled as free publicity.

Boomer's Groomers occupied a storefront in a small strip mall that also housed a deli, a dry cleaner, a stationery store and a pizza joint. The parking lot was barely adequate for the number of people these businesses attracted, but since no one lingered there for more than ten minutes, finding a space wasn't much of an issue. Rory turned into the parking lot as a minivan was backing out of a spot. Perfect timing. Now, if her interview with Eddie worked out as well, she might just learn something useful for the case.

Even before she opened the door to Eddie's shop, she heard a muffled chorus of barking and yipping from dogs of various sizes and lung capacities. The tape recorder she'd brought along would be useless with that much background noise. It was a good thing she always carried a pen and pad in her handbag. She wished she'd also brought along some aspirin for the headache she was bound to have by the time she left.

Although the noise was louder inside, it was to some extent still muted. Rory assumed that was because the grooming area was located beyond the partial wall toward the rear of the shop. There was an unmanned counter with a cash register to her left and narrow aisles radiating out from the entryway stocked full of every dog accoutrement one could imagine. She was getting quite an education in just how big the dog business had become.

She was about to call out to let Eddie know she was there, when she spotted a man hurrying down one of the aisles toward her. Opening the door must have triggered some sort of buzzer in the back that alerted Eddie when someone entered the store.

As he came closer, the words "odd duck" flashed through Rory's mind. It was one of her mother's pet phrases that she hadn't really understood before. But somehow she was sure that Eddie Mays would qualify for "odd duck" status in her mother's opinion. His brown eyes were magnified by thick glasses, and his head was shaved, although not recently, dark stubble sprouting across his pate like a randomly planted crop. A little silver hoop dangled from one eyebrow and a silver stud marked the center of his chin. His faded blue tee shirt stuck to his chest in wet splotches, and soapsuds twinkled like sequins in the dark hair of his forearms.

"What can I do you for?" he asked, wiping his hands on the sides of his jeans as he approached her.

"Lois Brady," she said, using the name that had popped into her head when she'd visited Anita. "I spoke to you about an interview?"

"Right, right." Eddie nodded. "I'd shake your hand, but I'm still pretty wet. Look, it's like I told you on the phone, we'll have to talk while I work." He turned and started back the way he'd come without waiting for her to respond.

Rory assumed she was supposed to follow. The noise level increased as they made their way to the back, until the din of dog complaints reached a crescendo at the doorway to the grooming area. She had all she could do not to plug her ears and run for cover. Eddie didn't even seem to notice.

The room was small for the number of dogs in it, which helped explain the dense noise that fell around them like a curtain. Eddie went straight to a steel table, similar to the one Rory had seen in the vet's office, where a miniature schnauzer was standing, tied to a retractable arm. The animal was soaking wet and shivering with either cold or nerves, or more likely a combination of the two, its dark eyes darting back and forth between Eddie and Rory, its stumpy tail offering a sluggish wag.

Having never been inside a grooming facility, Rory spent a moment checking out the place. There was a second steel table not presently in use a few feet away and at the other end of the room, a bathing tub with a ramp for large breeds and a smaller tub at counter height for their more portable brethren. A dozen cages of various sizes hugged the available wall space, two tiers high in places. Half the cages were occupied by dogs who'd already been groomed or by those still awaiting their turns. None of the dogs looked happy to be there. A few appeared downright miserable. Rory made Hobo a silent pledge to tend to his grooming herself, although she wasn't at all sure how she would manage that.

There was a little white dog yapping away in one of the cages who looked just like the Sugarmans' Falcon. When Rory remarked on this, Eddie told her she was looking at Falcon himself. Larry had dropped him off to be groomed that morning. Given how much Marti doted on her dog, Rory figured her patronage was the equivalent of a five-star rating.

Eddie was busy snipping away at the schnauzer's fur, so Rory took out her pen and paper and positioned herself beside him, doing her best to block out the cacophony around them.

"So, Eddie, tell me a little about yourself and how you got started in this business," she said, finding that she had to shout to be heard.

"I like dogs and I needed a way to make a living." He shrugged without pausing in his work. "So after my mom passed, I took the money she left me and bought this place from the last owner."

He didn't sound at all passionate about his career choice, but Rory doubted that anyone would be, given his present staff problems and workload. She asked him a short roster of questions that seemed appropriate for the article she was supposedly writing. Eddie answered her without embellishing on his life or accomplishments, which raised him several notches in her esteem. She was glad that she wasn't actually writing an article about him, though, because it would have been a short and boring one.

He finished trimming the schnauzer, clipped his nails and dried his short coat, topping it all off with a blue bow he tied to the dog's collar. Then he placed him in one of the cages to wait until someone came for him.

"I'm gonna take a ten-minute lunch break," Eddie announced, and without further comment he led the way to the front of the store.

Rory could have nominated him for sainthood. Her head throbbed from the incessant barking and her throat hurt from the strain of shouting to be heard. The muted noise at the front of the store now felt like a peaceful sanctuary compared to the hell of the grooming area.

Eddie reached behind the front counter and pulled out a brown bag dotted with either grease or water stains. He set it on the counter, then, using his hands, levered himself up there as well.

"Feel free to pull up a piece of counter," he offered. "Chairs take up too much retail space."

Rory thanked him, but chose to remain standing.

Eddie opened the bag and withdrew a can of Coke and a thin sandwich that had escaped its plastic wrap. "PB&J," he said, holding half of the sandwich out to her.

"That's very kind," she said, "but I have a lunch meeting right after I leave here." She didn't actually have a meeting, unless you counted potentially talking to Zeke, and that certainly had nothing to do with lunch, but it seemed like the most courteous way of declining the sandwich.

"Yeah, I'd pass on the PB myself if I had a better offer," Eddie said, already biting into the second half.

In an effort to adopt a more casual, "we're pals" kind of posture for her next round of questions, Rory leaned back against the counter a couple of feet from where Eddie was seated munching away on his sandwich. She needed to seem completely nonthreatening if she wanted him to confide in her.

"Listen, Eddie," she said, "can we talk off the record?" She set her pen down to show him that she'd stopped taking notes.

Eddie bobbed his head. "Yeah, why not."

"Good. I'd love to get your take on the recent rash of dog thefts. I mean, being in the dog business and all, I'm sure you've got your finger on the pulse of things."

He popped the last of the sandwich into his mouth and

washed it down with several loud gulps from the can of soda.

"Gotta get a fridge in here," he said, wiping his mouth with the back of his hand. "Warm soda just doesn't cut it." He paused to burp rather delicately. "Sorry, I gotta learn to eat slower and chew more. Turns out my mother was right," he said with a sheepish grin. "So, you want my opinion on the dog thefts, huh?" He gnawed on the inside of his cheek while he thought about it. "I don't know. Maybe the economy pushed some poor slob to do it, or maybe it's some nut job with a bone to pick . . . 'bone,' hey'd you catch that?" He laughed, enjoying his own cleverness. "I've always had a way with words."

Rory produced a smile, wondering what had ever given him that idea.

"Have any of your customers been hit?" she asked. Having seen the police reports from Leah, she already knew the answer, but she was interested in seeing if Eddie was going to be truthful with her.

"Yeah, six of them if you can believe it," he said glumly. "A real bummer. Means lost business for me too." After a moment of silence, during which he contemplated the linoleum, he raised his head and looked at her with his magnified eyes. "It's a good thing dog people can't stand to live without man's best friend," he said, perking up nicely. "After a couple of months, almost all of them bought replacements."

Rory managed to nod, although she was taken aback by his quick emotional U-turn. She couldn't imagine replacing Hobo as if he were a worn-out lightbulb. Of course, to be fair, the stolen dogs had not been Eddie's pets and he did have a business to run. There was no requirement that he love or mourn the loss of every dog who passed beneath his shears.

"Unfortunately Brenda Hartley won't be replacing her dogs anytime soon," Rory said, keeping it vague to see if Eddie was aware of her death.

"Not in this lifetime," he said with a low chuckle, to show her that he understood her meaning. "Not that I had anything against the woman. She paid her bills on time and almost never complained."

"But she did complain on occasion?" Rory prompted.

"One time. She said I didn't get all the knots and clumps out of her dog's coat. I spent more than an hour on that big mutt. So I told her I can't be expected to work all day on one dog unless she wanted to pay me by the hour."

"Some people think the world revolves around them," Rory commiserated, to see how much more she could get him to reveal. "Did she refuse to pay the bill?"

"Nah, nothing like that." Eddie slid down from the counter and brushed a few bread crumbs off his jeans.

Rory knew she should let the Brenda line of questioning go. She was trespassing on police turf. But how was she to know which questions might field valuable information for her own case until she'd asked them? Besides, anything she learned about the murder case she'd take directly to Leah. That sealed the deal. The last nagging voice of her conscience was stilled.

"Do you think she was killed by someone who came to steal her dogs?"

Eddie frowned at her, the hoop in his eyebrow lowering until it brushed through his lashes. "Wait a minute, what the hell's going on here? You seem a lot more interested in murder and dog thieves than you are in this article you claim to be writing."

Rory had overplayed her hand and he was calling her bluff. She straightened up and stepped away from the counter so that she was facing him. "I'm sorry," she said, going for sincerity with a side of humble pie. "I was laid off from my newspaper gig two months ago, and I'm having trouble letting go of the hard news angle. But the story about your business is great, and I promise to do it justice in the piece."

Eddie stared at her for a moment, as if considering whether he should believe her. "Yeah, whatever," he said finally. "I gotta get back to work."

Rory thanked him again and promised to send him a copy of the magazine when it came out, but she was speaking to his back. Eddie was already halfway to the grooming area.

# Chapter 16

Rory stopped at the supermarket on her way home. She'd been so busy lately that she'd been resorting to fast food and either her jeans were shrinking or she was gaining weight. She had to start eating better if she didn't want to buy a whole new wardrobe. She filled the cart with the makings of salad, fruit for snacking, yogurt for lunch and a rotisserie chicken for dinner and stoically resisted the siren call of the cookie and chip aisles. She was reaching for fabric softener when the air in front of her started to shimmer as if she were dizzy or seeing a mirage. But since she didn't feel light-headed and hadn't been wandering the desert dying of thirst, she quickly realized what was happening. In that same instant Zeke appeared, at least the top half of him, as if he'd been in such a hurry that he'd forgotten to bring his legs along. In spite of this deficiency, he was still mighty pleased with himself, judging by the grin on his face.

Rory immediately checked up and down the aisle to see

if anyone else was there to witness his impromptu magic act. With a sigh of relief she saw that she was alone.

"Get out of here," she said as fiercely as she could in a whisper. "Have you lost your mind? Get out now!"

Zeke's image wavered, faded, then disappeared bit by bit, like pixels in a television image, until only his grin was left hanging in the air, Rory's very own Cheshire Cat. Over the past few months she'd developed a real empathy for Alice; living with the marshal was a lot like living in Wonderland. Just before Zeke's smile winked out, an elderly couple turned into the aisle. Rory held her breath, hoping they hadn't seen it. No such luck.

"Oh my Lord," the elderly woman gasped, her hand flying to her heart as if that would keep the rebellious organ from jumping out of her chest. "Did you . . . did you see that?" she asked her husband, her eyes fixed on the spot where Zeke's mouth had been just a moment earlier.

The husband, who'd been trailing a few feet behind with their cart, came to an abrupt stop beside her. "You okay, Francine?" he asked, his forehead rumpled with concern. "You look like you've seen a ghost."

Rory had all she could do not to burst out laughing from nervous tension, but she kept a sober face while she put the bottle of fabric softener into her cart.

"I did. That's it exactly," Francine replied, unwilling to look away in case Zeke's mouth did an encore performance. "You didn't see it?"

"See what? All I see is you and that young woman up ahead. Maybe it's the new blood pressure medicine the doctor put you on. I think you'd better call him when we get home."

Francine finally turned to look at him with an exasperated scowl. "There isn't a damn thing wrong with me or my medicine, you old fool," she snapped. "If you'd just watch those programs about the ghost hunters with me, you wouldn't be so blind to what's going on right under your nose."

"Okay, here we go again," he murmured in the weary

tone of one who's already been down this particular path too many times. He started pushing his cart again, leaving his wife to either follow or stay behind without him.

Francine squared her narrow shoulders and marched along in his wake. As they approached Rory, who'd stopped to read the label on a bottle of stain remover, Francine couldn't seem to resist the chance to corroborate what she'd seen and prove her husband wrong.

"Excuse me, miss," she said hopefully, "by any chance did you happen to see something . . . well, something a bit strange a minute ago at the other end of this aisle?"

Rory was sorely tempted to tell her that she had. And more specifically that what she'd seen *was* a ghost, or part of one anyway. She would have loved to see the look of vindication on the older woman's face and the look of utter shock on her husband's. But after a quick assessment of the consequences, and with a silent apology to Francine, Rory chose to simply smile and deny that she'd seen anything out of the ordinary.

Rory set down the two grocery bags she was carrying and unlocked the front door, but when she turned the knob and tried to push it open, it wouldn't budge. It didn't seem possible that the door could have become warped over the past few hours. She looked at the hinges, but they looked the way they always looked. Not that she had any idea what she would be seeing if they were keeping the door from opening. Frustrated, she put her shoulder to the door and pushed again with all the power she could muster. This time it moved a couple of inches, before suddenly flying open the rest of the way. Rory lost her balance and stumbled inside, where Hobo was whirling in gleeful circles. So much for the mystery of the door. Hobo was a very effective doorstop. It would be great if all of her investigations were that easy to solve.

As she turned back to bring in her packages, she groaned. The wooden molding around the left side of the doorway had been ripped off and whittled down to a pile of toothpicks. Something must have happened to make Hobo more desperate than usual to escape and find her. And she had a good idea where to lay the blame. The problem was that she and Zeke hadn't had much to say to one another since their last fight. Their interactions had been minimal and only related to business matters, but Rory knew if they didn't patch things up, her family dinner could turn into a full-fledged disaster. Before the incident in the supermarket, she'd actually been on the brink of proposing a truce. Nothing seemed to please the marshal more than hearing her admit that she was wrong. But even though they'd have to come to an accommodation and soon, she was no longer in any mood to hoist a white flag. She grabbed up the groceries and stormed into the kitchen with Hobo plastered against her as if they were hobbled together in some strange five-legged race.

"Ezekiel Drummond," she fumed as she threw the perishables into the refrigerator, "we need to talk."

"Pleased to see you too, Aurora." His voice floated to her through the air. "I'm afraid I'm a mite indisposed. My little outing today used up more energy than I anticipated."

At the sound of Zeke's disembodied voice, Hobo tucked his tail and circled Rory, whimpering and trying to find a way to scale her body and climb into her arms.

"It also seems to have set Hobo back to day one," she raged as his claws sought purchase, scratching her thighs right through the jeans. She managed to push him down and herd him to the back door and an alternate form of sanctuary. As soon as she held the door open, he dashed outside.

"That was not my intention, but I suspect my efforts to travel cause some turmoil in the ether."

"We agreed that you wouldn't keep trying to do that,"

she said, pacing back and forth in the kitchen, since she had no specific focus for her attention. Not only was he invisible, but his voice didn't seem to be coming from any one direction. "You could have caused a panic in that store today. People could have been hurt."

"That agreement had two sides to it as I recall," Zeke said. "You were goin' to spend some time practicin' with me in the yard where there's no audience besides the mutt."

"I've been busy," she said defensively, her fury losing some of its steam. He was right. She'd been putting it off, hoping he'd forget. Who was she kidding? His refusal to move beyond the here and now until he had answers about his death was testament to the fact that when he set his mind to something he never let it go.

"Okay. Okay. You've made your point." She sank onto one of the chairs. "As soon as you're up to it, we'll get started." If she was going to ask for his cooperation with her family it was now or never. She wouldn't find herself in a better bargaining position anytime soon. "On one condition."

"You do like your rules and conditions, don't you?" There was a mocking tone to his voice, but Rory let the remark slide, more interested in moving forward.

"I'm going to have my family here for dinner next week. I want your word that you won't suddenly appear or cause any kind of problem or spectacle."

"I will be the very model of virtue."

"Never mind the flowery sentiment. Trust me when I tell you that they will not let me remain here if they think I'm in any danger. And as you may have noticed during the past hundred years, for most people, ghosts equal danger."

"Knowin' you, it's right hard to believe anyone could make you do what you don't choose to."

"Zeke . . ." She drew his name out as if it were a warning. Then the telephone rang, cutting her off. "Don't go anywhere; we're not done," Rory said, reaching for the handset.

BB was on the other end. "News flash, bulletin, hot off the presses," he said by way of greeting. "Reggie just handed me the results of the DNA tests."

"Great."

"Maybe yes, maybe no, it all depends on what you were hoping to find," BB said philosophically. "Both the letter and the envelope were clean, except for a few partial prints of yours. Since there was no DNA to match the hair sample to, all we can tell you is that the owner of the hair has no criminal record."

Rory thanked him and once again asked him to pass her gratitude on to Reggie. On a previous occasion she'd suggested that perhaps she should deal directly with him so that BB didn't have to play middleman. BB had assured her that he didn't mind and that his colleague preferred to remain in the shadows in a Deep Throat, undercover way.

Rory hung up the phone, frustrated. She wasn't any closer to knowing who'd sent the threatening letter. All she could say for certain was that the sender had done a top-notch job of not leaving any clues behind.

"Joe Kovack's DNA wasn't on the letter," she told the empty room. When Zeke didn't immediately respond, she had a fleeting image of herself old and gray, talking to invisible people, a legacy of her days with the marshal. Well, old anyway; she had no intentions of being gray.

"Then we can't eliminate him," Zeke said finally. He sounded happy enough with the results.

"We can't eliminate *or* accuse him," Rory pointed out.

"So, how did it go with Eddie Mays?" he asked, grabbing the reins of the conversation.

She figured he didn't want her backtracking to more ultimatums. That was fine with her; she'd said enough on the subject anyway. She had his word not to interfere with her family, and if she badgered him about it, she'd only succeed in changing his mind. Instead she related the details of her interview with Eddie.

"Sounds like a freak you'd see in a sideshow back in my day," he said after hearing Rory's description of the man.

"These days it's all a sideshow," she said with a laugh, glad to let go of the anger. "People like Eddie don't even raise eyebrows anymore. And though I wasn't crazy about his appearance or his attitude, as far as I could tell he was being honest with me."

"Then we're right back to where the bronc threw us."

"That about sums it up," she agreed, thinking that someday she ought to put together a book of the marshal's pithy observations and words to live by.

Zeke took his leave, promising to return as soon as he'd recouped enough energy. Rory was relieved to be alone. She and Hobo could use some quiet time themselves. She was trying to decide between peach and raspberry yogurt for lunch when the doorbell rang. She never had any stop-by visitors, unless she counted Aunt Helene, and she saw clients by appointment only, so she couldn't imagine who would be there in the middle of a workday. When she opened the door she found the mailman holding a manila envelope that required her signature. She'd completely forgotten about the information she'd requested from the U.S. Marshals Service.

# Chapter 17

Rory took the envelope back to the kitchen, disappointed by how light it felt. Hobo was standing at the back door waiting to be let in. When she held the door open for him, he sniffed the air and cocked his head, his ears like furred antennae trolling for ghostly noises. Once he was satisfied that there was no current danger, he bounded across the threshold. He stopped for a long, noisy drink from his water bowl and then ambled over to the table where Rory was seated. He took up his usual spot at her feet, dribbling excess water on her in the process.

Rory didn't notice. She'd opened the envelope and withdrawn the five sheets of paper that were inside. When she'd first thought of contacting the Marshals Service, she'd had, as it turned out, unrealistically high hopes of finding enough information to shed light on Zeke's killer.

The man with whom she'd spoken at the local headquarters in Brooklyn had entered her name and address into his computer along with her request for a Freedom of

Information application and immediately asked if she were related to a Michael McCain. It had taken her a second to realize that he was referring to Mac. Her uncle had only used his given name on official papers and it sounded as alien to her as if she were hearing it for the first time. Once she'd recovered her wits, she confirmed that Michael was indeed her uncle, now deceased. Apparently Mac had also requested an application from the Marshals, but according to them, he'd never returned it. One of the many pieces of his life that had been left hanging when he'd been murdered. She'd hung up the phone buoyed by the reminder that she was following in his footsteps and completing work he had started. It made her feel as if she were still bound to him by some fine cosmic thread.

Rory studied the papers in her hand. They were all photocopies of original documents held by the Marshals Service. Two of the sheets contained the statements given by Winston Samuels and his daughter Claire. These provided essentially the same information as the newspaper article Rory had found from that time. There was also a sketch of a man with a caption that read "John Trask, aka John Corbin" and a letter stating that Ezekiel Drummond's personal effects, i.e., his badge and billfold, had been returned to the U.S. Marshals Service in the Arizona Territory to be disposed of as they saw fit.

The final sheet of paper showed a picture of what appeared to be a ticket, the ornate printing on it badly faded and difficult to read. Dislodging her feet from beneath Hobo's rump, she went to the kitchen drawer where she kept a miscellaneous pile of items. After a minute of rummaging through it, she came away with a small magnifying glass.

The ticket was from the Pennsylvania Railroad. It had been purchased for travel from Philadelphia to Jersey City and was stamped with the date, September fifth, 1878. Beneath the image, someone in the Marshals office had

written, "recovered from the parlor of the Samuels residence September sixth, 1878." Since the ticket didn't bear
the passenger's name, its usefulness pretty much ended right
there. She couldn't go back and interview the ticket agent
who had sold it, unless she wanted to hold a séance. Her
only hope was that seeing the image might stir up some
memories for the marshal.

When she looked at the clock she realized that half the
afternoon had slipped away between grocery shopping and
dealing with Zeke. She only had a few minutes left before
her appointment with Joanne Lester. With any luck Holbrook's accountant would have a promising lead for them.

Hobo was still sleeping soundly, and Rory decided not
to wake him. He'd be fine alone in the house while she
commuted to her office in the backyard.

Joanne Lester arrived ten minutes late, full of apologies. She was a pale, fragile-looking young woman, several
inches shorter than Rory, who'd always considered herself
short at five-four. Joanne's brown hair fell straight and
blunt to her shoulders as if it had been cut with a hedge
trimmer instead of a hairdresser's scissors. Parted on the
left, it draped over the right side of her face, partially covering her right eye, like a curtain behind which she could
hide from the world.

"Okay, Joanne, how can I help you?" Rory asked once
her visitor was seated on the couch.

"Actually I think I may be able to help *you*," Joanne said
in a politely measured voice that was so soft Rory found
herself leaning forward to hear her.

"Well, you certainly have my attention." She smiled,
hoping to put the accountant at ease.

Joanne smiled back, then quickly looked down at her
hands as if she'd crossed some invisible line in interper-
sonal relationships. "Sorry," she said without looking up.
"I'm not very good with people."

Rory cast about for an appropriate remark that didn't

sound condescending or inane and came up empty. In the end she decided to simply skip over it and get on with the conversation. "How did you know I was investigating the dognappings?"

"I overheard some of the staff talking about it after you brought Hobo in," Joanne replied, looking up again, but fixing her eyes on the computer monitor to Rory's right. "Not that I eavesdropped," she added. "I would never do that."

"I understand," Rory said when Joanne didn't immediately pick up her narrative.

"Right. Sorry. I lost my place. Anyway, I thought to myself, 'Joanne, you really ought to go see this woman and tell her what you know.'" She risked an oblique glance at Rory, then looked away again.

"I'm glad to have any information that might help me solve a case," Rory encouraged her, thinking that Joanne had probably picked the perfect career, given her issues. She worked with numbers in an office populated with more animals than people.

Joanne stopped and took a deep breath as if she were summoning up the courage to dive into cold water. "I think Dr. Holbrook might be stealing the dogs." The words gushed out of her as she exhaled, and her whole body went a little limp, as if she'd been rigid with the effort of keeping the accusation tamped down inside.

Rory sat back in her chair, feeling like the air had escaped her as well. It was definitely not the sort of remark she'd expected to hear. She had no doubt that Joanne believed what she was saying. She was clearly not the type to seek out a conversation with a total stranger unless her conscience was making it hard for her to sleep at night. Even so, in all fairness to Stanley Holbrook, a person who lived as insular a life as Joanne probably did couldn't necessarily be counted upon to be a good judge of others.

"I'm sure you have strong reasons to believe that," Rory

said, wondering if one of those reasons might be the list that Holbrook hadn't wanted her to see.

"It just makes sense," the accountant said, her voice a bit more confident now that she'd unloaded the burden of her suspicions.

"I'm listening."

She cleared her throat as if she were about to address a gathering. "I guess I'm a little nervous."

"That's okay, go on."

"Well, I've been taking care of Dr. Holbrook's finances, personal as well as business, for almost five years now. He has an expensive lifestyle. Up until two years ago that wasn't a problem. His income supported it. But he got divorced at that time, and between child support and alimony for his ex-wife while she went back to school, his practice just wasn't covering the bills anymore. I know he tried to cut back, but I guess that's not so easy to do when you're used to the finer things. I'm sorry," she interrupted herself, "I know that must sound like I'm trying to make excuses for him, but really I'm not. I just want you to get the whole picture."

Rory nodded.

"Then about five months ago the money problems disappeared. I didn't see any upswing in revenue from the practice, and Dr. Holbrook never explained how there was suddenly enough money in his bank account for everything again. So I was trying to figure out where he was getting the extra money. That's when I realized that he's in a perfect position to steal dogs. You'd be amazed by how many dogs come through that office."

Rory remembered thinking the same thing during Hobo's visit there, but she refrained from commenting, because it sounded like Joanne had memorized her little speech and might have to start at the beginning again if she lost the thread of her narrative.

"Now, I'm not saying he's doing this all on his own. I

think maybe he's just selling the information to the real thieves. They probably pay him in cash so he doesn't have to declare the extra income or explain where it came from." She looked at Rory again, as if trying to assess her reaction, and this time she managed to maintain eye contact for a moment before dropping her gaze to her clasped hands.

"Have you ever seen a list with the names of Holbrook's clients, their pets and phone numbers?" Rory asked.

Joanne shook her head, but continued to stare at her hands as if she were afraid they might do something awful if she wasn't vigilant.

"I saw a list like that when I was in his office," Rory explained, "and there was a letter notation next to each of the names—either a 'T' or an 'M.' Any idea what that might mean?"

"No," she said. "I'm sorry I can't be of more help."

Rory assured her that she'd already been very helpful. She rose from her chair and held out her hand to say good-bye, hoping it didn't seem too abrupt. But if she heard Joanne apologize once more, she might just have to wash her mouth out with soap.

Joanne stood and shook her hand. "You won't . . . I mean you'll keep what I told you in confidence, right?" she asked, looking deeply worried, as if it had only now occurred to her that Rory might not be bound by the same ethics as a doctor, lawyer or priest. "I can't afford to lose my job. I only wanted to do the right thing, you know. . . ."

"Discretion is my watchword," Rory assured her. Of course if Holbrook was involved in the dog thefts, he'd probably lose his veterinary license along with his need for Joanne's services, a possibility the accountant didn't seem to have considered. But there wasn't much Rory could do about her suspicions anyway, without some actual evidence. If Holbrook was guilty, he'd no doubt fed the list she'd seen to a shredder the moment she'd left his office that day.

* * *

"Welcome back," Rory said. She'd been sitting on the couch in the living room reading the newspaper, with Hobo beside her chewing on a stuffed toy, when the lights flickered and Zeke appeared in the chair kitty-corner to them. Hobo immediately dropped the toy and tucked his big head into the protective curve of Rory's arm, like a furry, four-legged ostrich.

"Glad to be back." Zeke grinned, a slash of dimples bracketing his mouth like exclamation marks. He appeared refreshed, even jaunty. And if he'd thought of any sarcastic remarks to make about Hobo's hiding skills, he courteously chose not to voice them. Rest was apparently as good for a ghost as it was for folks still hooked up to flesh and bone.

"I have something to show you," Rory said. With her free hand she reached for the manila envelope she'd left on the glass cocktail table, away from the threat of kitchen spills and stains. She shook the envelope until all the pages slid out, then picked up the sheet with the image of the railroad ticket and held it up for him to see. "Does this look familiar?"

Since Rory was still seated with the cowering Hobo for an anchor, Zeke stood up and came closer to get a better look at it. His eyebrows arched in surprise. "It surely does," he said, straightening to his full height. "That's a Pennsylvania Railroad ticket to Jersey City, New Jersey. Back in my day the train didn't take you all the way into Manhattan, it being an island and all. You had to take a boat for the last part. Where ever did you come by that?"

"The U.S. Marshals Service. It was one of the only pieces of hard evidence they had from the day you were killed."

"I'm impressed, Aurora."

In the spirit of good sportsmanship, Rory didn't chastise

him for using her given name. "I want you to know that before Mac died he'd also been tracking this down."

"I thank you for that," Zeke said, his smile ebbing into a gentle sadness. "I never did lose faith in his efforts to help me."

Rory wanted to ask him why he'd been giving *her* such a rough time about it then, but she snatched the words back before they could pass through her lips.

"Wait a second," Zeke said, hunkering down and frowning at the image of the ticket. "That's not my ticket."

"Are you sure?"

"Damn sure. Look at the date it was purchased."

Rory had seen the date, but it hadn't raised any questions in her mind. She shook her head. "I don't know what you're getting at."

"Well, I boarded the train for Jersey City on September the fourth. This ticket's dated the fifth. And Trask was workin' out here in Huntington for near on a month by then, so the ticket can't be his, neither."

"It belonged to the man who killed you," Rory murmured, the words no more than a whisper. Although she already knew that Zeke had died in this house, in this very room, she was suddenly swamped by the image of his dying moments, moments that had played out within inches of where she sat. A tremor flashed up her spine and spun out through her limbs, making her grateful she was still seated.

Neither of them spoke for a couple of minutes, Zeke as lost in his thoughts as she was in hers. Hobo finally broke the silence with a whimper of confusion. Rory ran her hand down his back to soothe him, but he wasn't buying it. The whimper grew into a round of anxious, high-pitched barking right next to her ear.

"This here ticket's the first link I've had to the coward who shot me," Zeke said, for once oblivious to the racket the dog was making.

Rory hushed Hobo back to a whimper. "The only trouble is that it might be the last link too. If that's all the U.S. Marshals Service could find back when the trail was fresh, I don't see how I can possibly come up with anything else."

"You didn't think you'd find this, until you found it," Zeke reminded her, undaunted by her pessimism.

Since there was nothing to be gained by belaboring the point, she decided to put the subject aside. "Have you got your traveling shoes on?" she asked him instead. The day was winding down and she had a promise to keep.

"I don't believe I have travelin' shoes," Zeke said with some concern. "I've always been partial to boots."

"Boots will do just fine," Rory assured him. "I'm going out to the backyard. Care to join me?"

# 1878

## New Mexico Territory

Drummond left Las Cruces barely two hours after he arrived there. He'd only lingered that long to give his horse a chance to rest and dine on fresh oats and hay. Part of that time the marshal spent wolfing down a meal of beefsteak, rice and beans at a narrow restaurant that looked as if it had been compressed over the years between the larger boardinghouse and general store that were its neighbors. After he'd eaten, Drummond made his way through the town, stopping to show Trask's picture to shopkeepers and people he passed on the dusty wooden sidewalks. Several of Las Cruces' citizens claimed to have seen the fugitive, but hadn't taken notice of which way he'd been heading when he rode out two days earlier. Drummond had the distinct feeling that some of them knew more than they were willing to let on, either due to an imagined fear of reprisal or a very specific threat of one. A young mother herding her two children home from school remarked that she'd been relieved to see him go.

"I'm a God-fearing woman, Marshal, and I don't like to talk ill of folks, but I believe I saw Lucifer himself staring out of that man's eyes." Her shoulders jerked with an involuntary shudder as if she'd intuited the horror that her family had mercifully escaped.

"You didn't happen to notice where he was headed, did you, ma'am?" Drummond asked.

"No, but I daresay no matter where he was headed, he's bound for the fires of Hell."

"I saw, I saw," the little girl chirped up, proud to be of help. "He went that way." She pointed north, up the road that led to Albuquerque. She couldn't have been more than six years old, with sunny blond hair and wide, guileless eyes. Looking at her, Drummond was struck by the random nature of tragedy. This child had crossed Trask's path and been left unscathed, but if he didn't stop Trask soon, there was another child somewhere who would not be as lucky. As soon as he restocked his saddlebags with provisions for himself and oats for his horse, he was back on the fugitive's trail.

The road to Albuquerque was well-worn and for the most part provided easy footing for the chestnut. As much as Drummond yearned to run the horse flat out and eat up the miles between him and Trask, he knew there was nothing to be gained that way. The horse had a loyal and willing nature and would no doubt try to accommodate him. But in the end, the animal would only wind up dropping in his tracks, leaving the marshal to finish his journey on foot. So he set a reasonable pace, stopping often to rest and water the horse while he did the best he could to still the demons that gnawed at his heart and haunted his dreams.

He was still several hours from Albuquerque, riding in the shade of the Manzano Mountains, when the bullet slammed into his left shoulder, knocking him backward like a fist and nearly unseating him. He was so stunned by the assault that he didn't immediately feel any pain, a blessing as he struggled to keep the terrified horse from rearing and throwing him. Once he'd regained control, Drummond slid down from the saddle, pulling his Winchester free of the scabbard that held it. By his best estimate, the shot had come from the high ground where the slopes of the Manzano Mountains rose to the east. Crouched low and holding tight to the reins, he made for the only source of cover in the area, an old barn half burned to the ground. Before he could reach it, another bullet whistled by, digging into the ground near the chestnut's front hooves. Eyes wild and nostrils flared, the horse reared, then bolted, tearing the reins out of Drummond's hand and racing off to some imagined refuge.

By the time the marshal reached the barn the pain had laid claim to him. It blazed through his chest, a red-hot branding iron that knocked him to his knees and forced up the remains of the hardtack and peaches he'd eaten for lunch. The pain crashed over him in waves, a relentless tide ebbing and flowing, and in the troughs a gentle darkness crept around the edges of his mind, calling to him, wooing him with the promise of a long and painless sleep. He fought off the darkness and forced his mind back to the business of survival.

There hadn't been another shot, which most likely meant that the gunman had left his position and was coming down to see if the job needed finishing. Drummond could only wait. Wait and hope that he was still conscious when the man reached him. Was it someone he would recognize? His mind sifted through the possibilities. An old enemy with a score to settle? Possibly a bandit. A lone Apache marauder? Not likely. Or had Trask heard that he was on his trail and circled back to set up the ambush? No matter. He needed to make a decision. After considering his limited options, he settled on playing possum. It was a dangerous game, one that could easily end with his death, but in his present state he stood little chance of overwhelming his attacker without some element of surprise.

He placed his rifle within arm's reach, where it might logically have fallen at the moment he'd succumbed to his wound, and drew the pistol from his holster. Thankfully he'd been hit on the left side so he still had reasonable use of his right arm. He lowered himself as gently as he could onto the hard-packed earth. Even so, all the moving and jostling spiked the pain beyond endurance. He clenched his jaw against the scream that was clawing its way up his throat, but he couldn't shut out the siren song that promised sweet oblivion. If the gunman walked in before he was properly settled, it would be over. Curiously that thought was no longer cobbled with fear. In a strangely removed state of calm, he tucked the pistol into the lee of his body where it would not be immediately visible and he set about the difficult business of waiting.

Time had little meaning. A minute might easily have been an hour. Drummond fought to stay awake and aware. Finally, after what seemed like a lifetime, he heard the crunch of boots on underbrush. The footsteps closed in on him, then abruptly stopped. He kept his breathing as shallow as possible, depending on the dark shadows in the barn to hide the subtle rise and fall of his chest. If his assailant were to simply shoot him again to ensure that he was dead, the game would be over.

As one second became two, Drummond thought he might still have a chance. He strained to hear any sound that would help him get a better fix on the man's location, but his heart was hammering too loudly. Since he couldn't risk opening his eyes, he'd have to make his play blind. But in the next instant the gunman launched a devastating kick to his gut. This time he didn't try to stifle the roar of pain, but used it as a warrior's cry as he rose up shooting. The first round went wide, but the second slammed into his assailant's throat, dropping him before he could get off a single shot.

Drummond wanted desperately to lie back down and

rest, but he knew that if he did, he might never wake again. He'd already lost a lot of blood. He had to find help. He holstered his pistol, picked up the Winchester and dragged himself up on legs that made no promise to hold him. The dead gunman lay sprawled a few feet away. Drummond looked at him hard, but he was as sure as he could be in his present state that he'd never seen the man before. He stumbled over to him and checked his pockets for something that might identify him, but he found nothing. He'd have to puzzle it out later. If indeed he had a "later."

His head spinning, his shirt plastered to his body with blood and sweat, he staggered out of the barn into the late afternoon sun. He saw the chestnut in the distance grazing tranquilly. He summoned up a painful breath and issued a thin whistle. The horse looked up at the familiar sound and came trotting toward him as if they'd simply paused to rest there on a perfectly ordinary day.

When the horse came to a stop beside him, Drummond immediately grabbed for the canteen that was hanging by its strap from the saddle horn. He tried to drink slowly, but his need overwhelmed him, and he was soon guzzling the water, letting it splash over his mouth and chin and down the front of his shirt. When the canteen was empty, he looped it back over the saddle horn and stepped into the stirrup. It took him several agonizing attempts to lift himself onto the saddle, but the chestnut stood there patiently. By the time he was seated, the bleeding, which had subsided to a trickle, was flowing freely again from his exertions. He took hold of the reins in a hand that was too weak to grip and headed the horse back onto the trail to Albuquerque. An hour later and still several miles from his destination, Drummond slumped forward onto the chestnut's neck, where he balanced awkwardly for a few seconds before tumbling to the ground.

# Chapter 18

Zeke practiced traveling from the house out to the back-yard until the sky was a dusky blue-gray. By then his energy level was so low that he could barely make it through the walls of the house let alone materialize. Rory was happy to pack it in. Even though she was wearing a cozy shearling jacket and had been running laps around the yard to keep warm, she was shivering well before the sun slid below the horizon. October was a fickle month on Long Island, one day as mellow as summer, the next as bitter as winter. In his permanent cloak of fur Hobo showed no signs of discomfort or fatigue. Content to have Rory nearby, he patrolled his domain, staunchly defending it against trespassing squirrels and the occasional cotton-tail rabbit. At times he was so absorbed in his work that he didn't seem to notice Zeke's attempted comings and goings, which gave Rory some real hope that a future of peaceful coexistence might be possible after all.

Zeke's practice session itself proved somewhat less

successful. It was a complicated business involving two different components—breaking through the bonds that kept him housebound, and then materializing once he was outside. Neither of these appeared to be even remotely possible unless Rory figured into the equation. Unless she was at the other end of his journey, he simply wasn't going anywhere. Even with her in place, leaving the house was the most difficult part of the process for him. Although he'd proven that he could travel to her at will when her life was in jeopardy, traveling at other times required such a deep concentration of energy and determination that when he did make it out of the house, he was too depleted to manifest completely in three-dimensional form. His first attempt, at Brenda's house, had been a dismal failure, but he had improved substantially by the time he tried it again at the grocery store.

The results that afternoon could only be characterized as bizarre. In one appearance Zeke had a head and legs, but just an empty space where his torso should have been. In another, there was a head-to-toe Zeke with no arms. And then there was a full-body Zeke with a neck, but no head. He actually appeared intact once, but only as a flat, partially transparent image that reminded Rory of some filmmakers' visions of what a ghost should be. Still, he'd managed these travels all in one afternoon with no rest between them. Based on such progress, there was every reason to believe that he would eventually learn how to travel and materialize whenever and wherever he wished. Not surprisingly, Zeke found even this limited success heartening, while Rory was considerably less thrilled by the prospect of what lay ahead.

"I can't believe I'm actually here having brunch with you," Leah said, taking a sip of hot chocolate and coming away with a whipped cream mustache. "And I can't believe you talked me into this evil drink." She licked the residue from around her mouth, not looking the least bit remorseful.

"Well, I've been craving it since the weather turned cooler and it's much more fun being bad with an accomplice." Rory grinned. "Besides, you're right about it being forever since we've enjoyed our little Sunday ritual. So consider it a celebration." She clinked her mug against Leah's.

"No doubt about it, kids and husbands take a real toll on a girl's social life." Leah chased a piece of crisp bacon around her plate with a fork, then gave up and snagged it with her fingers. "How goes the case of the purloined pooches?"

"Slowly. Ve-r-ry . . . slow-w-ly." Rory took a couple of minutes to tell her about the interview with Joanne Lester.

"Holbrook," Leah repeated, thinking aloud. "I guess if she's right about his involvement with the thefts, it's possible he went to snatch Tootsie and wound up killing Brenda in the process." She took a sip of her hot chocolate. "I actually have a little news for you too."

Rory put her English muffin down before taking a bite. "Start talking."

"I was at 'meet the teacher' night at my kids' school Thursday, and I bumped into a friend who's been working that case. We got to talking and she told me it seems that it's mostly breeders and pet stores who have reported stolen puppies. For some reason the thieves are not just targeting private owners for them."

"That is peculiar. Did your friend have any theories about it?"

"She thinks it has to do with the fact that puppies grow so quickly. She asked a number of breeders, and they told her that most people in the market for a puppy want one that's two or three months old. It's probably too difficult for the thieves to find one in that narrow an age range from a private owner, so they hit the nurseries, so to speak—breeders and pet stores."

"That makes sense," Rory said. She didn't know how much the information was going to help her, but at least it was one more avenue to explore.

"I also have a couple of new stolen dog reports for you," Leah said, already rummaging through a handbag the size of a briefcase. "One chocolate Lab and one sheltie. It's in here somewhere. Ah, found it." She pulled a sheet of paper from the recesses of the bag and handed it to Rory. "I noted the same type of information I gave you on the others."

Rory thanked her and deposited the paper in her own pocketbook. When she got home she'd cross-reference the new data with the information she had on the other dogs and see if there were any more commonalities.

"I don't get it," she said, after swallowing a piece of her muffin. "Either the thieves don't know I'm investigating these cases, which I doubt, given the speed of today's high-tech grapevine, or they think they're untouchable." She didn't mention the possibility that the thieves were depending on their threatening letter to scare her off. Since she'd never told Leah about the letter, now hardly seemed like a good time to bring it up.

"I pity the dognappers," Leah said wryly. "If they don't think you pose a threat, they don't know you like I do."

"I appreciate the vote of confidence and the new info. How are you guys doing on the Brenda Hartley murder?"

"I'm afraid we're not doing much better than you are." Leah forked the last of her scrambled eggs into her mouth. "Of course I shouldn't be talking about this with anyone outside the department," she said, lowering her voice, "but I'd trust you with my life, let alone some fairly useless data."

"I'm listening."

"Well, Brenda's only family was a sister by the name of

Eileen who lives upstate in Duchess County with her husband and two daughters. She told me she and Brenda were
close growing up, but after she moved off the island in the
early eighties, they only got to see each other on holidays.
Now here's where it gets interesting. Eileen told me that
she talked to Brenda a few days before she was murdered,
and Brenda was extremely depressed over a relationship
that had gone sour."

"Does Eileen know the name of the guy?"

"Of course not. That would make my life way too easy,"
Leah said wryly. "Whenever she asked, Brenda would
only give her a first name—Bob. Eileen doesn't think
that's even his real name, because during one conversation
Brenda called him Jim instead, and then got all flustered
and defensive when Eileen pointed out the discrepancy."

Rory drained the last of her hot chocolate and blotted
her mouth with a napkin. "Married guy."

"That's what Eileen thinks and I'm inclined to go with
that too."

"Did she know any other details about him or the
breakup?"

"About the breakup—nothing significant. But she did
say Brenda was always going on about how the guy was
wining and dining her, buying her gifts and all."

"If you could find out whom she was seeing, you might
have the murderer."

"No kidding. We've followed every lead and more than
a few hunches, but it hasn't gotten us anywhere."

"You've spoken to the other women in that photo on
Brenda's mantel?"

"Several times."

"I guess you've got more pull than a lowly PI. I haven't
been able to pin them down."

"You haven't missed much. They both had alibis that
checked out. One of them was out of the country at the
time Brenda was killed, and the other one was on jury duty.

We've also canvassed every restaurant, diner and deli in a ten-mile radius and shown them Brenda's picture in the hope that she might have been seen there with the guy. We've sent her picture to every precinct on the island and asked them to do the same. So far—*nada*. But enough about work," she said firmly, "I don't get to see you all that often and I don't want to spend all our time talking shop."

Rory was in complete agreement. Half an hour later they were still chatting about everything and nothing, just glad to be in each other's company, when Leah glanced at her watch.

"Oh, crap, I'm late." She dug into her purse for her wallet and handed Rory a twenty-dollar bill. "You don't mind if I run? I promised my son I'd get back for his soccer game. Being with you is like being in a time warp." She slid out of the booth. "You know I mean that in the best possible way."

Rory assured her that she did. She hadn't realized how long they'd been sitting there either. She motioned to the waitress to bring the check. She had to get home too, before Hobo destroyed any more of her house.

# Chapter 19

"Stop looking at me with those pathetic eyes," Rory said. "I'm already late." Hobo had raced ahead of her to the front door and was now sitting there blocking her way. He was a quick study. By his second day with her, he'd learned that when she picked up her handbag it meant she was leaving. He'd also learned that if he beat her to the door and looked forlorn enough, he could sometimes persuade her to take him along.

"Okay, okay," she relented, "I'll get your leash." She went to the closet beneath the stairs and plucked it off the hook she'd put there to hold it.

Hobo was still sitting at the door, his tail swishing merrily at the sight of the leash in her hand. "You'd think I was going to leave you with a dog-eating monster," she scolded gently as she pushed aside the thick fur at his neck to attach the leash to his collar. Then they were out the door and into the car. Hobo took up his usual position directly behind her on the backseat, his head out the window, hair blowing back from his face like a model on a photo shoot.

They arrived at the bakery less than ten minutes later. Rory pulled into a spot from which Hobo could watch her through the store's plate glass windows. It was two o'clock and nearing the end of the Sunday crowds, so she didn't have to wait long for her turn. The teenage girl she drew quickly located her order for a dozen assorted dinner rolls and a chocolate and raspberry mousse cake that read "Happy Birthday, Dad."

When Rory was trying to schedule the family dinner, the earliest date they were all free had turned out to be the Sunday before her father's birthday. That made selecting a dessert easy. Mousse had long been his favorite and her mother and aunt were also big fans.

She put the cake and rolls on the floor of the front passenger compartment where Hobo wouldn't be tempted to sample them. With any luck she'd make it home before her family arrived so they wouldn't have to sit in their car waiting for her. While she knew it wouldn't matter to them, it mattered to her. This was her first dinner party in her own house and she wanted everything to go right.

She turned into the driveway. No other car yet. She'd timed it perfectly, Hobo's neuroses notwithstanding. When she walked around to the far side of the car to retrieve the baked goods, he gave her a questioning little bark as if to ask why she'd cut their lovely outing so short.

"Sorry to disappoint," she said as she passed his window on her way to the front door. "I'll be back for you in a minute." She'd learned a valuable lesson the last time she'd tried to take him and groceries into the house at the same time. He'd probably caught a sudden whiff of ghost, because he'd plowed through her legs in a mad dash back to the sanctuary of the car. Rory and the groceries had hit the flagstone walk at the same time, breaking eggs, bruising

peaches and leaving her with assorted abrasions and con-
tusions. Since that day she left Hobo in the car until she'd
brought everything else into the house. She was a quick
study too.

The boeuf bourguignonne she'd left simmering in the
slow cooker had filled the house with a warm, inviting
aroma that brought back childhood memories of cozy winter evenings when her mother had prepared the same meal.
Now if Zeke could just be counted upon to keep his word,
the day should be enjoyable for everyone.

She stowed the cake in the refrigerator, set the rolls on
the counter and was headed back outside for Hobo when
she noticed the envelope lying on the floor in the entryway.
When she'd walked in, the packages she'd been holding had
blocked it from her view. She picked it up by one corner,
determined not to compromise any potential fingerprints or
DNA. There was no address, just her name written in sten-
ciled letters. No return address, no postmark. No surprise.
She thought about opening it, then changed her mind. The
odds favored it being another threatening note, and she had
no intentions of letting the creep who'd written it spoil her
day. Whatever it was, she'd deal with it later when she was
good and ready. She backtracked to the kitchen and shoved
it into a drawer her mother and aunt weren't likely to look
in if they were helping her clean up after dinner.

When she walked outside she found her family clus-
tered around the left rear door of her car, introducing
themselves to Hobo, who was lapping at cheeks, arms,
noses and whatever else he could reach through the partially open window. So far so good. No traveling marshal
as self-appointed welcome wagon. But as she let Hobo out
of the car and ushered everyone into the house, something
elusive was niggling at her. Unable to pin it down, and with
a dinner party to attend to, she banished it to the back of
her mind.

"Your mother was thinking you were never going to

invite us over," Rory's father said with a wink. The four of them were sitting in the living room, talking and nibbling on the stuffed mushrooms, mini quiches and artichoke dip she'd prepared as hors d'oeuvres.

Rory looked at her mom and laughed. "Seriously?"

"No, of course not," she said. "I know you've been busy getting your new career going and all. Dad just likes to turn my words around and needle me."

"But with the best of intentions," he pointed out, reaching for another mushroom, "only with the best of intentions."

Being together in the house that had been Mac's, it was inevitable that the conversation should find its way to memories of him. Time had been working its quiet magic, though, and the memories they shared were good ones. Memories that made them laugh without pangs of guilt for the joy they felt. Memories that assured them that Mac was woven as tightly as ever into the fabric of their lives.

The timer rang for the rolls that were warming in the oven. With dinner ready and everything still quiet on the supernatural front, Rory was actually starting to relax. They were seated at the dining room table, toasting the success of her new career with the bottle of red wine her parents had brought for the occasion, when Hobo jumped up and bolted out of the room making a horrible sound that was somewhere between a bark and a shriek.

"Is he okay?" her father asked as he ladled chunks of beef and vegetables onto his plate. "I didn't know dogs could make noises like that. Could you pass those egg noodles, Helene?"

"Maybe he had a bad dream, the poor dear," she said, handing him the requested bowl.

"But he wasn't sleeping," Rory's mother said. "He was just sitting here between Rory and me waiting for handouts."

Rory shrugged. "He acts a little strange sometimes. No reason to be concerned." Unless you happen to be a federal marshal with a death wish. A moment later Hobo came tearing back into the room, executed a neat pirouette as if he were thinking of chasing his tail, then ducked under the table, trampling everyone's feet until he landed against Rory's legs with a dull thud and a groan.

"He's trembling something awful," Helene said when she reached under the table to pet him. She looked at her sister. "Remember Snuggles, that little dog we had when we were kids? Whenever there was a thunderstorm he'd shake like he'd swallowed a vibrator."

"Except there's no storm," Rory's father said. "And the expression is 'shake like a leaf,' not a vibrator." He broke off a piece of a roll and used it to sop up some of the gravy on his plate. "Great stew, Rory, great stew."

"So now you're the word police?" Helene came back sharply.

"Who sees a dog shaking and thinks 'vibrator'?"

"Someone with a bit of imagination."

Rory didn't pay attention to the little skirmish taking place beside her. As far back as she could remember her father and aunt had enjoyed sparring with each other.

Their sniping no longer even registered on her mother's radar. "Maybe you should speak to a vet or a trainer," she said to Rory.

Having had the last word, Helene claimed victory by refilling her wineglass and toasting herself. Then she turned to Rory and her sister and hopped aboard their conversation. "My neighbor swears by her vet. I can get you his name if you want."

"Thanks," Rory said, propping her lips into a smile, "but I know exactly who to talk to."


"Zeke!" Rory thundered. She was standing in the entryway after saying good night to her family. Not yet over his earlier trauma, Hobo was pressed against her like a bizarre conjoined twin. When she moved, he moved.

When she stopped, he stopped. He'd become so proficient at matching her steps that they could probably do a dance routine for one of the talent shows on TV.

The hanging lamp above her blinked and a moment later the marshal appeared wearing a perplexed expression. "You're sounding a mite vexed, Aurora," he said. "Didn't your dinner party go well?"

Hobo was caught in a conundrum. Although he wanted desperately to get away from the marshal, he was equally desperate to stay with his savior. His solution was to press his body more tightly against her leg, nearly knocking her over in the process.

"It went very well," she snapped, once she'd regained her balance, "in spite of your efforts to undermine it."

"My efforts?" Zeke managed to sound both surprised and indignant. "I just stopped by to get the feel of your family again. Surely I can't be blamed for simple curiosity. It's been a while since I've seen them."

Rory applauded, causing Hobo to flinch. "Nice performance, but I'm not buying it. You promised to behave yourself."

"I did. No one had any idea I was there."

"Except poor Hobo, who might have to be surgically removed from my leg. I don't even want to know what you did to make him flip out like that."

"In case you've forgotten, Hobo has a tendency to overreact when it comes to me," Zeke pointed out. "But I'm more than willin' to put that aside and talk about more important things, like that letter you got earlier."

Rory didn't want to let him off so easily, but she'd made her point and there was little to be gained by harping on it. She took a deep breath and changed gears.

"You didn't happen to see who slipped it under the door, did you?" she asked as a matter of course.

"Yes, darlin', I sure did." Zeke's mouth stretched into a grin as he waited for her reaction.

It took Rory an extra moment to absorb what he'd said. Then her brows arched up in amazement. Was this finally the break they'd been waiting for? "Give me a minute," she said, already on her way up the stairs. When she returned with her sketch pad and pencil, Zeke had relocated to his favorite chair in the living room.

"Okay, fire away," she said, perching on the edge of the couch, pencil poised to begin.

"He was a young fella, twenty tops. A couple inches shorter than me. Brown hair, real short the way soldiers wear it these days. His eyes were sorta squinty."

"Thin or heavyset?" Rory prompted. "Tell me about the shape of his face, his ears, his mouth."

"He was thin, gangly thin like he'd just got finished growing. Long face I guess you'd say. His ears stuck out from his head some, but that might have been because of that haircut. His mouth? Can't say that I noticed, him not being a woman and all."

Rory glanced up long enough to shoot him a disapproving look. "You need to focus. Any distinguishing marks or features?"

"Nothin' that I can . . . no, hold on. He had a tattoo on his right arm. I only saw a piece of it stickin' out between the sleeve of his jacket and his gloves, but I'm pretty sure it was the tail of a snake."

She nodded. The gloves were pretty much a given, since there hadn't been any prints or DNA on the first letter. "Regular leather gloves or the thin, latex ones I use for handling evidence?"

"Black leather gloves."

She drew for another minute, then turned the picture around for him to see. "Tell me what needs fixing."

Zeke issued a low whistle of appreciation. "I know this ain't the first time I've seen you draw, but it's a downright amazin' thing."

"Thanks," Rory said, more taken by his praise than she

would have expected to be. "But you need to help me fine-tune it. Tell me what's wrong."

He stared at the picture for a while and then had her make adjustments to the hairline and the thrust of the chin.

"Yup, that's him all right," he said when he saw the final product.

"Did you get a look at his car?"

"There wasn't any car, at least none I could see."

"The odds are he had one. Getting around the island is too difficult otherwise. Plus he had to be watching, waiting for me to leave. He probably parked down the street where we wouldn't notice him." She sighed. "I guess a license plate number would have been too much to hope for. First thing in the morning I'll drive out to Yaphank and give this to Leah to run through the database. With any luck this guy is in the system, and she'll be able to give me his name and last known address."

"What will you tell Leah when she wants to know who gave you his description?" Zeke asked.

Rory hadn't thought that far ahead yet, but he was right. She needed to have her answer ready if she didn't want to say a ghost was her resource.

"I'll tell her I saw him hanging around near Boomer's Groomers the day I was there," she said. That would have to do. If she said she'd gotten the description from someone else, Leah might want to interview that person too. They were both scraping the bottom of the barrel on their cases.

"What about the letter?" Zeke asked. "What did it say?"

Rory jumped up from the couch. "Damn, I got so caught up in drawing the guy, I haven't opened it yet."

Zeke beat her into the kitchen, since he didn't have to deal with the inconveniences of gravity and friction. He was standing at the center island, arms folded as if he'd been waiting an hour for her to arrive. Rory pulled on a pair of latex gloves, then took the envelope out of the drawer and tore it open. In all likelihood the sender had been as careful not to leave prints or DNA this time either, but a girl could dream.

The writing on the sheet of paper inside was done in the same neat stencils as her name on the envelope. The last note had been pieced together using words from magazines and newspapers. Apparently her pen pal liked variety. Rory read the two short lines out loud. "Drop the investigation now. This is your final warning." The words had no real impact on her. Like the previous note, it sounded like it had been lifted straight from the script of a hammy old movie. But taped to the bottom of the page was a grainy four-by-six photo of Hobo in her backyard with a large "X" drawn across him in permanent black marker. The nonverbal message slammed into her gut like a steel fist. If she'd harbored any doubts about the depth of her affection for Hobo, this threat put them to rest. No way was she going to let anyone lay a hand on him or disturb a single hair on his lovable, shaggy head.

She transferred the note to a plastic bag, hoping Reggie would still be willing to donate his time. Then she looked Zeke squarely in the eye. "I know what you're thinking, and I'm not going to have this argument with you again. I can't run to the police every time some thug tries to scare me off. If I do, my reputation and my career will be over in a heartbeat, and you'll find yourself haunting some new home owner's life."

Zeke's jaw was tight, his words measured. "I get what you're sayin', but I don't know that you've been in the business long enough to know the difference between what's prudent and what's downright foolish."

"Given your current status, you're hardly the right one to teach me," Rory reminded him as she stalked out of the kitchen.

"That's where you're wrong, Aurora," he said, cutting her off at the staircase. "I'm the perfect one to teach you, precisely because I got it wrong."

Rory didn't bother to reply. Determined not to let him block the way, she squeezed past him and continued up the stairs to her room. It wasn't late, but she was tired. She undressed, pulled on her nightgown and crawled into bed without bothering to wash. Yet sleep didn't come easily. In the stillness, the nagging feeling that she'd missed something important came back to her. Like an itch too deep to scratch, it kept tugging her back from the brink of sleep until well past midnight.

# Chapter 20

Rory arrived at the Huntington Dog Park in the early afternoon accompanied by Hobo. The plan was for him to get exercise while providing her with instant entrée into the social network of dog owners there. It was a cool day made colder by a blustery wind that chased clouds across the sky and juggled the russet and gold leaves it plucked from the trees.

Rory had bowed to the weather and hunted down her short winter jacket for the excursion. After searching for half an hour, she'd finally found it on the floor in the back of the guest room closet. As much as she loved the renovations Mac had made to the old Victorian, her one quibble remained. There was too little closet space. Mac hadn't felt the need to increase it. In his line of work he'd lived in chinos or jeans that he paired with tee shirts for summer and sweaters for winter. He had one good suit that he'd adapted to every occasion, from weddings to funerals, by simply changing the shirt and tie. Since it had been late spring when Rory moved into the house, she'd simply stuffed her winter clothing into whatever nook or cranny she could find, certain there'd be plenty of time to organize her wardrobe before the first chill. So much for certainty.

As she pulled into the parking lot of the dog park, Hobo started whining and dancing around the backseat as if he knew exactly where they were. Pavlov would have been proud of him. When she turned off the engine, he jumped into the front prepared for a quick exit. Rory grabbed his leash and ordered him to sit down. It took several tries and the addition of a menacing tone before he obeyed. But even then Rory could tell by the way he was wiggling around that she had a window of maybe twenty seconds before he came unglued again. She managed to open the door and jump out before Hobo launched himself after her. Some obedience training was definitely in order.

She closed the door and locked the car. She'd already decided to leave her sketch pad behind, so she could get a sense of the people there before she let on that she was investigating the dognappings.

The dog park occupied several acres of open field that were well maintained and complete with benches for the owners and waste bag stations so that they could clean up after their pets. The area was divided into two sections, one for small dogs under twenty-five pounds, the other for their larger kin. There was no ambiguity about where Hobo belonged. Rory opened the first of the double gates into the big dog enclosure. Like an airlock on a spaceship, the two-gate system prevented dogs from escaping when someone entered or left. Hobo was bouncing up and down with excitement by the time Rory led him through the second gate and unhooked his leash. He immediately took off across the open field, barking as if to announce his arrival.

By Rory's count there were close to a dozen people in the enclosure, most of them women, either sitting on the benches or standing and talking in small groups as their dogs raced around making the most of their freedom. Rory turned her collar up against the wind and set out for the two middle-aged women standing nearby. They stopped their conversation to say hello as she approached them.

"Hi." Rory smiled. "Is it always this windy here?" Thank goodness for weather, the universal conversation starter.

"Today's a little over the top even for this place," the shorter of the two women replied. Her hair was pulled back in a ponytail and her nose was red from the cold. "Was that Hobo with you?"

"Yeah, I guess he's used to coming here. I had no clue."

"See, Jean, I told you that was him," the taller woman said. She had on a red knit hat and oversized sunglasses. "There's only one Hobo, the original class clown. I'm Susan." She nodded to Rory, but kept her hands tucked into her pockets. Given the weather Rory understood perfectly. She'd shoved her own hands into her pockets as soon as she'd let Hobo loose. She introduced herself as Hobo's new owner.

Jean shook her head. "It's terrible what happened to Brenda, so terrible."

Susan wagged her head in agreement. "Did you know her?"

"Barely," Rory said. And not while she was actually alive, but they didn't need to know that yet.

"It was really good of you to take him," Jean said. "He's as lovable as they come, but a bit of a handful."

"So I've been finding out."

"Just between us"—Susan lowered her voice and leaned in to them—"I don't buy the idea that Brenda was killed when she got in the way of the dognappers. I'm willing to bet she was killed because of that affair she was having. When it all gets sorted out you'll see I'm right. I'm intuitive about these things."

"If you don't mind my asking, what makes you think that?" Rory asked. She'd planned to reroute any conversation about Brenda into a fact-finding mission about the dog thefts, but she couldn't resist hearing what Susan had to say. She told herself she was only pursuing that line of questioning so that she could pass any worthwhile information to Leah. The trouble was that she didn't believe it any more than Leah would.

"Well," Susan said, "we used to hang out a lot, you know, see a movie, get dinner. She was single like me. But for the past six months she was always, quote, 'busy.' No explanation. She used to confide in me when she had a man in her life, but this time—nothing. I think it's because she was seeing a married man and I think he was somebody we know. She was probably afraid that if she told me, I'd slip and spill the beans to his wife."

"Is that it?" Jean asked. "The entire basis for your theory is that Brenda didn't talk to you about a guy she was seeing?"

"A couple of times when I called her I heard a man in the background and I heard her trying to shush him."

"Come on, now. That's hardly proof she was having an affair," Jean said skeptically. "For all you know the guy was her brother."

"Except she doesn't have a brother," Susan replied, a testy snap to her words.

"I'm just saying, I don't think we should be spreading rumors when even the police don't know for sure what happened or why."

"So you think Brenda's death was the result of a lovers' quarrel?" Rory asked.

"Either that or the guy's wife found out and decided to take matters into her own hands," Susan said in a huffy tone aimed at Jean.

Rory was starting to feel responsible for the escalating tension between the two friends. It was time to change the subject. She was about to admit her real purpose in being there when a man shouted, "Heads up! Incoming!"

The three women automatically ducked as a Frisbee soared by, inches above their heads.

"Sorry, the wind caught it," the Frisbee thrower called to them. "Baxter, no!" he shouted. "No! Stop!"

Before Rory could turn to see what was happening, she was knocked to the ground by a brick wall that apparently went by the name of Baxter. The black Lab raced on to retrieve his toy oblivious to the casualty he'd left in his wake.

Susan and Jean were helping Rory to her feet when the Frisbee thrower reached them. "I am so sorry," the young man said. "Are you okay?"

Rory brushed off a few leaves that were clinging to her legs. "It's nothing my own dog hasn't done to me," she assured him.

"I feel terrible. Baxter's usually better behaved than that, but when he's going for a Frisbee he has no manners at all." He extended his hand to her. "I'm Pete Dowling, by the way. You'll need to know that if you decide to sue."

"Rory McCain," she said, laughing and shaking his hand as the Lab with a neck like a linebacker ran up to them, the Frisbee in his mouth. "And this I presume is Baxter."

"The one and only. I saw you come in with Hobo, right?"

Rory nodded. "He needed exercise and I needed information." As she told Dowling and the women about her investigation, she could see that they were regarding her with renewed interest.

"Have you noticed anyone hanging around the park here, checking out the dogs, maybe taking notes?"

Pete and Susan shook their heads.

"I think I did," Jean said. "There was a man standing outside the gate last Thursday. I saw him here once before too. He watches the big dogs here for a couple of minutes, then he goes over and takes a look at the smaller ones before he leaves. I didn't see him taking notes, but he was holding some paper in his hand."

"Would you be able to describe him?" Rory asked.

"I think so."

She excused herself and ran back to the car for her sketch pad. When she returned, she saw that one of the benches was now empty so she asked Jean to sit there with her. Pete and Susan followed them and Susan sat herself down on the other side of Rory.

Before beginning, Rory took a moment to check on Hobo. He was over on the far side of the enclosure still cavorting like a loon, the other dogs following his lead. He was definitely the life of the party. If there were a lampshade to be had, she had no doubt that he'd be the one sporting it. Satisfied that he was safely occupied, she opened the sketch pad to a clean page and took her pencil out of her purse.

"I hope I get this right," Jean said, rubbing her hands together from nerves or the cold, or both.

"There's no right or wrong," Rory assured her. "All you have to do is tell me what you recall. I understand that memory isn't a digital camera and that even the sharpest memories fade with time. But whatever you give me will be a lot more than I have now."

Jean smiled, clearly relieved. "Where should I start?"

"Why don't you estimate his height and weight first. Even though I'll be concentrating on his face, knowing body proportions helps."

Jean took a deep breath. "Okay, he was average height or a little under. I'm not good at guessing weight, but he was maybe a hundred seventy-five."

"Good, that's good," Rory said. "How old do you think?"

"The older I get, the younger everyone else seems to me." Jean gave a self-conscious little laugh that was loudly echoed by Susan. "I'd say he was in his late thirties."

"Okay. How about the shape of his face, the cut of his hair, the set of his eyes?"

Jean thought for a minute. "His face was more round

than anything else and he was bald. I was too far away to tell if he was really bald or just shaved his head the way a lot of guys do. I can't tell you much about his eyes either, except for the fact that he was wearing glasses with a dark frame."

"You're doing great," Rory told her, although expectations of a viable sketch were fading quickly. Unless this guy had some striking feature, her drawing wouldn't be specific enough to check against the police database. "What about his nose and mouth? Take your time and try to visualize him standing over there where you saw him."

Jean focused on the place where she had seen him, the skin between her brows bunching with concentration. After a minute she turned back to Rory, looking defeated. "I'm sorry, but I don't remember anything special about his nose or mouth. I think they were just ordinary." She shook her head. "I didn't realize how hard this is. I guess I don't have as good a picture of him in my mind as I thought I did."

"You're not alone. Most people are surprised by how little they actually notice about an individual, especially if it was just a casual observation." Rory put down the pencil and flexed her fingers, which were beginning to feel stiff and a little numb from the cold. Jean looked uncomfortable too. Her arms were crossed, her shoulders hunched forward as she huddled to keep warm.

Some of the other owners had wandered over to see what was going on, but Rory barely noticed them. Working with the police, she'd learned not to let onlookers distract her.

"Do you mind a few more questions?" she asked Jean, unwilling to walk away without the best sketch she could get.

"Not if you think it'll help."

"I'll make it quick. Did he have any facial hair?"

"No."

"Were his ears flat against his head or did they project at all?"

"Flat I think."

"Any scars?"

"Hey." A young woman who'd been watching spoke up. "I think I know that guy."

Rory looked up at her. "You know his name?"

"Yeah, that's Eddie Mays."

The man standing next to her told her she was nuts. Rory was inclined to agree with him. The Eddie Mays she'd interviewed had a very distinctive, identifiable face, while the man in her sketch was far too bland and ordinary.

"Could you make the eyes kind of buggy, the way thick glasses can make them look?" the young woman asked.

Rory was happy to oblige.

"And the nose should be thicker, fleshier at the tip."

As she made the requested changes, Rory was beginning to recognize the owner of Boomer's Groomers too. Without being told, she added the little hoop to his eyebrow and the silver stud to the center of his chin. There was a really good chance that the face staring back at her was Eddie Mays after all. What the drawing had been lacking most of all was the attitude that informed Mays's features. Now that she knew her subject matter, her pencil flew over the page, paring down the roundness of the cheeks, closing the distance between the eyes, adding shadows and lines and refining the set of the mouth.

"Damn if she ain't right," the man murmured. "That's him. I used to take my dog to his place to get groomed."

It was all very well and good that Rory's sketch now looked like Eddie Mays, but if this face was no longer the one Jean remembered seeing at the park, it was worthless. She held the drawing up for her appraisal.

"Okay, what do you think? Is this the man you saw here? Don't let yourself be swayed by what anyone else is saying."

Jean stared at the sketch and chewed on her lower lip.

"If you saw this man in a police lineup, would you pick him out as the man you saw here?" Rory prompted.

"Yes," she said finally, her voice shaking a bit from the cold. "Yes, I'm almost positive that's him."

"Well that's close enough for me," Rory said. She thanked her for the help and apologized for having kept her out there in the cold. Then she flipped her pad closed and tucked the pencil back in her purse. "You should probably go home and have something hot to drink," Rory told her, craving a big cup of hot cocoa herself, whipped cream piled high.

She looked up at the people standing around her. They all resembled refugees from a blizzard, eyes tearing, cheeks and noses raw from the wind. She thanked the young woman who'd identified Eddie. Without her help, the sketch would have been largely useless. Instead Rory had a face and a name, and tomorrow she'd be paying Eddie Mays another visit.

# Chapter 21

"You know it's possible Mays was just out there takin' a walk, or what folks today call 'gettin' some fresh air,'" Zeke said after Rory gave him the rundown on the dog park and showed him the sketch of Eddie. As if by mutual consent they'd both moved on from the impasse of the previous night without the need for apologies, for which Rory was grateful. She didn't have the time to waste dealing with bruised egos, his or her own.

The marshal leaned his shoulder against the doorjamb between the kitchen and the small laundry room where Rory had gone to transfer a load of towels from the washing machine to the dryer. "I mean he owns a dog groomin' place so I'm guessin' he likes dogs. Why wouldn't he hang out at the dog park from time to time?"

"Well, for one thing," Rory replied, tossing a fabric softener in with the clothes, "I'm not sure he loves dogs all that much. I doubt he even has one of his own. If he did, he'd take it to the shop with him and to the park. For another, if you're working on other people's dogs all day long, why would you spend your free time watching other people's dogs run around? That's what my dad would call a real busman's holiday."

"What does a bus have to do with anythin'?" Zeke asked in the exasperated tone he reserved for modern expressions that made no sense to him.

Rory almost fell into the trap of trying to explain it to him, but she caught herself in time. It was never worth the energy it required, because he'd already passed judgment on it and wasn't likely to change his mind.

Zeke wasn't waiting for an explanation anyway. "I suppose you could be right about Mays," he said, "but I'm assumin' that even these days the police can't arrest a guy for just standin' there watchin' some dogs play."

"No, we haven't sunk that low yet," she said. "Look, I know this may not be a great lead, but it is a lead. And in case you haven't been counting, we're not exactly buried under dozens of them. So I'm going to follow this one wherever it takes me. And tomorrow morning it's taking me back to see Eddie." She started the dryer and turned to leave the laundry room, but she found Zeke occupying half the doorway. She could either chance squeezing past him or she could ask him to move. Recalling Hobo's hysteria after bumping into the marshal, Rory went with a polite "excuse me."

Zeke moved out of the way without a single taunt about her lack of courage. Either he was totally focused on the Eddie Mays issue or he'd decided not to say anything that might push her into proving her courage in other, more dangerous ways.

Rory walked past him into the kitchen and picked up the coffee she'd left on the counter. She'd stopped for it at a local deli on her way home, and it had gone a long way toward removing the chill from her bones. When she'd set it down on the counter earlier, Hobo had promptly fallen asleep on the floor below it, a strategy no doubt meant to

keep him informed as to her whereabouts. But he hadn't
taken sheer exhaustion into account. Practically comatose
from his romp in the park, even Zeke's appearance and
voice had failed to rouse him. Rory stared at him with some
concern until she saw the gentle rise and fall of his chest.

"What did you do to the mutt?" Zeke laughed, stepping
over him as if that were the only available route through
the kitchen.

Rory held herself in check and said nothing, even though
she could imagine the hullabaloo if Hobo chose that moment
to wake up. But Zeke completed his transit, and Hobo snored
on blissfully unaware.

"You shouldn't go makin' an appointment with Mays
this time," Zeke said, straddling one of the kitchen chairs
and looking at Rory over the back of it.

"I can't anyway." She shrugged. "I've played out my
welcome as a journalist, and I'm pretty sure he wouldn't
agree to see me again if I did call ahead. So I'm just going
to drop in on him and hope he doesn't throw me out. All I
have to do is come up with a different excuse for wanting
to talk to him."

Rory sat down at the table, and in one quick blur of
motion Zeke turned himself and his chair around so that
he was facing her again. Thankfully Hobo wasn't awake to
witness Zeke's little performance of legerdemain.

"In my time I had some success usin' the least likely of
approaches with suspects," he said with a nostalgic smile.
"Like the time I went to Texas to help out some friends with
a cattle spread there. They'd been losin' a lot of their animals
to rustlers. After a few days nosin' around, I had me a pretty
good hunch who was doin' the rustlin', but they turned those
cattle over so quick I couldn't catch them with the goods. So
I sat myself down at a table in the local saloon and waited
for those boys to get thirsty. Two of them came in that very
afternoon. Once they'd had a couple of drinks, I went over to
them and told them I had it on good authority that a marshal

was coming to shut them down. They were real interested, and we got chummy quick." His smile deepened into a grin. "It didn't take me long to find out what I needed to know in order to catch them and their boss red-handed."

"So, make it seem like I'm on his side and just trying to give him a heads-up," Rory said, a possible scenario taking shape in her mind.

"Just don't let this Mays fella get you into the back of that store. You stay up front where you can be seen and heard in case he decides you're a problem he doesn't need."

"You know I'm really not as dumb as those rustlers," Rory said evenly, proud of herself for taking the high road when she actually felt like slugging him. It never failed to amaze her how helpful he could be one minute and how exasperating the next.

"Maybe I should try to meet you there," Zeke muttered, raking the hair back from his forehead, a gesture that generally meant he was feeling frustrated or helpless. Rory knew that "frustration" didn't come close to explaining what it was like for him to exist on the outskirts of life all these years. Surely it had changed him from the man he'd once been. Not for the first time she wished she could have known him before his long tenure in her house. Yet in spite of all the empathy she had for his plight, she had to keep him reined in now that his actions affected her life too.

"No way," she said firmly, "no traveling. You're not close to mastering it, and I can't concentrate on Mays if I'm waiting for pieces of you to suddenly pop out of thin air."

Zeke was shaking his head as if he already regretted telling her the story.

"I'll be fine. I'll have my gun with me, and besides, I'm pretty sure I can outrun Eddie." She'd added the last in hopes of getting him to lighten up and smile again.

"This is serious business, Aurora," he said, a smile nowhere in sight, "and you need to treat it as such."

The telephone rang before Rory could reply. Just as well;

her store of patience was bankrupt. When she answered the phone, Leah was on the other end.

"I ran the sketch of that guy you saw outside Boomer's Groomers," she said, "but there was no match. Whoever he is, he's managed to stay out of the system so far."

Another dead end. Rory thanked her and they spent a few minutes chatting about their cases. Leah wasn't having any more success finding Brenda's killer than Rory was having tracking down the dog thieves. For that matter, they still didn't know if they were looking for the same doers. Rory told her about Susan from the dog park who was sure Brenda was murdered because of the affair she was having. On its own, it didn't seem to be worth much, but it did tie in nicely with the information from Brenda's sister.

Rory didn't bother mentioning the sketch of Eddie Mays or her plan to visit him again. She told herself she'd let Leah know if anything came of it. Her conscience was stirring up a pot of guilt porridge over the omission, but not enough to change her mind. As she'd told Zeke on more than one occasion, she had to do right by her clients, and that meant not letting anyone tie her hands behind her back. For all of her fabulous qualities, Leah could be too maternal and protective of the people she loved.

When Rory walked into Boomer's Groomers, Eddie was behind the counter helping a woman who was there to pick up her dog, a miniature poodle that had been groomed and pruned into a canine topiary with a pink bow at each tasseled ear flap.

Eddie managed to keep his pleasant business face on until after the woman and her dog left. The minute the door closed behind them he came out from behind the counter, scowling at Rory from beneath recently shaved eyebrows. Added to his shaved head and piercings his appearance had morphed from merely odd to menacing.

"You're not welcome here," he said in a tone that matched his expression. "I called that magazine you supposedly write for, and they never heard of you. Who the hell are you? And why are you so interested in me?"

"Okay, here's the deal," Rory said, laying on a heavy dose of sincerity, "you've heard of neighborhood watch groups, right?"

"Yeah, so?"

She could hear his anger start to give way to wary curiosity.

"Well, I'm a member of PAW, Protect Our Animals Watch. The police haven't been able to find the thieves who are stealing our pets, so we've decided it's up to us to do whatever we can to protect them."

Eddie skewered her with his owl eyes. "What's that got to do with lying and pretending to do an article about me?"

This wasn't going to be an easy sell. "Give me a minute," Rory said, "I'm getting to that. PAW meets every week to share information, theories, suspicions. Last week your name came up."

"My name? What're you saying?" The scowl was back, blacker than before. "You accusing me of something?"

Rory's feet were itching to backpedal, but she held her ground. "Take it easy. Let me finish," she said more calmly than she felt. "A few of the members reported seeing you down at the Huntington Dog Park."

Eddie surprised her by chuckling. He held his arms out straight as if he were waiting to be arrested and cuffed. "You broke me. I confess. I was at the dog park." Then he turned abruptly away from her with a dismissive wave of his hand. "You're mad as a hatter," he muttered. "Leave now before I call the police to haul your ass outta here." He started to walk toward the back of the store.

"They thought you were taking notes, possibly targeting certain dogs to steal."

Eddie stopped and turned back to her. "Yeah? And how was I supposed to know where any of those dogs lived?"

"By following the owners home."

Eddie retraced his steps until he was standing toe-to-toe with her. "Get outta here!" he growled.

"I stood up for you," Rory said staunchly. She saw the rage ebb from his face and leave his features strangely blank. "I told them it wasn't possible. That I knew too many people who loved Boomer's Groomers and that you were a businessman with a good, solid reputation. I even said I'd check you out myself. That's why I lied and said I was writing an article."

"So you got what you wanted. Why're you here again?"

"They weren't sold by what I said. They still think you're involved, because one of them saw you holding papers at the park as if you were taking notes. Between you and me, I think they've gone off the deep end," she said, trying Zeke's gambit of aligning herself with her quarry. "I just wanted to let you know what's going on. You've got a reputation to protect and all."

Eddie didn't respond. He leaned over the counter and pulled a stack of paper from a shelf below the register. He held it out to her. "Here. Do these look like sinister notes or plans to you?"

Rory looked at the top paper on the pile. It was an ad for his store with a coupon for a free bag of dog treats with a grooming.

"I went down there to put these flyers on the windshields in the parking lot. I do that from time to time. It's called advertising. When you report back to PAW, you can tell them for me they're all certifiable." Eddie walked away muttering something unintelligible.

Rory left the store thinking that if he was lying, he was doing a mighty fine job of it.

Then again, prisons were full of criminals who were every bit as accomplished in that art.

# Chapter 22

"Jean got the flyer," Rory said, setting the phone back on its base. "It was on her windshield when she left the park. So I guess Eddie's story checks out."

Zeke was seated at the kitchen table. He rocked his chair back onto its rear legs and hefted his boots up on the table, a position that always made Rory cringe even though she knew the dirty boots weren't actually there.

"Just because his alibi checks out, it don't necessarily mean he was tellin' you the whole truth. I've been derailed myself by that kind of assumption. It's possible, and sometimes downright easy, to hide a criminal activity inside a perfectly innocent-lookin' one."

"It was you who suggested Eddie might have been at the park to 'get some fresh air' in the first place," she said with an edge of exasperation. "You can't keep switching sides of the debate."

Zeke laughed. "Of course I can, unless that's another one of your rules." When Rory didn't give him so much as a smile in response, he dropped the humor and switched on a serious expression again. "Listen, you've got to keep reevaluatin' a case as the investigation goes along; otherwise you're just hog-tyin' yourself."

"Lord knows I wouldn't want to be hog-tied," she said, glancing out the kitchen door to see if Hobo was ready to come in. Ever since she'd received the letter threatening him, she'd been afraid to let him out of her sight for long. She located him in the back of the yard blissfully rolling on his back in a pile of leaves the wind had raked into one corner. She'd be finding leaf particles all over the house for days. No matter, as long as he was okay.

"We can't seem to make any progress in this case," she said, sighing in frustration as she took a seat across from Zeke. "I'm going to have to speak to Tina and see if she wants me to continue. She certainly hasn't seen much benefit from the retainer she gave me, and I'm not in a position where I can work for free."

"You've spent so much time on the case, it'd be a real shame to give up on it now."

"I know. I just wish we had a solid direction to go in. It feels like we're chasing our tails, pardon the pun, and what do we have? I can't honestly imagine Marti Sugarman stealing other people's dogs, except maybe Tootsie. The woman's too much of a nervous Nellie. That only leaves Stanley Holbrook and that list of his, Eddie Mays and Anita Callaway, winner of our Miss Congeniality award. If we're not counting Marti, the motive for a crime like this has to be money, right? Joanne Lester seemed to think Dr. Holbrook was in particular need of some, but who doesn't need money these days? It's too broad a motive to help us eliminate anyone."

"I beg to differ," Zeke said with a grin. "It would eliminate me."

"There's no solid evidence that points to any one of them." Rory went on refusing to be sidetracked. "In fact, we have no evidence at all, except for the two letters I received. And according to Reggie, they were both completely clean."

"You're forgettin' a couple of suspects," Zeke reminded her. "Tina's husband Joe and the fella I saw deliverin' that last letter."

"Joe's not on *my* short list," she said, "and there's no way to track down the delivery guy. Not without a license plate or a criminal record or something. To tell you the truth, I'm worried that the real thieves may not even be on our radar yet."

"Now, don't go gettin' all discouraged. There were times when I was clean out of leads and hunches only to find the answer was right under my nose. It's like that children's game where you gotta connect the dots in order to see the picture."

"I really don't see how that helps."

"Maybe not yet, but you will. All I'm sayin' is you gotta keep on keepin' on, darlin'. The only cases I didn't solve were the ones I gave up on."

Rory supposed there was a strange kind of upside-down logic to what he was saying. In any case she didn't feel like discussing the point any further.

"Hell," Zeke went on, "you've got more gumption than any woman I've known; more than most men too. There ain't a quittin' bone in your whole body."

"I'll try to keep that in mind," she said, giving in to the smile that was tugging at her mouth. The marshal really knew how to pay a girl a compliment.

She saw that Hobo was standing at the back door, so she went to let him in. Instead of racing through the kitchen at warp speed when he saw Zeke, the dog padded cautiously past the table and on into the dining room. Once he'd made it to safety, he gave his coat a vigorous shake that produced a mini whirlwind of dust and leaves. Then he settled onto the floor with a weary sigh.

Rory watched in wide-eyed amazement. "Did you catch

that? I think we may at least be making progress on the home front."

"I wouldn't go claimin' victory just yet," Zeke grumbled, clearly unwilling to adjust to life with a dog, even if Hobo was making an effort to adjust to life with a ghost.

"Well, I choose to be optimistic," she said, thinking that Hobo was showing more maturity than the marshal.

"I've often found optimism to be a direct path to disappointment," he said.

Rory was about to suggest that he'd enjoy life more with an attitude adjustment, but since he didn't actually have a life anymore, she decided that it would be tactless of her to harp on the fact. Instead, she let the subject expire and went over to the cabinet beneath the sink to take out Hobo's brush. Armed with the brush and a scissor in case she came across matted fur, she joined the dog on the dining room floor.

"Can we get back to business now?" Zeke pulled his feet off the table, setting his chair down with a loud thump that gave Hobo a start. Rory had to grab the dog's collar and sweet-talk him back down again. She sent the marshal a withering glare.

"If direction in the case is what you're needin', I believe I can help you out there," Zeke said as if he hadn't noticed the dog's reaction or hers. "I've hunted down some questionable newspaper ads."

"Seriously?" Rory looked up as she pulled the steel bristles through Hobo's shaggy coat. "I could really use some good news about now."

"I aim to please," he said with a smile. "Far as I can tell there are two types of ads. First you have the more particular ones where an owner is tryin' to find a new home for a pet. Then you have the general type that just says things like 'all breeds, lowest prices, we won't be undersold.' It's that second type I've been concentratin' on like you suggested. If the ad mentioned a website, I checked that out too."

"And?" she asked, the brush suspended in midair.

"I found three that fit the bill. I left the names and phone numbers on your computer in case you want to call the places. Sorry I couldn't do that part for you," he added.

"Hey, no need to apologize," Rory said. "You did the research to get me the numbers. Calling is the easy part." At least it was for her. For some reason, Zeke's energy didn't translate well through the phone lines. The person on the other end was treated to an ear-splitting screech of static, which she'd discovered the hard way when Zeke had tried to call her cell phone from the landline in the house.

"In fact," she said, "I'm going to do just that as soon as I've made Hobo here a bit more presentable."

Hobo chose to stay behind in the dining room for a little snooze while Rory went up to the study to make the calls. The marshal was perched on the edge of her desk fidgeting impatiently with a button on his shirtsleeve when she walked into the room. She supposed it was easy to get bored when one was always waiting for mortals who had to rely on the traditional form of locomotion.

She sat down behind the desk and picked up the phone. Although she'd had a new business line installed when she'd opened her agency, she'd also kept Mac's existing home number. Since it was unlisted, it allowed her to make outgoing calls that didn't come up on caller ID. Perfect for calls like the three she was about to make. She found the names and numbers from the ads on the computer screen as Zeke promised.

"Wish me luck," she said.

Zeke gave her a wink and a thumbs-up.

Two of the lines were answered by women, the third by a man. Unfortunately none of their voices sounded like any of her suspects, but she'd known that was too much to hope for.

On the off chance that one of them had heard of her, Rory had decided to use an alias. Better safe than sorry. When she inquired as to who supplied the dogs they sold, they all said they worked exclusively with legitimate breeders, and that they would refund her money if she wasn't fully satisfied. She told them she was interested in a Jack Russell puppy and asked if she could have the name of the breeder they would be using, since she wanted proof the puppy didn't come from one of the notorious puppy mills. They were all reluctant to provide her with that information, until she made it clear that their refusal was a deal breaker. In the end, two of them gave her the names and numbers, but emphasized that the breeders had signed contracts preventing them from selling directly to the public and undercutting their prices. The third one, It's a Dog's World, refused to give her the information and hung up when she tried to press for it.

Rory set down the phone and turned to Zeke with a smile. "I think we have ourselves a winner."

"Yes, ma'am." He smiled back at her. "Sounds like you got yourself some of that direction you were lookin' for. How are you fixin' to handle this?"

"I'll wait a couple of days so they don't connect the two calls, and then Dog's World is going to hear from a new customer. A lovely customer who's willing to pay in cash and doesn't ask too many questions."

"You still plannin' to ask for a puppy?"

She nodded. "The puppies aren't being stolen from private owners, only from breeders and pet stores. Even though I'd return the dog right after it's delivered, I couldn't stand causing someone else so much pain and anxiety."

"I know you don't think I understand," Zeke said softly, "but I do."

Rory nodded. "I'm really glad to hear you say that."

An awkward moment of silence stretched between them, and Rory found herself oddly at a loss for words with which to bridge it. That brief exchange had been among the most basic and honest they'd ever shared. In the past, whenever Zeke had revealed something of himself it had been in the heat of anger, as if it were wrenched from him against his will.

It was Zeke who spoke first. "So, what kind of puppy is it goin' to be?"

It took Rory a few seconds to round up her meandering thoughts and refocus. "I don't want to pick a dog that's too hard for them to find or this will drag on forever. I think I'll go with a beagle. They seem to be popular. After I order the dog, I'll let Leah know, and if there's a report of a stolen beagle puppy, we'll know we've probably targeted the right company. It's not a foolproof plan, but it's the best we can do for now.

Zeke nodded. "Sounds fine. Of course, we'll have to work out the details of how they're gonna get the dog to you, and how you're gonna nab them."

"Well, some of that's going to depend on how they usually do the deliveries. If I make too many demands, it could tip them off."

"I wouldn't mind bein' with you when it goes down," he said.

Rory could tell he'd picked his words carefully to avoid an argument, but the delivery couldn't be at her house. If the dognappers knew her, using her address could be just as damaging as using her real name. And Zeke simply wasn't ready for his traveling debut.

"I know I don't quite have the hang of it yet," he said as if he'd been reading her mind, "but there's still time to get in more practice beforehand."

"We'll have to see what kind of time frame we're dealing with. They could tell me I have to wait a month for the dog, or they could say they'll have one for me tomorrow."

"I suppose," Zeke allowed grudgingly. "But we'll do the strategizin' about it together, right?"

"You have my word on that," she promised.

# 1878

## New Mexico Territory

When Drummond opened his eyes he found himself in a room he'd never seen before. Sunlight was pouring in through a window directly across from the bed in which he lay, and his eyes ached from the brightness as if they'd been shuttered for too long. Hard as he tried he couldn't remember how he'd come to be there. He couldn't even recall what day it was, although he had the disquieting feeling that he'd lost a large parcel of time along the way.

Squinting against the light, he took stock of the room. This was clearly the home of a man of means. The wooden wardrobe and matching dresser had been made with careful attention to detail and were polished to a fine glow. Lace curtains framed the window, and a dozen leather-bound books filled a small bookshelf in the corner. From his position on his back, Drummond could just make out the edge of a braided throw rug below him on the shiny planked wood floor.

To the right of the bed there was a small nightstand and

atop it a glass, a decorative pitcher presumably containing water, and lengths of bandaging material. The bed itself was comfortable; the linens, smelling mildly of lemon, were soft against his skin. That realization led him directly to wondering where his clothes were. He peeled back a corner of the blanket and sheet to check beneath them. Whoever had undressed him had not even left him the dignity of his drawers, though to be fair, they hadn't been in the best of condition given his time on the trail.

He was still sorting through the jumbled images in his mind, trying to reconstruct how he'd come to be in this bed, wherever it was, when the pain in his left shoulder roared back to life. For the first time since he'd awakened, he was aware of the tightly bound dressing that immobilized his left shoulder and upper arm. He remembered being shot and then killing his assailant. He was pretty sure he'd managed to mount his horse. From that point on, his memory was lost to a black haze, illuminated only by the jagged flashes of pain that had ripped through him.

How many more miles had Trask put between them, while he lay senseless in this bed? He needed to find his clothes and his horse before any more time passed. He threw back the covers and with great difficulty managed to draw himself up until he was sitting on the edge of the bed. His head was wobbling on his neck, the room dancing merrily around him. Then somehow he was lying in a heap on the rug, the injured shoulder bearing the brunt of his fall. He heard himself scream as if it had come from someone else's throat. Surely he couldn't have made a sound like that.

A young man, not yet out of his teens, came running into the room. "Papa, he's fallen," he called out as he bent to help Drummond up from the floor.

The marshal allowed himself to be supported and deposited back in the bed, mortified by both his weakness and his state of undress, but grateful that it was a young man who had come to his aid and not a young lady.

After he was once more settled beneath the covers, the pillows propped behind him, the young man introduced himself as Henry Abbott, eldest son of Dr. Walter Abbott. He said his father's name and title with deference.

"I'm to be a physician myself," Henry added, his shirt buttons nearly popping with pride. "I've been helping my father with your care. You're one lucky man, I'd say. Lucky that Thad Redmond came across you when he was driving his buckboard into town for supplies. And luckier still to have had my father as your doctor."

Drummond supposed that was all true, but he was too breathless from the pain to say so. Before Henry could expound any further on his great luck, a distinguished-looking man with graying hair and spectacles entered the room. Without a word he bent over his patient and started touching and prodding the injured shoulder until Drummond was on the verge of blacking out again.

"I don't think you did it any grave damage in the fall, Marshal," he said finally, "but you would be wise to take more care in your actions. You're terribly weak from loss of blood. And you haven't eaten in days. When you were brought in here you had a nasty infection and a raging fever. It was all we could do to get sips of water into you. I wouldn't have taken bets on your ability to survive. But happily, here you are," he added with a smile, as if he were a teacher approving of a student's efforts.

"I thank you kindly, Doc," Drummond said. "If you'll tell me what I owe you for the excellent care, I'll be happy to pay my bill. But first, I'd appreciate knowin' where I am and what day this is."

"Of course, of course. It must be disturbing to wake up in strange quarters having lost the thread of time. You're in Albuquerque. Today is the eighteenth of June."

Albuquerque. At least he'd wound up where he'd been headed. As for the days he'd lost, they might prove to be his undoing. But there was no point dwelling on what couldn't be changed.

"I'd be much obliged if I could have my clothes back," he said. "And I'll be needin' my gun and badge as well as my horse. Is he—?"

"You cannot be serious, Marshal," Abbott cut him off, his face cinched with concern. "Please, give yourself at least a day or two to recover some strength, or I fear it's your corpse someone will come across next."

"I don't have the luxury of time, Doc. I'm after a fugitive, the worst sort of man. He abducts young girls, assaults them, then kills them. I mean to find him before he takes another life and destroys another family."

The color had drained from Abbott's face. "I'm reluctant to tell you this, Marshal, but you may already be too late. A ten-year-old girl was taken from her bed, even as her parents slept in the next room. A posse's been out looking for her close to a week now."

"Then there's no time to waste." Drummond swung his legs over the side of the bed, steeling himself against another bout of vertigo. Hanging on by sheer determination, he rode it out. "Your posse has no idea how John Trask thinks or acts. I may be the only one who does. Now, do I get my clothes back or do I go after him naked as a jaybird?"

Abbott shook his head in defeat. "Henry," he said, turning to his son, "go ask your mother to cook up some eggs and biscuits for the marshal. Pack up food for him to take along as well. I'll see to his clothes."

"Thank you," Drummond murmured.

"Don't thank me, Marshal. I just know enough not to fight a battle I've already lost. Though I wish you well, I don't think you're going to survive this quest of yours. And that's a downright shame. We can't afford to lose a fine lawman like you."

"No need to worry on that account, Doc," Drummond said with a rueful smile. "I'm a whole lot stronger than you think and a lot less deserving of your praise."

# Chapter 23

Rory called It's a Dog's World and placed her order for a beagle puppy. The woman who took the order said she'd be notified as soon as they had her dog. Then Rory called Leah to let her know the sting was on.

When a week went by without a word from anyone, Rory found herself pacing restlessly around the house. Hobo had marched along at her side, until it became clear to him that she wasn't actually headed anywhere.

"You're gonna wear a rut in the floors if you keep that up, darlin'," Zeke said, watching her from his perch half-way up the stairs. Hobo seemed to echo the thought with a "woof" from the comfort of the living room couch where he was keeping tabs on both of them.

"I can't stand the waiting," she said, stopping at the base of the stairs. She'd caught up on her other cases, cleaned the house until it reeked of furniture polish and ammonia and brought some order to the overstuffed closets. It wasn't in her DNA to just sit around and wait for Leah or

Dog's World to call. Besides, if she and Zeke were wrong, and Dog's World proved to be a legitimate enterprise, she'd have wasted valuable time.

"I made an appointment to see Tina Kovack this afternoon," she said, looking at her watch and sighing. "But apparently this morning is never going to end."

"Believe me, I know how hard waitin' is," Zeke sympathized, "but I don't think you should be givin' Tina the 'I haven't made much progress, so you may not want to keep me on the case' speech until we see how this sting of ours pans out."

"Not to worry. I've tucked that speech into the 'for future reference' folder. Today I'm just going there to get her feedback on our top suspects. I'll bring along the sketch of the messenger too. Maybe she'll recognize him. She's got a good perspective on all things dog related. Who knows, she might come up with a piece of the puzzle that makes all our other pieces fall into place."

"Sounds like a lotta wishful thinkin'," Zeke said, "but I've always preferred workin' to bein' idle, myself. Of course, wearin' out the floors hardly qualifies as work."

"Well, I've done everything there is to do around here. The house is spotless. Even Hobo's shaggy hide is tangle free."

"Then I have a suggestion to take up that excess time you have on your hands."

"I'm listening."

"We could go out back and work some on my travelin'."

Rory hesitated while she groped around for a good reason to decline or postpone such a session. The sooner Zeke became a free agent, the sooner her life was guaranteed to become crazier. Unfortunately she'd made the tactical error of admitting she had nothing else to do before her appointment.

"You said yourself I need the practice," he pressed her. Bravo. He'd waltzed her gracefully into a corner of her own making. When would she learn to be more careful about what she said to him?

"Let me grab my coat and gloves," she agreed, trying to pump some eagerness into her voice.

W ith the sun still high in the sky and virtually no wind, it was far more pleasant outside than the last time they'd practiced. Rory took along a ball she'd bought for Hobo, and after he'd seen to irrigating the trees and bushes, he played an enthusiastic game of fetch. From time to time a section of the marshal would appear, causing the dog to drop the ball and cower at Rory's side, head down, ears flattened against his skull, tail tucked securely between his legs. By Zeke's fourth try, Hobo had decided that whatever was going on didn't directly affect him and he went about retrieving the ball without further interruption. It was the kind of progress that gave Rory's heart a lift.

At the half hour mark, Zeke also had a breakthrough. He materialized completely, looking every bit as three-dimensional as he did inside the house. He even managed to say, "We're gettin' there," before exhaustion quite literally undid him, and he winked out of sight. Not surprisingly, Rory wasn't nearly as thrilled with *his* progress.

S he pulled into the Kovacks' driveway and parked beside a silver Jeep with Jersey plates, a Jaguar XK8 in British racing green and Joe's work van. Since it was still early afternoon, Rory thought he might have stopped home between service calls to have lunch with his wife. It was Joe who opened the front door when Rory rang the bell. He ushered her inside and explained that a customer had arrived late to pick up her new puppy—something about traffic on the Garden State Parkway. Tina was just finishing up the transaction and would be with Rory shortly. Joe led the way to the family room, where they settled themselves in easy chairs across from one another.

"Who belongs to the beautiful Jag?" Rory asked to make conversation. "That's always been my dream car."

"Mine too," Joe said with a sheepish grin. "Twentieth anniversary gift from Tina."

"Wow, I guess I picked the wrong occupation."

"Don't go quitting your day job," he said. "Breeding and showing dogs doesn't bring in that kind of money. My Tina girl does it because she loves it. But the money for the fancy stuff—she was born to that. I almost didn't marry her on account of it. You know how that is."

Rory wasn't sure that she did, but she nodded politely anyway.

"Yeah, I was from the blue-collar side of the tracks, and Tina came from the big old mansion on the hill, so far from the tracks that she couldn't even hear the train whistle."

"What changed your mind, if I might ask?"

"She convinced me that the money would never come between us. That she'd make a bonfire of it before she'd let that happen."

"Before I'd let what happen, hon?" Neither of them had heard Tina come in through the kitchen door. The three household Maltese accompanied her, weaving in and out of her legs as she walked. It seemed nothing short of miraculous that she didn't trip over them or accidentally punt one across the room.

"Rory was just admiring the Jag," Joe said, getting to his feet. "Hey, you okay, babe?"

A tear wobbled on Tina's lower lashes before spilling onto her cheek. Others crowded her eyes ready to follow. "I'm fine," she sniffled, even her voice congested with tears. Joe pulled her into a bear hug. Since Tina was a couple of inches taller, she had to scrunch down in order to rest her head on his shoulder. It looked like an awkward position, but it didn't seem to bother her in the least.

From the comfort of her husband's arms she gave Rory a tremulous smile. "I'm sorry. I'm afraid this happens every time I send one of my babies off to a new home," she explained at a substantially slower speed than Rory was accustomed to. Apparently tears had a salutary effect on the tempo of her speech.

Joe kissed Tina on the forehead and held her out at arm's length for inspection. "You going to be all right now?"

Tina nodded, pulling a crumpled tissue from the pocket of her pants. She dabbed at her eyes and delicately blew her nose.

"Okay, I'm going to let you ladies get to your business. I've got a dozen oil burners waiting for me." He gave Tina a quick peck on the cheek.

"Don't forget to call Larry back," she said.

"Will do."

He was already out of sight, making his way down the hall to the front door when she called to him to wait. Asking Rory to excuse her, she hurried after him, the three-dog entourage at her heels. A moment later Rory heard Tina's muted voice.

"I don't know where my head is these days. I keep forgetting to give you the money for that retirement dinner. How much do you need?"

"Fifty should do it." Joe's voice was softer, the words harder to pick out.

A minute passed and then Rory heard him say, "Thanks, babe, see you later." There was the whisper of the front door opening, then the thud of it being closed. When Tina returned to the family room, she settled herself in the chair where Joe had been sitting.

"Sorry for the interruption," she said, "it seems to be one of those days."

"No problem," Rory assured her. "Forgive me if I'm being too nosy, but was that Larry Sugarman, Marti's husband, you were talking about?"

"Yes, why?"

"Nothing really. I didn't realize the Sugarmans were more than just customers."

"Most of our local customers become our friends too. We don't buy the theory that you can't mix business with pleasure."

"I guess the dog community is one big, happy family."

Tina laughed. "Well, like most families we're not always happy." As if to underscore that point, two of the dogs tried to jump into her lap at the same time and had a midair collision that knocked them both to the ground. A nasty little squabble ensued, punctuated by snarling and growling, which Rory found comical coming from such little powder-puff dogs. Tina wasn't at all amused. She reprimanded them and ordered them all to lie down on the floor and be quiet, which they did without further protest.

"Sibling issues," she said with a mother's loving smile. "Just like children."

"They're more obedient than most kids," Rory said, laughing.

"You've got a point there. They certainly listen better than my own kids. Now, I know you didn't come here just to talk about my dogs," she said, gunning up to full speed. "Can I get you some soda? Coffee? It'll take no time to get a pot brewing." She inched closer to the edge of her chair, prepared to fly into action if Rory accepted her offer.

"Thanks, but I'm fine. Like I said on the phone, I just want to get your feelings, your insights about some of the people I've been interviewing. Without actual evidence to tie anyone to the case, I'm pretty much stumbling around in the dark."

"Absolutely," Tina said. "Fire away."

"Let's start with Stanley Holbrook," she said, watching Tina's face for her initial reaction. Leah had taught her the importance of observing a person's expression immediately after receiving unexpected news. There was a moment, often less than a second, when their reaction was purely visceral, straight from the gut. To the untrained eye it vanished too quickly to read, replaced by the reaction that came from the brain in all of its multilayered splendor.

There was no doubt about it; Tina was shocked by the suggestion that Holbrook might be stealing the dogs.

"That's not possible," she said firmly. "I've known the man for close to twenty years. Don't get me wrong, he's a bit of a prima donna, and he's always running late, but dognapping? I've never met a vet who cares more about the animals and their owners. That's why I keep going to him."

Rory waited for her to throttle down before she told her about his accountant's visit. This time Tina's first reaction was bewilderment. A crack was developing, a fault line in her hard certainty about Holbrook's innocence.

"Are you sure this Joanne wasn't lying?" Tina asked breathlessly, as if the accusation had knocked the wind right out of her.

"No, I can't be," Rory admitted.

"I mean, what if she's an unhappy employee?" Tina had recovered enough to plead Holbrook's case. "Maybe she didn't get the raise she expected. Or maybe she was in love with him, but he wasn't interested."

"Look, anything's possible. But if Holbrook's been having money problems, he has a motive, and opportunity is as close as his patient files. He knows the age, breed and condition of hundreds of dogs, and he knows exactly where they live."

"I see your point," Tina murmured reluctantly. "I sure hope it's not him, though. I don't know where I'd find another vet of his caliber around here."

"There's no need to go looking for one yet," Rory reminded her. "This is all still conjecture."

Tina nodded and took a deep breath.

"Okay," Rory said, "moving on—what's your take on Eddie Mays?"

"I used to take my dogs to Boomer's Groomers. I know a lot of people who still go there. Mays just got too moody for my liking, and he couldn't seem to hang on to employees. Every time I went in there he had a new groomer. I never knew what to expect, so about a year ago I started doing the job myself." She smiled. "It's messy and time-consuming, but at least that way I have no one to blame if I'm not satisfied."

Rory jotted down a few lines before looking up again. "What about Anita Callaway?"

Tina shook her head. "The name doesn't mean anything to me. Who is she?"

"She runs a doggie day care out of her house. When I stopped by there it looked like a pretty slapdash arrangement."

"That's not a service I'd ever need," Tina said. "But it's strange that I've never heard anyone mention her name." She paused for a moment, a frown working across her forehead. "You know, a doggie day care would be a perfect façade for hiding stolen dogs."

"That crossed my mind too."

"You didn't happen to see any Maltese there?" she asked hopefully.

"No, but I never got past the front door. In fact, she didn't seem all that interested in selling me on her service. It was more like she wanted to get rid of me."

Tina sat up straighter, on full alert. "Can't we get a warrant or something to make her let us in so we can see if my dogs are there?" She was getting worked up enough to storm the house that afternoon.

"We'd need to have some real evidence, probable cause, to get a warrant, and then it would be the police who'd have to execute it."

"Oh." She slouched down in her seat again, deflated. "But you'll tell them to look for George and Gracie if that happens?"

"Of course. And I'd let you know immediately."

Tina recovered enough to produce a little smile. "Is there anyone else you want to ask me about?"

"Just one," Rory said, opening the manila envelope she'd brought with her and taking out the sketch of the messenger. "Any chance you know this guy?"

Tina studied it for a good twenty seconds before shaking her head. "Who is he?"

"I think he's working as a 'go-fer' for the dognappers. He may not even be aware that he's abetting in the commission of a crime. But then again, I may be giving him more credit than he's due." She slid the sketch back into the envelope without mentioning the threatening notes she'd received. Tina was already on full alert and Rory didn't see any point in causing her anxiety level to redline.

They talked for a few minutes about how Hobo was adjusting to his new home, and then, with a promise to get back to her soon, Rory left. She'd hoped for enlightenment, but it appeared that enlightenment would have to wait for the sting to play out.

# Chapter 24

Rory parked in front of the dry cleaner's and scooped up the two sweaters and the corduroy pants from the passenger seat. Even though she'd be close enough to keep an eye on the car, she locked the doors and left the rear window open for Hobo to stick his head out. They'd already stopped at the deli for Rory's kick-start coffee, as well as the drive-through window of the bank, where she deposited a check for a minor case she'd recently closed. After the cleaner's, Rory planned to drop Hobo off at home before going to see Jill Feeny and Beth Feeny-Blake, the two other women in the photo on Brenda's mantel. She'd all but given up on interviewing them, since they never returned her calls.

According to Leah, who'd had a similar problem trying to pin the women down, Jill was busy house and pet sitting for clients who were out of town, and Beth was a jet-setting widow. At first Leah had left polite, businesslike messages on their cell phones. When they didn't return her calls she discarded the amenities and told them bluntly that she'd have them hauled into the police station for questioning if they weren't available to be interviewed at home.

Without a badge, Rory had no such leverage, so she was nearly rendered speechless when she received a call from Jill, weeks after Leah had cleared them as persons of interest in Brenda's murder. Jill said that she and her sister would be at home the next day if Rory was still interested in speaking to them. She made it clear that this was a one-time offer. Rory found out later that Leah had "suggested" they call her.

When Rory emerged from the cleaner's she found a young man in a brown UPS uniform standing at the rear window of her car. He was holding a package in one hand and scratching Hobo's head with the other, while Hobo gave his cheek a thorough washing.

"Great dog you've got here." He grinned as Rory approached the car.

"As long as you're a fan of doggie saliva," she said.

"Hey"—he shrugged, wiping his face—"what's a little drool between friends? I'll tell you, it's a nice break from the greeting I usually get from dogs. Even if they don't take exception to the uniform or the packages, they're really clear about not wanting me anywhere near their house or their car."

"Yeah, I guess Hobo wouldn't make a great junkyard dog."

"That's okay. The world could use a few more Hobos in it." He wished Rory a great day and walked off to deliver his package.

"I don't know, Hobo, I leave you alone for two minutes, and I find you romancing someone else." Rory laughed as she got back in the car. Hobo gave a sharp little woof as if to deny the accusation.

"Tell it to the judge, pal; it's not like this is your first offense."

They were halfway home when Rory realized what had been nagging at her ever since her parents' visit. Not only did Hobo love every living soul at first sight, but he didn't have a territorial bone in his big, furry body, regardless of what her dog book claimed. When her family had congregated around Hobo at the car that day, he hadn't so much as chuffed at them although he'd never met them before. And he didn't even issue a warning bark when the UPS guy approached her car. The only time she'd heard Hobo sound like one of the hounds of Hell was when she'd left him in the car at the Sugarmans' house and Larry had come home. But Larry Sugarman wasn't a stranger to him. In fact, he'd known Larry for years. What could have turned a sweet dog like Hobo into the snarling, vicious animal she'd heard from Marti's kitchen that day? The answer made her pull over to the side of the road and stop.

How on earth had she missed it before? Larry had murdered Brenda, and poor Hobo had been an eyewitness. Several different scenarios immediately occurred to her. Either Brenda had come home and caught him stealing Tootsie, which wasn't likely since the evidence indicated she'd been sitting at the kitchen table paying bills, or Larry had come by unannounced, and she'd let him in because she knew him. This possibility also ended with Larry killing her so that he could take the dog. Rory didn't put that one high on her list either. All the other dogs had been stolen when the owners were out. Why suddenly change MOs?

In a third scenario, Larry was Brenda's mystery man, and he'd killed her during a lovers' quarrel. That was the one Rory was betting on; she still didn't believe the crimes were related. The fact that Zeke thought they were had only hardened her to that view. If it turned out Zeke was right again, he was going to be difficult to live with. Make that more difficult to live with.

Rory's first instinct was to call Leah. She pulled the cell phone out of her pocket, intending to do just that, but she changed her mind before the call went through. How could she make such an outrageous claim based solely on a dog's behavior? That kind of evidence was no evidence at all. Lawyers weren't in the habit of putting dogs on the witness stand. She'd have to find a way to test her theory before she told Leah or anyone else. But even that would have to wait. For now she had an appointment to keep with the elusive Feeny sisters.

R ory had a harder time pushing Larry Sugarman out of her mind than she'd imagined. Truth be told, she'd already decided it was unlikely that the Feeny sisters were involved in the dognappings. Still, now that Rory finally had the opportunity to speak to the women themselves, she felt she owed her client due diligence by following through.

It turned out that the Feeny sisters lived in a grand house in the exclusive Lloyd Harbor area of Huntington, a locale that had known the likes of Billy Joel and Twisted Sister. The house stood on top of a sizeable hill that made it appear even grander. It resembled a fieldstone castle straight out of the Middle Ages, complete with turrets, balconies and a picturesque bridge that spanned a narrow moat. Rory found it both magical and disorienting, as if she'd made a wrong turn and crossed an invisible boundary into the past. As she drove over the bridge she half expected to see a giant crocodile's head break the surface of the water.

The tree-lined driveway led to a parking area large enough to accommodate a dozen cars, but presently holding only three. Most likely staff. Presumably Jill and Beth kept their own cars in a garage that could be accessed from inside. Rory parked and walked the twenty yards to the house. She passed an Atlas Oil van parked where the circular driveway wound past the front door. No service entrance for the Atlas Oil man.

When Rory rang the doorbell she heard a trumpet's clarion echo inside. No detail had been overlooked. She wondered if it would be a maid or a butler who came to answer the trumpet's call. When the massive, arched door opened she was surprised to see one of the sisters standing there. She recognized her immediately from the photo on Brenda's mantel. As the woman ushered Rory inside, she introduced herself as Jill, clearing up the question of which Feeny she was.

As much as Beth and her deceased husband seemed to have enjoyed medieval architecture, they were also clearly fans of modern amenities. No cold stone and drafty corners inside their castle. Instead plush fabrics and warm tones gave the interior of the house a gracious, welcoming charm.

Jill led Rory into a large study where built-in bookcases lined the walls. A stately desk, with a computer, anchored one end of the room. At the other end a robust fire crackled in the fireplace. A fine leather couch and two armchairs, showing exactly the right amount of genteel wear, were grouped in front of the fireplace. Beth was sitting in one of the chairs reading the newspaper when they walked in. She put the paper aside and rose to greet her guest.

If Rory hadn't known the women were identical twins, she would never have guessed it by their appearance. Leah had told her they were fifty-two, but Jill appeared to be at least a decade older than her sister. Her brown hair was liberally threaded with gray, while Beth's was a flashy blond without a telltale root in sight. Jill wore no makeup, but Beth's eyes were meticulously outlined and shadowed, and her cheeks glowed with a subtle blush. No one would have trouble telling the sisters apart, and perhaps that was exactly their aim.

Beth invited Rory to make herself comfortable and asked if she'd like tea or coffee. Rory politely declined the refreshments. She took a seat on one end of the couch and withdrew a notepad and pen from her purse. Beth went back to her chair, while Jill settled herself in the other one so that they were both angled toward Rory.

"You have an amazing home," Rory said, both because it was true and because she wanted to put the two women at ease.

"Actually I'm a guest here," Jill said, "but it is an amazing place."

Beth frowned at her sister. "That's ridiculous. You live here every bit as much as I do."

"Well, yes, but the house is certainly not mine. I don't want to give Miss McCain any false impressions."

Beth was shaking her head. "Okay, full disclosure— technically my sister's name is not on the deed. After my husband passed away, it seemed silly for her to keep paying for a condo when she was practically never home. And it was just as silly for me to be the only resident of this enormous place, since I'm not here very often either. In any case, since Charlie and I never had children, when I die Jill will inherit this house along with everything else I own."

"You're not dying, so stop talking like that," Jill said. She seemed genuinely distressed by the turn the conversation had taken. "We were born together and with any luck we'll die together."

Rory couldn't help thinking that Jill had a first-rate motive for murdering her sister, but not much of a motive for stealing dogs, since her livelihood depended on them.

"Fine," Beth said wearily, as if they'd had this discussion numerous times before. "You be sure to let me know when you work out the details with fate." She turned her attention back to Rory.

"Forgive us for wasting your time, Ms. McCain. Detective Russell told us you were investigating the dognappings. How can we be of help?"

Rory sent her a silent thank-you for sidetracking the Maudlin Express her sister had hopped on with a week's worth of baggage. "I imagine you've heard that when Brenda was murdered, her Maltese went missing."

The sisters nodded in unison.

"Now, Tootsie might have escaped through an open door, but if she was stolen, it was probably by the dognappers who've been operating around here. Did Brenda ever mention to either of you that she had a particular concern for Tootsie's safety? Or that she'd noticed any strangers hanging around the neighborhood watching her comings and goings?"

The sisters took a moment to consider the question. Rory noted that they didn't glance at one another, which she took to mean they weren't worried about some shared secret.

Beth was the first to speak. "I haven't seen much of Brenda since I became a widow two years ago. When my Charlie died so young, I decided not to waste a moment of my life. I've made it my goal to see the world. I wish my sister would ditch her business and join me. Charlie certainly left me with enough money for two to live in high style."

"I could never do that," Jill protested. "I'd feel like a total leech. You know you'd feel the same way if you were in my shoes."

"Jill, what about you?" Rory asked, trying to pull her back from the edge of another tangent. "Had you been in touch with Brenda?"

"I hadn't seen her in six months or more. We e-mailed each other maybe once a week, but I don't recall her mentioning she was worried about anything like that. In fact, her last e-mail didn't even mention her dogs. She was pretty consumed by the fact that her boyfriend had just broken it off with her."

"Did she ever mention who he was?" Rory asked. She knew she was crossing the line from the dognappings to Brenda's murder again, but she told herself she was simply hoping for some corroboration of her new theory.

"From what I understand nobody knew who he was. She refused to say anything beyond the fact that she was seeing someone."

"Excuse me, ladies," a male voice said from the doorway of the study.

Rory knew that voice. When she turned her head she saw that she was right. "Hi, Joe."

"Hey there." He nodded, a smile pumping up his cheeks.

"We keep bumping into each other," Rory explained in answer to the question on the sisters' faces.

"With my job I get around a lot," Joe said.

"Did you find everything in working order?" Beth asked. The woman clearly liked getting right down to business.

"Absolutely, Mrs. Blake." He gave her a thumbs-up. "And I cleaned out the system, so you're good to go for the winter. No need to get up, Ms. Feeny," he said as Jill started to rise from her chair. "I can let myself out. Good to see you all."

Once Joe was gone, Rory picked up the conversation where they'd left off. "If Brenda was that upset about being dumped, I'm surprised she didn't expose the guy, out of revenge if nothing else."

This time Jill looked across at her sister and raised her eyebrows in a silent question.

Beth gave a little shrug, hitting the ball back into her court.

"There's something I didn't tell Detective Russell when she interviewed us," Jill said, picking absently at one of her cuticles. "It didn't seem important, and it would have cast a shadow on poor Brenda, who can't even defend herself. But it's been bothering me. I don't want to be accused of withholding information from the police."

Rory could hear the rising anxiety in her voice.

"My sister has a conscience that works overtime," Beth said lightly. "Detective Russell even gave us her card in case we thought of anything else that might be germane to the case. I told Jill to just call her and stop being such a worrywart. No one's going to cart her off to jail because she 'forgot' to mention one thing. Am I right, Ms. McCain?"

"If you come forward on your own, I'm sure it'll be fine," Rory agreed. "And believe me, the information will be appreciated. You never know which detail might be the key to solving a case."

Jill nodded and managed a weak smile. "Okay. In her last e-mail, Brenda did mention that she had a plan to even the score with her boyfriend. I didn't think too much of it at the time. People say all kinds of things when they're hurting."

"What did you think she meant by that?" Rory asked.

"That he was married, and she was going to tell his wife what was going on, but I'm just guessing."

"You should definitely call Detective Russell and tell her about this," Rory said.

"I will. I'll call this afternoon." Jill's voice was stronger, more poised now that she wasn't concerned about being locked up for her little lapse in judgment. "Is there anything else you wanted to ask about?"

"Actually there is one more thing. I know you take care of dogs while their owners are away. Have any of your clients' dogs been stolen?"

"None of my regulars. I do sit for others that I only see once or twice a year, though. If I hear anything in the future I'd be happy to let you know."

Rory tucked her notepad and pen back in her pocketbook and thanked the sisters for their time. Jill accompanied her to the front door. Answering the door and escorting guests in and out appeared to be her job, probably one of many she'd taken on so she could feel that she was earning her keep.

Rory drove home thinking about her conversation with the twins. She was glad she hadn't bailed on the interview. There was a good chance that Jill had just handed her the last piece in the puzzle of Brenda's murder.

# Chapter 25

By the time Rory arrived home, she'd made two important decisions. Decision one: she and Hobo were going to pay Larry Sugarman an impromptu visit. Her meeting with the Feeny sisters was instrumental in helping her reach that decision. According to Jill, Brenda intended to even the score with her boyfriend for leaving her. Then, out of the blue and after years of not speaking, she'd called Marti Sugarman and invited her over. If two plus two didn't equal four in this situation, they never did. Marti may have thought Brenda called to apologize and revive their friendship over a cup of coffee, but what Brenda planned on serving her ex-friend was a mixed grill of betrayal, adultery and revenge. Unfortunately Brenda made one huge tactical error. Probably because she wanted to enjoy Larry's misery, and because she didn't think he was capable of violence, she'd told him what she planned to do. Afraid that his whole world was about to collapse around him, Larry had gone straight to Brenda's house to talk, plead or threaten her into dropping that plan, and when she proved intractable, he'd killed her. As certain as Rory was about this scenario, she wanted some corroboration. If Hobo went for Larry's throat, she'd have exactly that.

Decision two: she wasn't going to tell Zeke about her plan. He would either demand to accompany her or he'd pre-empt her by sending Leah an e-mail, prematurely spilling the proverbial beans. He might not be able to manage phone calls, but she'd seen for herself that he'd developed quite an aptitude for working the computer keyboard and mouse.

When Leah called the next morning to let her know that a beagle puppy had been reported stolen from a pet shop in Bay Shore, Rory didn't bother mentioning the plan to her either. Of course it would have been difficult to talk about, since Zeke was there with her. Who was she kidding? She'd had no intentions of telling Leah anyway.

"The pet shop was able to give us a photo of the puppy," Leah said. "They post photos of their inventory on their website."

"A photo—that should come in handy."

"It'll definitely make it easier to prove that the thieves are trying to resell a stolen dog. I'll e-mail it to you right now."

Then Leah had to run, and Rory was happy to end the conversation. She didn't like deceiving her friend even by the sin of omission.

"From your conversation, I take it that things are finally startin' to percolate along," Zeke said once she'd hung up the phone.

You have no idea just how much, Rory thought, as she rummaged through the pantry. She came away with a cereal bar and resumed her seat at the table where she'd left her coffee when the phone had rung.

"Do you ever eat food that requires cookin'?" Zeke asked, frowning at her.

"Don't knock what you haven't tried," she said, tearing off the wrapper and taking a bite.

"Eggs or a hot bowl of oatmeal, now, that's a breakfast that'll stick with you."

Rory nodded and chewed, sure that any other response would have earned her a lecture on the merits of "honest-to-goodness food" back in the day. She washed the bar down with a swallow of coffee and, before he could say anything else, launched into a report on her meeting with the Feeny sisters.

Zeke agreed with her that Brenda's killer was most likely her boyfriend. He went on to say that while that was inter-esting, the murder case was not the one they were investi-gating. Since he hadn't posed a question, Rory didn't bother commenting. Nor did she share her epiphany with regard to Hobo and Larry or the fact that she was convinced Larry was the boyfriend in question. With that much information there was a good chance the marshal would figure out what she planned to do next, and he'd never understand why she wanted to be more certain of her theory before she took it to the police.

In the early afternoon, Zeke bid her good day, citing the need for further recuperation from his last traveling ses-sion. That worked for Rory. At five thirty she put her plan in motion. She grabbed Hobo's leash from the bench, along with the jacket she'd left there when she'd planned their escape. They were out the door and into the car in seconds. Indy 500 pit crews had nothing on her.

Rory found the side streets clogged with commuters eager to get home to dinner and their favorite programs. She was banking on Larry being a typical nine-to-fiver who was out the office door as soon as the workday ended, but when she reached the Sugarman house at five forty there were no cars in the driveway. There was no way to tell if Marti's car was in the garage or not, but Rory suspected she was home at this hour, busily whipping up dinner. She would have preferred confronting Larry alone, but that would have been difficult to arrange.

She drove around the block and parked at the curb two houses down from the Sugarmans' to wait for Larry's homecoming. She left the engine running, because Hobo got antsy when she shut it off and remained in the car. They didn't have long to wait. At five fifty Larry drove past them and swung into his driveway. Rory gave him another ten to put down his briefcase and unknot his tie. A relaxed suspect was preferable. She didn't pull into the driveway, since that would immediately have set Falcon off. Instead she and Hobo walked up to the front door, so the Maltese wouldn't alert his humans until he heard the bell. The less prepared the suspect, the safer the PI. Rory pressed the bell, and Falcon started his high-pitched yapping on cue, which set Hobo to do some woofing of his own. She tried to hush him, worried that Larry might not open the door if he had a chance to think about who was waiting on the other side of it and why.

After several moments, it was Marti she heard telling Falcon to be quiet, to no effect.

When the door opened, Marti stood in the doorway with the Maltese still barking from her arms. Hobo fell silent, more interested in sniffing the air that wafted out redolent of something roasting.

"Ms. McCain," Marti said, looking from her to Hobo and back again. "Why are you here?" It wasn't the most gracious ŏf greetings, but then Rory had caught her by surprise again.

"Actually I was hoping to speak to your husband briefly, if I may," she said, pouring on the syrup.

"About what?" Marti asked warily.

"It would just be quicker if I could talk to him," Rory tried. She had to get Hobo into the same room with Larry, or the visit would be pointless. "Of course you're welcome to be there."

Marti bristled. "I should hope so! This is my house too."

Rory gave her a sweetly innocent smile. Then a timer rang back in the kitchen, and Marti's attention was sorely divided between Rory and her need to get back to the roast.

"Well, all right," she said, backing up so Rory would have room to enter. "Can't Hobo wait in . . . ?" It finally occurred to Marti that she hadn't seen an extra car in her driveway or parked at the curb. "Where is your car?"

"We'll only be a minute," Rory promised, entering the house with Hobo before Marti could start quizzing her further.

The timer beeped again, causing Marti to adjust her priorities. "Just keep him away from my Falcon," she said as she toddled off in the direction of the kitchen with the Maltese peering over her shoulder and growling at Hobo.

As far as Rory could tell, Falcon was the one with issues. Hobo padded quietly along beside her, no longer showing any interest in the little dog.

"You can have a seat," Marti said grudgingly as she went to the oven to baste what looked like a rib roast. "Larry's just changing his clothes. He'll be down in a minute." Falcon was still in her arms, trying to dive headfirst into the pan with the roast.

Rory sat down at the kitchen table. Hobo lay down next to her, intoxicated by the smells, strands of drool hanging from his mouth. When Rory heard Larry on the staircase she stood up, ready for action. He came around the bend into the kitchen as Marti shut the oven door.

When he saw Rory and Hobo some of the color drained from his face, but he did his best to act normally. "Hi, it's Rory, right?" He held out his hand to her, at which point all hell broke loose in the Sugarman kitchen.

No longer anesthetized by the smells, Hobo jumped up snarling, ears flattened back against his skull. Rory had never actually seen him this way. If she didn't know him better she would have been scared even on her end of the leash. She tightened her grip on him just before he lunged for Larry and nearly pulled her off her feet.

Marti shrieked, crushing Falcon against her chest to protect him as Larry stumbled backward. "Get that dog out of my house!" He screamed in a voice approaching falsetto range. "Get him out of my house now! What the hell are they doing here, Marti?"

Marti uttered some syllables that never quite made up a whole word.

"What have you done to make him hate you so?" Rory demanded. As soon as the words left her mouth she knew she probably shouldn't have said them. The plan had been simple. She was just going to see if Hobo reacted badly to Larry a second time. Well, mission accomplished. And exactly why was she still standing there?

"How dare you come into my house and let your dog attack me? I'm calling the police." Without taking his eyes off Hobo, Larry started edging over to the phone that was hanging on the wall just inside the kitchen entrance. "You and that mutt belong in prison or in a mental ward."

"When you get the police on the line you might want to save them some time and tell them why you killed Brenda Hartley." Okay, she *definitely* shouldn't have said that, but her temper had gotten the better of her.

Marti went from looking terrified to looking bewildered and terrified. "What . . . what's she talking about?" she sputtered.

"Get out of here, Marti," Larry ordered. "Get out of here before you and Falcon get hurt."

Marti didn't move. She seemed rooted to the floor, as incapable of motion as a potted plant.

Larry bypassed the phone to grab the knife that Marti had left on the counter for cutting the roast.

Things were escalating rapidly. Rory regretted her decision to stow the new .45 in her handbag instead of in a holster on her hip. It had made sense at the time. Of course that was before she'd accused him of murder and more or less asked to be silenced.

"Marti!" Rory shouted to get the woman's attention. She needed to neutralize her to help balance the odds. "Do you know what Brenda wanted to tell you the day she was murdered?"

Larry was circling to Rory's right. With the knife in his hand he sounded almost jaunty. "Open your mouth again, bitch, and you're going to be saying your last words."

"What's she talking about? What's she talking about?" Marti repeated like a one-trick parrot.

Rory pivoted to keep Larry in full sight. "She wanted to tell you that she and Larry were having an affair."

Marti's eyes popped to twice their normal size. Then her lower lip quivered like a child's, and tears started pumping out of her eyes. Rory had been hoping for anger, but beggars couldn't be choosers. What mattered was that Marti wouldn't be helping her husband anytime soon.

Larry must have come to the same conclusion. His eyes narrowed and jaw hard with purpose, he came at Rory and Hobo, the knife tight in his fist. Hobo strained at the leash, growling like a thunder roll. Rory released him so he'd be able to maneuver and protect himself. But defense wasn't on his agenda. The first thing he did was lunge at Larry, who managed to step aside at the last moment, although with somewhat less grace than a matador. Hobo kept going on his original trajectory, obeying the law of inertia until he slammed into the lower cabinets. He picked himself right up without a whimper. He was accustomed to hard landings courtesy of a certain deceased federal marshal. Marti was screaming again, but it had lost its initial impact and was fast becoming as tedious as elevator music.

Rory ordered Hobo to go, to run, to leave the room, but either Hobo didn't understand the words or he was playing deaf and dumb. While she was still trying to shoo the dog out of danger, Larry saw his opportunity. He covered the distance to Rory in a couple of long strides. Rory grabbed one of the kitchen chairs and held it before her like a lion tamer under the big top. After several hectic seconds, Larry managed to wrench it out of her grasp with his free hand.

Rory backed away from him until she was up against the refrigerator, her future dependent on how well she'd learned to feint and parry back on her high school fencing team. At that critical moment Hobo launched himself at Larry from a point just beyond the man's peripheral vision. The unexpected, ninety-pound dog missile knocked him off his feet. His head hit the ceramic tile floor with a sickening crack, and the knife skittered to a landing near Marti's feet.

As Rory ran to retrieve her purse from the kitchen table, she warned Marti not to touch the knife, not to even think of trying to help her husband, or she'd be facing jail time as well. She needn't have worried. Marti's face was nearly as white as Falcon's fur, and both woman and dog were absolutely silent, probably for the first time in either of their lives.

By the time Larry came out of his stupor, Rory had her gun trained on him and her cell phone in hand. Ordering him to stay where he was, she called 911 and then Leah at police headquarters. Hobo, who had appointed himself to guard the prisoner, paced back and forth in front of him, snapping at the slightest twitch.

Police from the local precinct pulled up to the house within minutes, along with an ambulance for Marti, who had screamed her way into palpitations. Leah and her partner arrived from Yaphank half an hour later. Larry was read his rights and loaded into a police cruiser. Marti was carted off to the hospital, still clutching Falcon and threatening anyone who tried to pry him away from her. Then Leah pulled Rory aside and calmly inquired when it was that she'd completely lost her mind.

# Chapter 26

The game was already into its final period when Rory arrived at the soccer field. She found Leah on the sidelines cheering loudly for her eight-year-old son and his team. Her husband, the team coach, was on the far side of the field, keeping pace with the players as they ran first toward one goal, then toward the other as the teams lost or gained possession of the ball. It was a mild day, a teaser that felt more like spring than fall. The parents and grandparents watching the game had traded in their parkas for lighter jackets, and some of the men had already shrugged off even those.

Leah had asked Rory to meet her at the field so she could give her an update on the Larry Sugarman case. Her weekend was a marathon of running to each of her children's sporting events; she wasn't free for brunch or even a cup of coffee.

"Sorry to drag you out here," she said, giving Rory a quick hug before turning back to watch the game.

"Hey, the weather's great, and I get to spend some time

with you and find out what's happening with our murdering scum."

"Well, for one thing, he's an arrogant, murdering scum," Leah said. "Excuse me, I mean person of interest. Didn't even blink when I told him we had his prints on the knife that killed Brenda. He just sat there with this little smirk and demanded to see his lawyer. You have no idea how much I wanted to rearrange his face with—way to go, Jake!" she shouted as her son maneuvered the ball away from an opposing player and headed for the goal. "Go, Jake, go—go—go—all the way!"

Jake took a shot on goal. For a moment it seemed like the goalie would be able to deflect the ball, but it flew by him just out of reach. A cheer erupted from half the onlookers, while the coach from the other team called out encouragement to his players.

When Leah picked up the narrative, she was going hoarse from all the cheering. "We had to wait for his lawyer to get there before we could finish questioning him."

Rory shook her head in disgust. "Let me guess—he's claiming he killed Brenda in self-defense."

"Bingo! A lovers' quarrel. He'd broken it off with her; she was distraught and came at him with a knife. In the ensuing struggle the knife found its way into her chest. Trite, but it works more often than it should."

"I'm surprised he told you that much."

"Sometimes they're so full of themselves and so sure you can't touch them, they like to dangle their 'get out of jail free' card in your face."

"If Hobo could talk, Larry wouldn't have a prayer."

With her briefing finished, Rory took the opportunity to apologize for trampling on police turf. "You have my word that it won't happen again," she said.

"Really?" Leah asked skeptically.

Rory thought for a moment before she replied with a sheepish grin, "Well, I'm pretty sure."

"That's what I figured. But joking aside, Rory, you've got to curb your impulsiveness. Preferably before it gets you killed."

"That's number one on my 'to do' list."

"It certainly ought to be."

Then Jake had the ball again, and Rory joined in to cheer him on.

"Hey, I almost forgot," Leah said. "We found some scabbed-over bite marks on Larry's arm, bites that came from the mouth of a large dog."

Rory issued a low whistle of amazement. "So heroism isn't a new concept for Hobo."

"That's one hell of a great dog you have there."

Rory couldn't have agreed more. She stayed on to watch the last minutes of the game, but declined an invitation to join Leah and her family for a pizza victory lunch. As much as she loved pizza and spending time with Leah and her energetic little tribe, she had some unfinished business to attend to back home.

She'd decided that she had to tell Zeke about the events at the Sugarman residence. As unpleasant as that conversation was likely to be, Hobo deserved his due. The marshal needed to know about the dog's heroic efforts on her behalf. She was trying to work out a sanitized version of the truth, one in which she hadn't egged Larry on, when the telephone rang. The woman on the line introduced herself as "Debbie from It's a Dog's World." But Rory had already recognized her voice and shifted gears. If she wasn't careful with what she said she could compromise the sting.

Debbie said she was pleased to let her know they had her beagle puppy. Rory was thrilled. It was barely twenty-four hours since the puppy was reported stolen. Either it was an amazing coincidence or Dog's World was in the "steal to order" dog business. Of course she and Zeke still didn't know the names of the thieves or whether the suspects on their list were among them, but they finally seemed to be headed in the right direction. In one day they'd made more progress than in all the weeks before.

Rory asked the questions that she thought a prospective owner would ask, like what kind of food to buy for the puppy and whether he'd been given any of his shots. When she'd run out of questions, Debbie asked if they could deliver the puppy the next day. Rory said that would be fine, and they agreed on a time of two p.m. Debbie repeated the time to someone else, after which Rory heard a man in the background give his approval. Apparently Debbie had her on speakerphone. In a tone that was far from pleasant, the man reminded Debbie to get the address right this time. Rory thought his voice sounded familiar. If he would just continue talking she might be able to place it, but instead she heard a door close, and then Debbie was speaking directly to her again.

Flustered and stumbling over her words, she apologized for the interruption. Whoever the man was, he certainly had enough clout to make her nervous. Her voice still wobbly, she asked Rory for her address.

The address Rory gave her was Helene's. She'd decided to take delivery at her aunt's house to avoid the possibility that someone at Dog's World might recognize her own address. When she'd talked to Helene about it, the conversation had been more trying than arranging for the stolen puppy.

"I don't see why I have to leave," Helene had said, as if Rory were borrowing her house to throw a party that she wasn't invited to attend.

"It's too dangerous," Rory told her. "I can't take the chance."

"You wouldn't be taking the chance," Helene pointed out. "I would."

"Semantics aside, the result would be the same. I'd rather not have to explain to my mother why I let you get killed. That kind of thing is hard on family relationships."

Helene ignored her attempt at humor. "I'm sure you're exaggerating. It's not like this is a drug bust. They're going to drop off a puppy. What could possibly go wrong?"

It occurred to Rory that her aunt was a lot more naïve than she'd realized. "You read the papers and watch the news, Aunt Helene. Things that shouldn't go wrong, go wrong every day."

Helene had begged to differ. That sort of thing was actually rare if you took population numbers into account. Rory stood her ground. She couldn't remember ever arguing with her aunt before, and, though she didn't like it, she refused to give in and put her at risk. She finally had to threaten to use her parents' address, before Helene would agree to leave.

"And that includes the immediate area," Rory had added firmly. "No lurking behind bushes or parking across the street to watch."

Helene's huffy sigh told her she'd been entertaining thoughts of doing exactly that.

# Chapter 27

With the delivery arranged and Helene given notice that she had to be out of the house well before two the next day, it was time for Rory to bring her partner up to speed. Maybe the news about the puppy would help distract him from asking too many questions about her little set-to with Larry. Zeke's name was barely out of her mouth when he appeared in his customary seat at the kitchen table, eyebrows hitched up with curiosity.

"What can I do for you?" he asked.

"Actually I want to fill you in about everything that's been happening," she said brightly. No problems here. She dashed through her epiphany about how Hobo loved everyone but Larry, and that she'd taken him to see Larry to test that theory. In her revamped version of the event, Larry became unhinged the moment he saw her and Hobo in the kitchen with Marti. One minute Rory was trying to calm the dog and the next she was fighting for her life. She wouldn't be standing there if not for Hobo's heroism. He'd defended her without hesitation and without regard for his own survival.

Although the basic elements of the story were true, Rory could tell by the furrow working between Zeke's eyes that he wasn't buying the total package she was selling. She decided that as long as he understood how courageously Hobo had acted, she'd accomplished what she'd set out to do. Zeke's issues with the way she lived or conducted her business were academic. She had zero intention of changing them. At some point he would learn that he couldn't whittle her into a shape that fit his idea of a proper woman. Of course, that might take a while, since he'd proven that change wasn't easy for him. He'd been wrestling with death for over a century, yet here he was still managing to have a life of sorts from beyond the grave.

He looked like he was about to start lecturing her, when Rory preempted him with an enthusiastic "Hey, guess who called less than ten minutes ago? Debbie from Dog's World." She steamrolled on before he could respond. "They have our puppy. We did it. I mean *you* did it. You found the right ad. Dog's World is the one stealing the dogs."

She watched the conflict play out across Zeke's face. He didn't want to let go of the events at the Sugarman residence before he'd had his say, but neither could he ignore the excitement of their plan finally moving ahead.

"Okay," he said somewhat grudgingly, "when's the delivery set for?"

"Tomorrow at two. I'm going to get there early, though. I don't want to take a chance on missing them." Rory gave herself a quick pat on the back. Zeke had hooked into the Dog's World news as she'd hoped he would.

"Okay, so someone will deliver the dog to you," he said, thinking out loud. "With any luck it'll just be one guy."

"One guy who has no reason to expect trouble."

"Right. But he will be expectin' payment, and I'm assumin' you don't have twelve hundred bucks in cash just sittin' around."

"Not a problem," Rory said. "As soon as he comes in with the dog I'm going to detain him and hold him until the police arrive."

Zeke ran his hand over the stubble on his chin, a gesture Rory had come to be wary of, since it was often the preamble to an argument. "I think you need a plan B," he said. "You know, just in case the delivery guy takes exception to plan A."

"I've got my plan B loaded and ready for action." She smiled. "It's a good thing you suggested the upgrade when you did. The .45 will be perfect for the job." She might have ducked the Larry issue, but there was already another debate staring her down. She was going to need every ounce of the marshal's goodwill to win the coming battle with him over the sting. And this time it wouldn't be as easy, since it involved his actions as well as hers.

"Have you given any more thought to lettin' me tag along?" Zeke asked, effectively firing the first shot across her bow.

Rory had not only given it more thought, she'd weighed it down with an anchor and thrown it overboard to a deep, watery grave. Wondering if and when the marshal, or various parts of him, might make an appearance would only distract her and put her in more jeopardy.

"I could stay out of sight unless you need me," Zeke pressed on, anticipating her objection.

"You don't have enough control of the process yet," she said. If she'd had any hatches, this would have been the time to batten them down.

"Maybe not." Zeke's tone had grown testy. "But I'll bet it's good enough to save your neck again."

"Let's not be so dramatic. I'm perfectly capable of saving my own neck if it comes to that."

"Is that how Hobo sees it?"

Rory had known that by expounding on the dog's help, she would leave herself open to that sort of remark. It was a trade-off she'd been willing to make. She didn't even bother with a reply, since she didn't have a good one. She'd let him have this round.

Zeke vanished from his seat, muttering something unintelligible under his breath. He popped up a moment later near the door to the backyard. Rory had taken to leaving it open, with just the storm door closed to keep out the cold, whenever Hobo was outside. That way she could easily check on him. She'd become a lot more vigilant in the wake of the last threatening letter.

She waited to see what Zeke's next move would be. Since he hadn't disappeared, she assumed he had more to say on the subject. But she wasn't expecting what came next.

"Rory, you need to get out there," he shouted. *"Right now!"*

The marshal knew better than to bark orders at her, so it was immediately clear that there was a serious problem outside, a problem that most likely involved Hobo. She flew past Zeke and out the door without bothering to grab a coat. Hobo was near the gate that opened to the side yard. His whole torso was chugging back and forth as if it were in the grips of an alien being. As she ran to him, he started vomiting violently, spewing up chunks of undigested raw beef along with mucus and blood. Rory didn't know what to do for him. She tried to soothe him, to rub his back. He didn't even seem to realize she was there.

When there was nothing left in his belly, he kept on retching, bloody spittle hanging from his jowls. Then he staggered a few steps before collapsing onto his side. His breathing was noisy and labored, each respiration an enormous effort. She had to get him to a vet and fast. As she was trying to work out the logistics of lifting a ninety-pound dog off the ground and carrying him to her car, Zeke appeared beside her, looking a whole lot more solid than she felt.

"Get the car goin'," he said.

Rory ran into the house to get the keys. Ten seconds later she was opening the rear door of the car. She looked toward the side gate and what she saw wasn't possible. Hobo was still lying on his side, but he was floating toward her, hovering several inches above Zeke's outstretched arms. She could see the strain on Zeke in his tightly clenched jaw and in the blood vessels standing out along his neck. By the time he'd reached the car, his lower body had vanished. Hobo lay perfectly still, a sculpture of a dog. His eyes were barely open, the thin inner lid all that was visible. If he knew how close he was to the marshal or how he was being transported, he was too ill to care.

Rory jumped into the car and started the engine while Zeke maneuvered Hobo onto the backseat. A moment later the marshal disappeared. Rory knew the effort had cost him dearly. She had no idea how long it would take him to recuperate, how long it would be before she'd be able to thank him properly. Then Hobo moaned pitifully from the backseat, wiping every other thought from her mind.

She drove through the winding side streets as fast as she dared. When she reached Jericho Turnpike she tramped down on the accelerator, praying she wouldn't attract the attention of the police. Right then she decided that if that should happen she wouldn't stop. They could chase her all the way to the vet and arrest her there if that suited them.

"Oh my God," she cried aloud. "What am I doing?" She'd automatically headed for Stanley Holbrook's office, because he was the only vet she knew in the area. But what if he was the person who'd sent the threatening letters? The person who'd arranged for Hobo to be poisoned? Well, she had no choice. There was no time to call around and get another recommendation, no time even to look in a phone book and locate another vet. It would be okay, she told herself. After all, Holbrook had a reputation to maintain. She'd insist on staying with Hobo, and she'd watch every move Holbrook made. It was one thing to pay someone to poison a dog miles away, quite another to fail to help an animal brought to his office. If his aim had been to scare her into dropping the investigation, she'd convince him that he'd succeeded. Of course, she could be getting ahead of herself. Holbrook might not even be the guilty party.

She pulled into the parking lot and took the last open spot. Promising Hobo she'd be right back, she ran into the office. There was a woman already speaking to the receptionist, but this wasn't the time for waiting her turn or other social amenities.

"I need help—my dog is dying," she blurted out. "I think he was poisoned. He's in the car, but I need help to get him in here. Please."

The receptionist pressed a button and called for the veterinary aide, stat. A man in the waiting room asked the woman sitting next to him to hold his dog's leash. He hurried to offer Rory his help as the aide came running from the back. Together they raced out the door to Rory's car.

Even before they opened the back door, they could hear Hobo's tortured breathing. He's still alive, Rory told herself. At least he's still alive. She was close to tears as she watched them struggle to get the dog's limp body out of the car. She hated feeling so helpless, but there was no room for another person in such tight quarters.

Hobo looked like a big, furry rag doll when they finally pulled him out. As they rushed him inside, the aide told Rory to stay in the waiting room, but she made it clear she was going wherever Hobo went. She followed them into an empty exam room, where they laid him gently on the steel table. Holbrook walked in a moment later.

He nodded briefly at Rory, no flashy fluorescent smile this time. He put his stethoscope to his ears and frowned as he listened to Hobo's heart and lungs. He palpated the dog's abdomen and looked in his mouth. Rory watched him as if he were a jewel thief browsing in Tiffany's. Holbrook sent the aide for oxygen, and after he'd fitted the mask to Hobo's snout, he asked her what symptoms the dog had exhibited before falling unconscious.

Rory recited everything she could remember, which wasn't difficult. The horrible scene was indelibly etched into her brain.

"Could be a number of things," Holbrook said, shaking his head, "but if I had to pick one, I'd pick cyanide—his trouble breathing, the way he collapsed. For that matter it could have been a poison cocktail."

"What are his odds?" Rory asked, afraid to hear the answer, but unwilling to hide from it.

"I'm not going to sugarcoat this," he said. "You have a very sick dog here. The good news is that he seems to have vomited up most of the poisoned meat. The bad news is that some of the poison clearly made it into his blood-stream. I'm going to get an IV started to hydrate him. We have a doctor who's on the premises overnight, so we'll be able to monitor him closely and deal with any complications that might arise. If Hobo makes it to the morning, I'd say he's got a pretty good shot."

"I'm going to stay with him," Rory said in a tone that dared anyone to argue with her.

Holbrook started to do just that until he caught the look in her eyes. "We don't permit that as a general rule, but given the circumstances we'll try to accommodate you. I'm afraid the most we can offer you is a chair."

"That's fine," Rory said, thinking that would be far more comfortable than walking the floors back home.

They transported Hobo by gurney to a critical care room with Rory one step behind. The aide shaved the lower part of his left front leg, after which Holbrook ran an IV. Rory kept watch, trying to stay out of their way and willing Hobo to open his eyes and wag his tail as if this were all some strange misunderstanding. But the dog remained chillingly still.

"Any idea who might be to blame for this?" the vet asked, stepping back from Hobo once he'd adjusted the rate the IV fluid was flowing into him.

"Someone who wants me to stop investigating the dog-nappings," Rory said bluntly.

Holbrook wagged his head. "It's one hell of a convincing argument. Personally, I wouldn't be able to pursue the case if something like this happened to one of my animals."

And that's exactly what the thieves are hoping for, she thought. Still, it was hard to tell if Holbrook was speaking from honest sentiment or just trying to protect his sideline. Too bad life wasn't more like TV, where the guilty party breaks down and confesses and all the loose ends are tied up by the end of a sixty-minute episode.

"Believe me, I'm done with this case," she said, going for the Emmy. "Tina can have her retainer back. Nothing's worth causing Hobo to suffer like this, or worse, losing him altogether." The tears that sprang into her eyes were as real as they come.

Holbrook pulled a tissue from a box on the counter and held it out to her. She'd won his vote. "There's coffee in the small kitchen we have in the back," he said. "And the deli down the block delivers until eight p.m. I'll be in to check on Hobo between my other patients, and I'll introduce you to Dr. Rosen when she gets here for the night shift. Meanwhile I'll get a chair in here for you."

Rory nodded and thanked him. Without proof that he was involved in the poisoning, she had no choice but to keep up the pretense of civility.

"Now, we're going to have to put Hobo into a crate for his own safety," Holbrook said, with a "here's where I draw the line" firmness. "And it doesn't matter that you're going to be right by his side," he added as Rory started to object.

"We can't take the chance that he might move suddenly and fall off the gurney." He motioned to the aide, who wheeled over a large steel cage that had been standing in a back corner of the room. The cage was on high legs that brought it up to waist height.

The two men maneuvered Hobo off the gurney and onto the soft palette in the crate and then closed the door. Hobo was still unconscious, but his breathing had become more peaceful.

After Holbrook left, the aide brought in a padded desk chair for Rory. She pushed the chair up against Hobo's crate and sat down. She was weary to the bone, but wired with adrenaline. She reached through the bars to put her hand over Hobo's paw and settled in for a long night's vigil.

# Chapter 28

Rory awoke with a start. It took her a moment to remember where she was. Her neck was stiff and her lower back ached like a bad molar, but her spirits soared when she realized it was Hobo pushing against her hand with his oxygen-clad muzzle that had roused her.

He was still lying on his side, but his eyes were open and when she smiled at him he rewarded her with a thump of his tail. The tears she'd managed to control until then flooded her eyes and spilled down her cheeks from sheer relief. As she scratched behind his ears, one of the spots he loved best, she told him how happy she was to see him awake and how sorry she was to have been the cause of so much misery. After a few minutes, she tore herself away to find Dr. Rosen and give her the good news.

When Rory opened the door and peered into the corridor, she found it empty. The building was eerily quiet. She glanced at her watch and saw that it was barely dawn. Too early for appointments or for the regular staff to be in yet.

Before she could start searching for Dr. Rosen, she saw the
vet turn into the corridor from the direction of the kitchen,
a steaming mug in her hand. She picked up her pace when
she saw Rory standing there.

"What's wrong?" she asked, trying to keep the hot liq-
uid from slopping out of the mug as she hurried toward her.

"He's awake." Rory practically sang the words. "He
even wagged his tail."

The vet's expression changed from concern to guarded
happiness. When she reached Rory, she handed her the mug.

"Untouched," she said, as she went straight to Hobo's
crate. "You're welcome to it if you don't mind milk and
sugar. I'll get more later." She opened the door to the crate
and smiled when Hobo wagged his tail for her. Rory was
aglow with pride, like a proud parent whose child has shown
signs of genius.

The vet listened to his lungs and gently explored his
abdomen with her fingers. Then she took the oxygen mask
off his snout and turned to Rory. "I think we're out of the
woods," she said.

"Thank goodness. When can I take him home?"

"We should watch him for another couple of days. With
a possible cyanide poisoning we need to check his blood
regularly so we can monitor his organs. If he has no set-
backs, we can talk about discharging him."

Rory was running through her options as she listened
to the vet. She could ask her aunt and her parents to take
turns staying there to guard Hobo during the day so that
she'd be able to keep her appointment for the delivery of
the puppy. And if she got in a nap and filled her tank with
some industrial-strength coffee, she should be able to make
it through another night shift.

After a couple of phone calls, Helene and her folks were
on board. She had to be discreet when explaining why
Hobo needed to be watched around the clock in a place
that was supposedly doing just that. Helene was twice as

happy with the assignment once she heard the undercover
aspects of it.

"I won't even leave his side to go to the bathroom. I'll
stop taking fluids right now."

Rory tried to convince her that dehydration wasn't a
good idea and that it might land her in an adjoining crate.

An hour later her mother arrived for the first shift.
When Dr. Holbrook balked at the idea of a continuing presence by the McCain clan, Rory had an explanation ready.
She told him that since Hobo had saved her life, she and
her family felt this was the least they could do in his time
of need. Holbrook's expression told her that he thought
they were all crazy, but he didn't say so. He just shook his
head and reminded her they'd have to stay in the room with
Hobo and out of the way.

Rory left for home, hoping more than ever that Holbrook wasn't involved in the dognappings. Finding another
vet who'd accommodate an emotional, possibly irrational
owner might not be easy.


The first thing Rory did when she arrived home from the
vet was to take a long, hot shower. Then she crawled
into bed for a nap. The puppy wasn't going to be delivered
until two in the afternoon, but she set her alarm, afraid
that she might oversleep. She couldn't remember having ever been quite so tired before. Zeke didn't put in an
appearance, which was fine with her. No doubt he was still
recharging from providing Hobo's transportation to the
car. She owed him a huge thank-you, but that would have
to wait until they were both in better shape.

When the alarm woke Rory at one o'clock she was
momentarily disoriented. She was in her house, in her bed,
but why was she wearing jeans? And what day was it anyway? She groped through the fog in her brain like someone
groping in the dark for a light switch. Then, as if she'd

flicked that switch, the fog cleared and everything came back to her—Hobo! the sting!

She jumped out of bed and pushed her feet into the loafers she'd left on the floor. Then she loaded the .45, tucked it into the holster suspended from her belt and made sure she had a set of plastic handcuffs in her purse. She was pulling a comb through her hair when her stomach started grumbling about neglect. She realized that she hadn't eaten a thing since lunch the day before. To appease her body, and because she couldn't afford to faint in the middle of the sting, she grabbed an apple and ate it while she drove to Helene's. As it worked out, Rory didn't have to worry about her aunt hiding in bushes or on rooftops to watch the delivery of the puppy. She'd arranged the shifts at the vet so that Helene would be watching Hobo instead.

She let herself into her aunt's town house at one thirty. She had half an hour to wait. She settled herself in the living room near a window that faced the street, so she'd know as soon as the deliveryman arrived. She started reading the newspaper, but gave up when she realized she wasn't absorbing a thing. She made two calls to check on Hobo, first to the front desk for a formal status report, then to Helene's cell phone for a more subjective and detailed view. Everyone seemed to think he was doing exceptionally well.

By three she could no longer sit still, so she started rearranging Helene's DVD collection alphabetically. At three thirty she'd completely run out of patience. She dialed Dog's World. Debbie answered the phone as usual, but when Rory identified herself, the woman's tone changed from cheerful to guarded.

"Is there a problem with the delivery?" Rory asked politely. She didn't want to get snippy with Dog's World, since she needed them a lot more than they needed her.

"No, well, yes, sort of," Debbie babbled. She clearly didn't cope well with stress. Rory couldn't imagine why they'd hired her. It was a good bet that a company in the business of stealing dogs and reselling them was a stressful place to work. Maybe she was the mother, sister or daughter of the head honcho. Nepotism in the workplace could be ugly.

"So there *is* a problem?" Rory asked, forcing her to choose one answer.

"Yes, a problem on the supplier's end."

So why in hell didn't anyone call to tell me that? she felt like yelling. But what she actually said was, "Oh no, you can't imagine how much I was looking forward to getting that puppy." She was going for devastated with a splash of vulnerability. "I went out and bought him a bed and toys and everything." She added a sniffle for effect. "What happens now? When will I get him?"

"I'm sorry. All I can tell you is that we don't presently have your puppy, and we don't know when we will," Debbie said without inflection. She'd either been given a script to read or she lacked the gene for compassion.

"Will you call me when you do?" Rory asked.

"Okay, but there's no way to tell how long that might be."

Rory thanked her and hung up. She was frustrated and angry. If there'd been something unbreakable to throw she would have thrown it. Debbie was lying. The beagle puppy had already been stolen. Either they'd sold him to another client for more money or they'd somehow gotten wind of who she was and pulled the plug on her. If they'd wanted to keep her as a customer, she reasoned, they would have called, apologized and made some excuse as to why they couldn't deliver the puppy as scheduled. Since they hadn't called, it was more than likely they wanted nothing more to do with her.

She went over everything in her mind from her first conversation with Dog's World to the one twenty-four hours ago when they'd called to tell her the puppy was available.

At first she couldn't see how or when things might have gone awry, but then it struck her and she couldn't believe she hadn't realized it before. If the man she'd heard over the speakerphone had sounded familiar to her, the odds were that she'd sounded familiar to him as well. Only, he'd been able to put a name to the voice in time to avert disaster. Score a point for the opposing team.

After dealing herself a harsh mental flogging, Rory decided there was still reason to be heartened. She'd known the man's voice even if she couldn't place it yet, and he had known hers. That meant there was a good chance he was one of her suspects. It was only a matter of time before she zeroed in on him.

Rory spent a second night in the chair beside Hobo's crate. She'd brought along a pillow so that she didn't have to rest her head against the metal bars. By now the entire veterinary staff thought she was mad as a hatter. They spoke slowly to her in sweet tones as if she were fragile and required special care. Rory didn't bother trying to correct their misconception. Hobo was doing well and that was really all that mattered.

Later the following day he'd recovered well enough for Dr. Holbrook to discharge him. He was back on solid food and loudly protesting his incarceration. Rory's father had taken the last shift, freeing her to buy groceries and run some other errands. When she walked back into what she now thought of as Hobo's room, her father was sitting beside the crate, listening to his iPod and conducting an imaginary orchestra with an air baton while he read a paperback. Hobo was lying with his head between his paws, looking lower than a pregnant ant, as her uncle Mac used to say. As soon as he caught sight of her, he jumped up, hitting the top of the crate in the process. Unfazed, he started yodeling his joy, while his tail went into hyper-drive. The racket made it past the music being piped into her father's ears and he finally looked up.

"Mission accomplished, ma'am." He popped out his earbuds and snapped her a neat salute. "One Hobo safe and sound as instructed."

Rory grinned, returning the salute.

Frustrated that no one was paying attention to him, Hobo let loose with another hearty round of Alpine vocals that brought Holbrook double-timing it into the room.

"Your dog's got an impressive set of lungs there," he said, flashing his overbleached smile as he went about setting Hobo free. "They can hear him out in the waiting room and halfway to Manhattan."

Rory laughed. If she'd known Hobo's serenade could bring the vet running, they wouldn't have had to wait so long the first time she'd brought him there.

While an ecstatic Hobo kept trying to jump into her arms, Holbrook went over some basic instructions with her. "Keep him hydrated and give him small amounts to eat several times a day instead of one big meal. I wouldn't let him run any marathons for a while either. In fact, he's probably going to want to sleep more than usual for a few days. Just take your cues from him. He's been through quite an ordeal."

Rory thanked him for saving Hobo's life, which he had. Of course there was still the question of whether he'd arranged to have the dog poisoned to begin with.

"Nice guy," her father remarked as they walked out to their cars.

"The best," she said, hoping that in fact it was true.

When they got home, Hobo took some time to sniff every corner of the house, perhaps to determine if there was still a ghost in residence. Then he curled up on the living room couch and fell fast asleep.

He slept a lot over the next two days, going from one of

his favorite snoozing spots to another. Rory stayed home, afraid that if she left him alone and Zeke made an appearance, it would be too much for him. When Tina called to see how the patient was doing, she mentioned that every dog she'd ever known adored chicken soup. Rory immediately called her mother for the family recipe that had been passed down from one generation of women to the next for at least a thousand years, if her grandmother was to be believed.

Hobo confirmed Tina's statement. He wolfed down the soup and chicken as if he hadn't eaten in a week, which was true to some extent, and then he begged for more. When he realized no more would be immediately forthcoming he ambled off to find his next napping place.

While Hobo whiled away the hours healing, and chasing rabbits and squirrels in his dreams, Rory spent much of that time at the computer in the study. She'd decided that the best way to thank Zeke would be to renew her efforts to find out who'd killed him and thereby give his restless soul some peace.

Unfortunately, in spite of her best efforts, she kept coming up empty. The train ticket was the only evidence that tied the killer to this house and that day in 1878, so she didn't have a lot to go on. As nice as the people at the Tucson and Phoenix historical societies were, they couldn't offer her much help. Yes, Ezekiel Drummond had been a federal marshal. And yes, his last case involved a fugitive by the name of John Trask who was wanted for raping and murdering five young girls. Rory was welcome to come down there and read through all the material they had from that time period to see if she could find out anything more. And no, they were sorry, but most of that material was not available online. With each website Rory visited, it became increasingly apparent that she'd have to make a trip to Arizona. In the meantime, an IOU of her intentions would be the best she could do by way of thanking Zeke.

She pushed back from the computer, plucked the dog-napping file off the desk and went downstairs. She found Hobo asleep on the living room floor, basking in the sunlight that was shining through the large front window. She sat down on the couch to review her notes, with the hope of spotting a new connection or lead she'd somehow overlooked before. Within five minutes her eyelids were drooping and she gave in to the luxury of a nap. It had been a rough few days for her too.

She awoke to find Zeke, or at least a washed-out, barely intact version of him, perched on the arm of the couch watching her and Hobo sleep.

"Hi," she said, sitting up. "How are you?" It struck her that as common and overused as that question was she'd never asked it of Zeke before. Death had made it seem pointless. Yet it had become increasingly obvious to her that her understanding of the discarnate state needed some rethinking.

"I've got a ways to go," he said so softly that she had to strain to hear him. "But I had to make sure you were all right." His mouth lifted in the barest of smiles. "I see the mutt made it."

"Thanks to you. If you hadn't helped . . ." Her voice tightened with emotion, making it hard for her to continue.

Zeke shrugged off the praise, but she could tell by his expression that he appreciated it. "How did the delivery go?" he asked. "Did we get the bad guys?"

Rory would have preferred to give him good news, but she couldn't change the facts. The sting had failed miserably. She explained her theory as to why and tried to put the best spin on it she could. At least they knew Dog's World was behind the thefts. It was just going to take a little longer to catch them. She was sure they'd be able to come up with a new plan.

Zeke didn't seem as disheartened as she'd feared, but

then it was difficult to tell, since he was fading more by the minute. "I'll think on it," he murmured.

The phone rang, startling them both and waking Hobo, who looked up and spotted the marshal less than three feet away. Rory braced herself for one of his lapdog impersonations. But Hobo stayed where he was, languidly wagging his tail. Then he put his head down and went back to sleep as if everything were perfectly normal. Rory glanced at the marshal and thought she saw her surprise mirrored in his face.

The phone rang twice more before Rory finally grabbed it off the base. After a brief conversation, she set it down again and turned to Zeke, who was on the verge of disappearing into the ether.

"That was a woman by the name of Julia Davenport." She raised her voice in the hope that he might still hear her. "She says she has information about the dognappings. Her friend Marti Sugarman told her to call me."

# Chapter 29

Rory didn't know if she was more surprised that Marti Sugarman had a friend or that she'd referred that friend to her. Of course Rory wasn't the one who'd done Marti wrong, but people had an unfortunate tendency to focus their anger on the messenger of bad tidings, and Rory had laid a dandy set on her doorstep.

With Zeke out of action for the immediate future, and Hobo still sleeping through his convalescence, Rory went out to her office alone to meet with Julia Davenport. Julia arrived at exactly three p.m., having come straight from the elementary school where she taught. She was thirty-something and pretty, with full, rosy cheeks and a tiny, upturned nose. In polite society of a different era, she would have been described as Rubenesque.

"How did you and Marti become acquainted?" Rory asked once they were both settled, she at her desk and Julia on the couch.

"Through my dog Lola," Julia said. She rummaged

around in her purse and withdrew a photo that she passed to Rory. "She's a Cavalier King Charles spaniel," she said proudly. The photo showed Julia holding a little black and white dog with long fur and tan markings over her huge eyes. "We met Marti and Falcon at obedience class."

Rory couldn't help thinking that was one class Falcon must have flunked, but she kept the thought to herself. "She's adorable," Rory said, handing back the photo.

"But Lola isn't why I called you," Julia said. "I just bought another King Charles, a male, so she wouldn't be lonely when I'm at work. Louis was delivered two weeks ago. He's the reason I'm here." She spoke slowly, in a pleasant singsong rhythm, as if she were still speaking to a roomful of second graders.

Rory took a pad of paper and a pen from the desk and asked Julia to please continue.

"Well, yesterday when I was brushing Louis, he whimpered and tried to pull away from me. I thought maybe he'd hurt himself, you know, running through the bushes in the backyard. So I looked through his fur to see if there was a cut or a scratch. What I found was a small cut that was almost completely healed. Only it didn't look like something a dog would get from a branch. It was too straight and healing too neatly, like a tiny surgical incision."

Rory could imagine her adding, what do you think of that, boys and girls? "Where did you buy your dogs?" she asked.

"Lola came from a breeder, but I got Louis from It's a Dog's World. Have you heard of them?"

Rory nodded, but didn't elaborate, having found over time that the less she said the more she was likely to learn during an interview. "Were they recommended to you?" she asked, hoping there was a trail she could follow back to the source.

"No, I just came across their ad in the newspaper. When I called they quoted me a price that was five hundred dollars less than what the breeders were asking." Imagine that, class.

So much for a trail. "Did you contact Dog's World when you found the wound?"

"Right away. But they said they had no idea what it could be. They insisted the dog was checked out carefully before he was delivered to me." Julia slumped against the back cushions of the couch as if her day in the classroom had finally caught up with her.

"Then you told Marti about it?" Rory asked, to prime the pump again.

"Yes. She's my only real 'dog person' friend."

Rory smiled. There was a time when she wouldn't have understood that comment, but now that she had Hobo in her life no explanation was necessary. With friends who weren't "dog people" there was a limit to how much you could go on about your pooch before they drifted off to sleep and eventually out of your life.

"I'm sure Marti was sympathetic," she said.

"Absolutely. She came right over to look at Louis. When she saw that the incision was in the scruff of his neck, she told me that's where ID microchips are usually implanted. The chips get injected under the skin, but to remove them you have to make an incision. Marti knows everything when it comes to dogs."

Rory was beginning to understand the appeal of Marti's friendship as dog mentor and confidant to the younger woman.

"That's when she told me that you're investigating the dognappings," Julia went on. "She said I should definitely tell you about this, because it might help you solve the case." Wouldn't that be wonderful, children?

Rory thanked Julia for coming forward and sent Marti a silent apology for all the unkind thoughts she'd harbored about her.

"Does it sound as suspicious to you as it does to Marti and me?" Julia asked.

"It definitely bears looking into." Rory set down the pad and pen and opened the bottom drawer of her desk. "I want to show you something." She withdrew the sketch of the man who'd delivered the second threatening letter and held it out to her. "Do you recognize him?"

"Yes, of course. That's the young man who delivered Louis. How do you know him?"

Rory put the sketch down. "I don't. I got his description from a witness who saw him making another delivery." Apparently he was an all-purpose deliveryman. She wondered how much he earned for aiding and abetting and whether he delivered poison as well as dogs and letters.

"Then Dog's World really *is* behind the dognappings?" Julia asked, stunned that she might actually be the victim of a crime. "Wait . . . wait a minute," she said before Rory could reply. "Does that mean my Louis belongs to someone else?" Tears welled up in her eyes as it hit her that she might have to give him back.

Rory plucked a tissue from a box she kept on her desk for just such occasions, a habit she'd developed when she worked for the police department. Investigating criminal activity often led to tears for a variety of reasons. She handed Julia the tissue. "How old is Louis?"

Julia took the tissue, but didn't use it to blot the tears that were threatening to overflow the banks of her eyes. "Ten weeks now. He was eight weeks when I got him."

"Then you probably don't have much to worry about. The thieves seem to steal the really young puppies from pet stores and breeders. It may just be a matter of working out payment if you want to keep him."

Julia sniffled and produced a hopeful little smile that further inflated her cheeks. "Excuse me for getting so emotional, but I already love my little Louis so much. And

Lola would be devastated if we lost him. She acts like his mother, you know, teaching him things and scolding him if he does something bad." Thinking about the dogs increased the voltage of her smile. "Is there anything I can do to help you?"

An idea was taking shape in Rory's mind. Dog's World had already completed a successful transaction with Julia and wouldn't have any reason to suspect trouble delivering another dog to her address.

"The problem we're up against now is that although we suspect Dog's World is involved, we still don't have the names of the people behind the organization. I've been trying to figure out a way to follow this deliveryman back to his bosses . . ." She let her words trail off, hoping Julia would pick up the ball.

"What if I ordered another dog from them? I could tell them how much I adore Louis and that I want another Cavalier as soon as possible so they can grow up together. The day they deliver the puppy, you could stake out my place, and then follow the deliveryman when he leaves." Julia had not only scooped up the ball, she'd dribbled it down the court and slam-dunked it.

"Do you think you'd be comfortable doing that?" Rory asked.

"I don't see why not. I'd like to help catch these thieves before they can cause any more grief."

Rory was still considering it from every angle. She didn't want to put Julia in any danger. On the positive side, she wasn't dealing with Helene. She adored her aunt, but it was no secret that her enthusiasm could get the better of her, and she could easily ad-lib any situation into a crisis. Julia was a novice in this arena, less sure of herself and more inclined to stick to the script she was given. And in spite of her tendency to speak like Mother Goose at story time, Rory could tell she had a quick intellect as well as a willing nature.

"The risk to you would be minimal," she said finally, "as long as you promise to abide by my rules."

"I'll do exactly what you tell me to, I swear," Julia said, placing her hand over her heart to emphasize her intent. "Oh dear"—her brow furrowed—"there is one problem. I'm short on money right now, what with paying for Louis and all. And Dog's World only takes cash on delivery."

"Don't worry," Rory assured her, "I'll provide the money." She wasn't exactly rolling in it herself, but she could take it out of her savings account or get a cash advance on a credit card. She couldn't expect Julia to front it, especially when she might already be out whatever she'd paid for Louis. If this second sting attempt worked, Rory could get her money back after the deliveryman and his bosses were arrested. Of course, if it was needed as evidence, she might not see it again until she was ready to retire.

She and Julia spent the next half hour fine-tuning the plan. They decided Julia should wait at least a week before she called Dog's World to place the order. Intellectually Rory knew that allowing more time to pass would make the request seem less suspicious, but a week was all her patience could endure. She impressed upon Julia the need to play it from the heart when she made the call. If she didn't sound convincing, they'd get suspicious.

Julia suggested it might help if she sounded a little unbalanced, like one of the people you read about who have a dozen animals in a two-room apartment. Dog's World would never be able to pass up potential future sales like that. Rory pointed out that it would be a fine line to walk. If Julia sounded too crazy they might just balk. So the women worked out a basic script for the conversation. By the time Julia left, Rory was confident they had a workable plan.

She crossed the backyard to the house, grateful that Zeke wouldn't be there to voice any objections. But when she entered the empty kitchen, her heart sank a little. She had good news that she wanted to share with someone.

She found Hobo asleep on the living room couch and sat down beside him. He hitched up an eyelid in response to her arrival, then fell back to sleep while she told him all about her meeting with Julia Davenport and how they were finally going to catch the bad guys.

# Chapter 30

Hobo was once again acting like the dog Rory had come to know and love. He chewed on his favorite stuffed duck with all of his normal enthusiasm and begged for a bite of everything Rory put in her mouth. After spitting out the piece of green olive she'd offered him from her lunch, he gave her a puzzled look that clearly said, "Why would you eat something so awful when you could have meat?"

Rory laughed and scratched his head, grateful for the company and the comic relief. It would be a few more days before Julia contacted Dog's World, and since Zeke hadn't yet returned from what Rory thought of as ghost rehab, life in the McCain household was quiet and serene and thoroughly boring. But all that changed in the time it took for the phone to ring.

She glanced at the caller ID screen before she answered it. The readout said "unknown caller." No big deal. She knew a lot of people with blocked or unlisted numbers. But when she said "hello," the voice on the other end was strange and high-pitched, as if the speaker had taken a hit of helium before placing the call. Rory's first thought was that someone she knew was having a little fun at her expense, but she quickly realized she was wrong. The helium was intended to further hide the caller's identity.

"You got lucky with the dog, McCain, but you're a slow learner. Keep your nose out of our business or . . ." The caller paused. The effect of the helium had started to wear off and Rory could discern a man's voice breaking through. When he came back, his voice was once again fully masked. "When it's your turn, trust me, you won't be so lucky." The line went dead before she had a chance to keep him talking long enough to blow his cover.

She set the phone down, her insides quaking with a little healthy fear and a whole lot of lethal anger. Giving Rory a command amounted to issuing a challenge. To her credit, she actually spent a minute or two storming through the house debating the pros and cons of calling Leah. On one hand, she was sure if someone wanted to kill her, they would have already made the attempt—and without the heads-up courtesy call. On the other hand, Leah would surely have pointed out that whoever was making the threats had already followed through on the one involving Hobo. True, Rory would have countered, but whoever was stealing dogs away from their loving homes already thought of them as nothing more than possessions, and expendable ones at that, whereas the legal consequences of homicide upped the ante exponentially. In the moot court of Rory's mind, the verdict had been reached. She didn't need to involve the police.

There was still one thing bothering her about the call, though. How did the dognappers know that she hadn't given up the investigation? She hadn't actively pursued the case since Hobo's brush with death. Only two possibilities occurred to her. Either they considered her call about the failed puppy delivery proof that she was still on their trail or Julia Davenport was working for them.

In the end, Rory decided to trust that Julia was on her team. She needed the teacher's help to lead her to the thieves or the investigation was dead in the water. Besides, if she'd so seriously misjudged Julia's character and intentions, maybe she ought to be in a different line of work. Of course, moving ahead with the plan didn't have to mean putting on blinders. She'd be on full alert for any sign of treason.

A second blocked call came that evening while Rory was trying to get interested in an old movie. Had "helium man" forgotten a crucial part of his threat the first time? She muted the TV before answering the phone. She didn't want to miss anything that was said.

"Rory McCain?" a man on the other end asked. No helium. And the voice was familiar.

"Yes?" she said, trying to place it.

"Hi, this is Dr. Holbrook. How are you doing?"

"I'm fine, thanks." Why was Holbrook calling her?

"Hobo's doing well?"

"He's great." It couldn't be about an outstanding bill; she'd paid in full when she took Hobo home. "What can I do for you?"

"Well, I've been calling all of our dog owners to explain our tattooing and microchipping procedures and to offer them a discount if they'd like to protect their pets in one of these ways."

"I appreciate the offer," Rory said, "but you told me I didn't have to worry about Hobo being stolen since he's a mutt."

"That's certainly true," Holbrook said quickly. "But if he were to get out of the yard or run out the front door when you answer the bell, a tattoo or a microchip would be useful in finding him."

"Only if the person who finds him wants to return him," Rory pointed out.

Holbrook gave a halfhearted laughed. "Yes, of course. But some protection is better than none."

Rory never responded well to the hard sell, and the vet was definitely headed in that direction. "Again, I appreciate the call," she said, "but Hobo's never shown any inclination to leave me. In fact, after the traumas he's suffered he's practically glued to my side."

To his credit, Holbrook knew it was time to save his professional dignity and say good-bye, which he did after wishing Hobo continued good health.

What he didn't know was that in the course of their five-minute conversation Rory had eliminated him as a suspect. The list of people, dogs and phone numbers that she'd seen the first time she'd taken Hobo to his office was apparently just a list of pet owners he was calling to promote the benefits of tattoos and microchips, the "T" or "M" noted beside each name. Those procedures were undoubtedly the source of his extra income. He wasn't up to anything illegal or nefarious in spite of his accountant's certainty that he was the dognapping kingpin. In fact, his effort to hide the list was probably an attempt to keep his clients' personal information away from prying eyes.

Two nights later Rory was awakened by Hobo, who was barking so ferociously that the bed shook like a rowboat in a squall. She sat up, adrenaline pumping, as the dog leaped off the bed and raced out of the room. She heard his nails tapping and skidding across the hardwood floors as he made his way down the stairs and toward the living room, roaring his displeasure all the way.

Rory tried to collect her thoughts, which wasn't easy

with her heart hammering away in her chest. She took a couple of slow, deep breaths and found that she could think a bit more clearly. The first thing that occurred to her was that the alarm should be wailing if someone had broken in, but it wasn't. Had she remembered to set it before going up to bed? She wasn't sure. It certainly wouldn't be the first time she'd forgotten since she'd been living there. No point in worrying about it now.

She grabbed the .45 from her nightstand where she'd been keeping it since Hobo was poisoned and followed him out of the room. Although he was all about announcing himself in the most menacing of terms, Rory preferred to leave possible intruders in the dark, literally and figuratively, as to her own presence until she'd had a chance to assess the situation.

The night-light outside the bathroom was a tiny beacon in the darkness. She moved quickly along the upper hallway to the stairs, confident that if intruders had been waiting in the shadows there, Hobo would have already found them. When she reached the bottom step she realized that she didn't hear him barking anymore. Had he stopped on his own or had someone stopped him? There hadn't been any noise of a scuffle, and if there'd been a gunshot she would have heard it. Even a silent knife would surely have caused the dog to howl in pain. Rory's mind recoiled at the mere thought of such a sound. Hobo had been through enough. She wasn't going to let anything else happen to him. Propelled more by fear for him than by concern for her own safety, she left the relative security of the stairs and followed the route he'd taken.

The living room was dressed in black as if in mourning for the day, the furniture and empty spaces indistinguishable from one another. No light of any sort breached the windows.

The street lamp must still be out. She'd meant to call town hall about it. She moved on, her back against the wall and her gun at the ready, trying to remember if she'd left a laundry basket or a pair of shoes in the middle of the floor where they could trip her. Too bad she hadn't thought to keep a flashlight beside the gun.

How much would she give right now to have Zeke call out to her from his chair by the window? She'd even forgive him his arrogant smile. Although she might not want to admit as much to him, a ghost was far better than a gun when it came to confrontations. Intruders might be willing to take their chances in a gunfight, but most of them would rather flee than take on a ghost. There was simply no way to win a fight against someone who was already dead.

As Rory approached the kitchen, she heard a familiar sound that lifted her heart with hope. She held her breath and listened closely to be sure she wasn't hallucinating or indulging in wishful thinking. No, there was no doubt about it. That was the unmistakable sound of Hobo snuffling, the sound he made when he was trying to pick up the scent of a squirrel who'd given him the slip or when he was foraging for crumbs he might have missed at dinner. A wave of relief washed through her, instantly turning her legs to jelly. She leaned against the wall for support until they felt solid enough to hold her weight again.

She reached for the light switch but stopped herself in time. If someone was outside, illuminating the kitchen would make her an easy target. Instead she made her way to the refrigerator by memory and touch, which included banging her shin against the garbage pail. When she reached the refrigerator, she quickly tugged the door open and crouched behind it. No shots rang out. No window glass shattered. It was probably safe to assume there wasn't anyone out there, at least anyone with a gun. The small bulb in the refrigerator cast enough light for her to see that Hobo was indeed fine. He was pacing back and forth at the kitchen door, which was still fully intact as well as locked.

When Rory flipped on the kitchen light, Hobo turned

toward her and gave one plaintive bark. Rory reset the safety on her gun before going over to him.

"I know you want to go after whoever or whatever is out there," she said to him, "but I can't risk you getting hurt again. It's not like you're a cat who still has eight lives," she added with a weak little laugh.

Hobo didn't seem to appreciate the humor in it. He turned away with a snort of indignation that as much as said, "This is ridiculous; you're not letting me do my job!"

"Sorry to pull rank on you, buddy. But as soon as it's light out you can come along and help me scout the perimeter." While Leah would have been pleased to know that she had enough sense not to go prowling around in the dark, it was patently clear that Hobo didn't share that sentiment. With a whimper of frustration, he sank to the floor. If he wasn't allowed outside to police the area, he seemed determined to remain on guard duty.

The clock over the sink said it was four a.m. Sleep was out of the question, and it was still a few hours until dawn. Rory put up water for tea, gave Hobo one of his doggie treats that claimed to taste like peanut butter, and the two of them settled in to wait.

# Chapter 31

When the sun came up, Rory was dressed in sweatpants and a heavy sweater. She had the .45 in her hand and an evidence bag in her pocket. Since Hobo hadn't so much as growled in the past few hours, she didn't really think she needed the gun. Whoever or whatever had spooked him was no doubt long gone. Still, the weight of the weapon in her hand felt wonderfully reassuring.

While waiting for daybreak, she'd had plenty of time to review the night's events from a somewhat calmer perspective. It was entirely possible that what Hobo had heard was just a raccoon on the roof looking for a room to let. With the car being their only predator on the island, the raccoon population was booming. Most of the people Rory knew had had one or more encounters with the animals, who often tore up roofing tiles and dug their way into attics and crawl spaces. The great American dream of owning a home seemed to extend to the four-legged species as well. And although Rory had no desire to go through the hassle and expense of hiring a trapper to remove one of these squatters, a raccoon was definitely preferably to a hit man.

As soon as the first rays of daylight sifted through the windows, Hobo's alert status ratcheted up several notches. The moment Rory headed toward the kitchen door, he jumped up, clearly determined to be the first one outside. She unlocked the door, but it wouldn't open more than a few inches with Hobo standing there doing his impression of a doorstop. She tried to push him out of the way, but he refused to give any ground. She tried ordering him to move and bribing him with a treat. No success. She even tried tugging him out of the way. The bottom line was that she had maybe ten or fifteen pounds on him, but he had a lower center of gravity and four sturdy paws that seemed rooted to the floor. They were at an impasse.

She was debating whether she could beat him to the front door, when he resolved the dilemma for her. By shifting his position, he was able to squeeze his snout into the opening between the door and the frame and widen it by another couple of inches. Then, using his body like a wedge, he wriggled in far enough to push the door open the rest of the way. With a triumphant bark, he glanced over his withers to see if Rory had witnessed his accomplishment.

She gave him a "way to go, what a good boy" cheer, thinking he must have sacrificed an entire layer of skin in the effort. She leaned over him to hold the storm door open so that he could be the first one out. It seemed like the least she could do under the circumstances.

With the last obstacle out of the way, Rory fully expected him to go barreling through the doorway, but he took two steps outside and started snuffling the immediate area around the door. Her pulse quickened; she'd never heard of a raccoon trying to gain entrance through a door. That was a much more human thing to do.

Hobo had moved away, nose to the ground as he followed the scent to the side of the house where the gate led into the backyard. He spent a few minutes investigating that area before he returned to the kitchen door. From there he widened his search until he'd scoured the entire yard.

Trusting Hobo's nose and instincts, Rory started looking for evidence of a would-be intruder around the door as well. It hadn't rained in several days, so the ground was hard and dry, not likely to hold footprints. She still took the time to examine the soil between each of the bushes that bordered the door and ran along the length of the house. Nothing. When she reached the gutter at the left corner of the house, she found the earth around it still damp. Since the purpose of leaders and gutters was to funnel and drain water away from the house, the ground around the gutters was always the last to dry out. And it was there that Rory finally found a set of tracks, animal tracks big enough to have been made by a raccoon or an opossum. The discovery seemed like a small victory for a moment, before logic came knocking. Animal tracks were nearly as ubiquitous as trees on Long Island's north shore. And if there weren't any human footprints, it only meant a trespasser hadn't crossed through the small area around the gutter. Rory also found it worth noting that Hobo had snuffled his way past the animal tracks without lingering or showing the least interest in them. Had his nose already told him the prowler wasn't an animal?

When they'd finished investigating the backyard, they went into the house, where Rory grabbed Hobo's leash and hooked it to his collar, after which they proceeded to check out the unfenced property in the front.

Hobo pulled her straight to the living room window, where he conducted a careful inspection of the flower beds beneath it, before sinking to the ground with a grunt of frustration. Rory's search wasn't any more successful. She found some broken branches on one of the azaleas there, but the frame around the window was intact. There was no chipped paint or other evidence that someone had tried to pry the window open from the outside. She finally gave up with no more information than when she'd started. Only Hobo knew what he'd heard or smelled during the night, and he wasn't talking. One thing was certain though: Rory wouldn't forget to set the alarm anytime soon.

Later that afternoon, while Rory and Hobo were wedged together napping on the living room couch, Julia called to report that she'd spoken to Debbie at Dog's World and ordered the second puppy.

"She didn't sound at all suspicious about the request?" Rory asked as she struggled to extricate her arm from under Hobo's head so she could sit up.

"Not at all. In fact, we had a nice little chat about the two dogs she has."

Listening to her, Rory couldn't help but smile. Julia was really perfect for the role she was playing. With her gentle singsong voice, who would imagine that she'd be involved in a nasty piece of police business? Sometimes the fates were kind. The fates and Marti Sugarman in this case. Rory would have to thank her for sending Julia her way, assuming everything went smoothly with sting number two.

"Did Debbie give you any idea when they might have the puppy for you?" she asked.

"No. I did try to press her on it, though." Julia gave a self-conscious twitter of a laugh. "I fibbed and said my birthday is in two days and that I'd love to have the puppy by then. Of course I don't normally condone lying," she added quickly, "but I thought in this case it might be forgiven?"

Rory didn't know why Julia was casting her in the role of confessor, but she did her best to assure the teacher that such a little white lie should certainly be forgiven, especially since it was done in the pursuit of justice and for the public good. Where had those words come from? Maybe she'd missed a calling in the ministry. Zeke would certainly have enjoyed overhearing that strange bit of conversation. Rory was surprised to catch herself thinking about him and, what's more, wondering when he'd be back. You'd better be careful what you wish for, McCain, she warned herself.

Regardless of where her comforting words had come from, they'd apparently struck just the right chord with Julia, since her tone had brightened perceptibly. "This is really quite exciting for me, you know. The high point of my day is usually a cup of tea and the newspaper when I get home from work. So, what's next?"

Rory reminded her that there wasn't anything to do until Dog's World called to set up the puppy's delivery. A sudden sense of déjà vu prompted Rory to run through Julia's role with her again to be sure there were no misunderstandings. She stressed that her involvement would be minimal—she was to open the door, accept the puppy, pay the deliveryman, thank him, close the door and stay put until she heard from Rory, no matter how long it took. Absolutely no ad-libbing permitted. The last thing Rory needed was another Helene in the making.

# Chapter 32

Three days later Julia received the call from Dog's World to set up delivery of her new puppy. Although Rory had made it clear that she could arrange it around her work schedule, Julia had insisted on doing it as soon as possible. She had plenty of sick days accumulated, and she didn't mind in the least using one of them for such a worthwhile cause. With that in mind, she arranged to take delivery the next morning. Rory was secretly thrilled. The sooner they proceeded, the less chance Dog's World could get nervous and once again pull the plug.

On the morning of the delivery, Rory didn't take any chances. She arrived at Julia's two hours early. The teacher lived in a tidy gray and white town house complete with a little front porch just south of Main Street in Huntington. Although the people at Dog's World had no reason to be wary of this particular transaction, they might have instituted safeguards across the board since they'd recently come so close to being duped by Rory. Sending a scout to check out each home and its environs before a delivery made good business sense if you were in the business of deception.

And Rory didn't want to be setting up her stakeout when someone might already be watching for such activity.

She'd borrowed her mother's beige sedan for the day, since she'd sold her Honda, and Mac's snappy red convertible, was too likely to attract attention. For her plan to work she needed a nondescript car in which to follow the delivery guy back to his boss.

Julia had asked her neighbors across the street if Rory could park in their driveway for a couple of hours. Since the couple were empty nesters and left for work before Rory planned to arrive, they'd been happy to oblige.

Rory backed into their driveway and parked with the car facing Julia's house. From this vantage point she could view the entire block. When she'd done a dry run earlier in the week, she'd been pleased to discover that the street was a cul-de-sac, which meant that the traffic was minimal and consisted mainly of residents' cars and the occasional delivery truck.

She spent a few minutes observing the activity on the block. A man dressed in a suit and carrying a briefcase exited one of the town houses, got into the car parked in the driveway and drove away. A woman in a bathrobe came out of another house to claim the newspaper lying on her walk. Only two cars were parked at the curb; both appeared to be empty. There was no sign of anyone who didn't belong there.

Rory had left herself time to check on her protégé and to give her the photo of the stolen Cavalier, once again compliments of Leah. Rory was acutely aware that this might well be her last shot at catching the dognappers. If anything went wrong they would surely curtail their operation or completely abandon it. While that might put an end to the dognappings, it didn't bring the perpetrators to justice.

And Rory wanted justice, not only for the people who'd suffered the loss of a pet, but for the animals themselves, especially Hobo, who'd come so close to dying at their hands. Julia opened the door before Rory had a chance to ring the bell. The teacher was beaming with excitement, her cheeks even rosier than Rory remembered them. As Rory was ushered inside, she heard the muted barking and whining of the two dogs in residence.

"Lola and Louis, I presume," she said with a smile.

"Yes, well, I decided it would be best to keep them in the bedroom, out of the way, what with a new puppy arriving and doors being opened. They're little, but they're fast."

"They don't sound happy about their incarceration."

"They're complaining because they're not accustomed to being cooped up. I'm afraid I spoil them terribly," she added with a shrug that as much as said she wasn't going to be changing her ways anytime soon. "Speaking of spoiled pooches," she went on enthusiastically, "have you heard about Marti's windfall?"

Rory shook her head. She had no idea what the teacher meant.

"Well," Julia said, grinning like a little kid with a secret to tell, "a family over in Greenlawn had Tootsie all this time. They say she didn't have a collar or ID tag when they found her, and they claim they never saw any of the flyers Marti stuck up all over town. I don't see how that's even possible," she interrupted herself to editorialize, "but once the flyers were brought to their attention, they called Marti, who told them to contact the police."

Rory was happy to hear that Tootsie was okay, but a bit surprised that Marti had done the right thing. She would have figured Marti to take the path of least resistance and simply keep the dog she'd coveted. Could she really have misjudged the woman so badly?

"Contacting the police was Marti's idea?" Rory couldn't help asking.

"I suggested it would be the right thing to do," Julia admitted, "but I'm sure Marti would have come to that conclusion herself."

I wouldn't bet the house on it, Rory thought, but she kept the thought to herself. If Julia chose to be naïve about her new pal, it wasn't Rory's job to educate her.

"Anyway," Julia went on, "since Brenda was gone, and her sister didn't want the dog, the police told Marti she could keep her."

"Marti must be ecstatic." Rory was actually glad for the woman who'd so recently learned that her husband was not only a liar and an adulterer, but also a murderer. Quite a guy she'd married.

"Oh, she is," Julia said, "ecstatic and then some. Now, may I offer you some coffee or tea before zero hour?"

Rory couldn't help thinking that "milk and cookies" would have sounded more natural coming out of Julia's mouth. She politely declined, adding that she kept liquids to a minimum when she wouldn't have access to a bathroom. She'd learned that uncomfortable lesson during her first stakeout.

Julia's brow furrowed as she considered this bit of information. "That never occurred to me. With my bladder, I wouldn't be at all suited to undercover work." She laughed her birdlike laugh. Rory joined in. One less applicant for the clandestine services.

She gave Julia the photo and told her to keep it out of sight until the deliveryman left. Once he was gone, Julia was to compare the new puppy to the photo and call Rory immediately. If the photo of the stolen puppy didn't match the puppy Julia was given, it would be pointless for Rory to continue following the van.

Rory spent a few minutes doing some role-playing with Julia, until she was satisfied that they'd left no room for error. She felt like NASA's mission control doing a final

systems check. Everything was A-OK. They were as ready
for launch as they would ever be.

She suggested Julia read or watch TV to pass the time.
With any luck that would keep her excitement from reaching critical mass and endangering both the project and her
safety. Then Rory made sure that Julia had her cell phone
number, availed herself of the bathroom facilities and
headed back to the car to wait.

She'd borrowed a curly blond wig from Helene in case the
deliveryman had been shown a photo of her. She would try
to stay out of sight, but that wasn't entirely within her control. She planned to slouch down in the driver's seat and take
a peek only when she heard a vehicle turn down the block.
If the deliveryman got suspicious and decided to check out
her car, she'd say she was waiting for her friend to get home
and hope that the wig threw him off. Although she intended
to stay at least two cars back when she was following him, if
the intervening cars suddenly changed lanes, the wig might
again be the factor that saved the day. She'd addressed whatever contingencies she could imagine, but she found herself
wishing that the marshal had been around to give her plan a
stamp of approval or to point out something she might have
missed. She'd grown accustomed to hearing another perspective, even if it was one she rarely agreed with.

"Come on, McCain, stop second-guessing yourself,"
she said as she pulled on the wig. She flipped open the
little mirror on the sun visor to see if she had it on straight.
The wig was on fine, but one thing was certain: blond was
definitely not her color. She scooted down in her seat and
prepared herself for a long wait.

A total of six cars came down the street in the next hour
and a half, along with a water delivery truck. Rory
was feeling nostalgic for the cars her parents had when she

was little, the kind with the bench-type seat in the front. Her back ached from the need to keep a low profile, and, no matter how she maneuvered, one part of her body or another was being jabbed by the gearshift in the center console. The cold added to her discomfort. Though she'd dressed in layers, the temperature was in the forties and it had worked its way into her bones. Heat was only a button away, but that would mean turning on the engine, and she couldn't take the risk, especially this close to the delivery time.

Two minutes before the appointed hour Rory heard another vehicle turn down the street. She counted to ten before risking a look. An unmarked white van had pulled into Julia's driveway. Rory instantly recognized the young man who stepped out of the van. The sketch she'd drawn from Zeke's description was amazingly accurate. Either he was assigned to the Huntington area or he was the only deliveryman Dog's World employed. She took note of the van's license number before she ducked down again. If she lost him en route back to his boss, at least she'd be able to track down the owner of the vehicle.

Unable to watch what was happening, she had to depend on what she could hear. She listened for the high-pitched yapping of a puppy or the sound of voices at Julia's door. Nothing. She hadn't even heard the van's door close. She wanted desperately to take another look, but managed to hold herself back. Then she heard Julia calling out a bit shrilly.

"Hello-o-o. Dog's World man, over here, over here." She'd probably been glued to the window like she was when Rory arrived. So much for reading or television.

"Just a minute, ma'am," the deliveryman called back to her. "I'll be right there."

Rory's heart double-timed it into her throat. There was only one reason Julia would be yelling those words—he was headed away from her, toward the car where Rory waited. He'd obviously been instructed to check out the area before any transaction went down. She had to hope that Julia managed to distract him enough that he forgot his initial concern about her car. She withdrew the .45 from the holster at her hip. She'd never been a Girl Scout, but she was a big fan of their motto.

"Hey, I don't have all day," Julia shouted with a healthy dose of attitude. "I have to get to work, you know."

Rory was surprised to hear this unexpected alter ego of Julia's take charge. Gone was the lilting teacher's voice. This Julia could do an award-winning stint in *Taming of the Shrew*.

"This'll only take a minute, ma'am."

Judging from the volume of his voice, Rory knew he was still coming her way.

"It's now or never, buddy," Julia replied. "I'm already late."

If the man replied, Rory didn't hear him. He might have been trying to decide whether it was more important to obey his orders or to please a repeat customer. Or her least favorite option—he might be slowly sneaking up on her car. Seconds ticked by as she waited for him to appear at her window.

"If you don't get over here right now, you can just take the dog back with you."

"I'm coming," Rory finally heard him say in disgust. "I'm coming." To her relief his voice was fainter than it had been. He'd recrossed the street and was on his way back to Julia.

Five minutes later Rory heard Julia's door slam shut, followed quickly by the sound of the van starting. Then she heard it back out of the driveway.

She risked a quick look to see which way the van turned when it reached the nearby cross street. Once it was out of sight, she started her engine and tucked the gun back in its holster. She was turning the corner when her cell phone rang. Julia was as certain as she could be that the puppy was the stolen one from the photo. Rory thanked her and promised to let her know how the sting played out. Now came the tricky part—pursuing the van without being detected.

# Chapter 33

Rory lost him twice. The first time because he was taking residential backstreets that twisted and turned with virtually no camouflaging traffic in which she could hide. She had to stay so far back that when she came out of one particularly sharp turn he was nowhere in sight. She passed several cross streets where he could have turned left or right instead of going straight. She had to make a decision and she had to make it fast. She didn't think he'd noticed her yet and, assuming he was still headed south, it would have made no sense for him to turn off the road they were on.

She was frustrated and disgusted. She'd been so careful. How could she come this close to cracking the case just to lose sight of him now? She was still debating whether to turn around and try one of the cross streets she'd passed, or just go home and take up drinking, when she spotted him a few blocks ahead of her stopped at a red light. Never before had she been quite so pleased to see a red light.

She was almost as happy to see that there was now a large SUV between them. She tucked her car in close behind it so she'd be less noticeable in the van's rearview mirror. She was back in business.

The second time she lost him when she took a calculated risk. She was following him south on Route 110 when he started changing lanes for no apparent reason. Left to right, right to left and back again, doing a slalom run around the other cars that earned him a chorus of angry horns. There was only one reason why someone who'd been driving sanely for the past twenty minutes would suddenly turn into Evel Knievel. He wanted to see if he was being tailed.

Rory stayed where she was in the left lane. On a two-lane road with moderate traffic it would be too obvious if she followed his every move. But she had to be careful not to let him out of her sight. There were too many places where he could turn off, either at office buildings, diners, hotels and strip malls or onto any number of side streets. She knew that when he made his move, he'd make it without warning. She just didn't expect him to make it from the left lane.

The traffic was moving along at a fifty-mile-an-hour clip when he cut off a pickup truck and exited onto the next side street. As it happened, there was room behind the pickup if Rory wanted to change lanes to follow the van off. She decided against it. That would have confirmed any suspicions he had about being tailed, and she would have blown her chance of finding out who was behind the dognappings, possibly forever.

Instead, she turned into the next strip mall she came to, drove through the parking lot to a side exit and started backtracking through the local streets, hoping her luck would hold long enough for her to find him again. If the place he was going to had a garage, their little game of cat and mouse was over. She'd be out the money with nothing to show for it.

She drove around for ten minutes that felt more like ten hours. She wasn't even sure if she was in Farmingdale or Amityville. It was a run-down commercial area with cement buildings and warehouses built on the cheap, the only architectural details limited to a few windows and a door. Every street she passed without a white van was a sucker punch to her gut. But she refused to give up. If she'd given up earlier, she wouldn't have caught up with him at that red light. She kept the pep talk going to drown out the negative thoughts that were trying to stage a mutiny.

When Rory found the white van, she could hardly believe it was the right one. It was parked out in the open for all the world to see, near the front door of one of the smaller buildings on the block. Apparently she'd convinced the deliveryman that he wasn't being followed. There were two other cars parked beside the van. She suspected one of them belonged to the boss of the operation, who was waiting for his money. The other could belong to the delivery guy or to Debbie. Further speculation would have to wait until later. Time was of the essence if she wanted to catch them by surprise. If anyone chose to leave before she made her move, she'd be the one at a disadvantage.

She backed her car into a slot beside the others so she wouldn't have to waste time turning around if she had to leave in a hurry. Then she picked up her cell phone and dialed Leah's extension at police headquarters. When Leah picked up, Rory told her briefly where she was and what was about to go down. In response to Leah's alarmed questions, Rory promised to call back later. She knew Leah would immediately contact the local precinct with a heads-up. They in turn would dispatch patrol cars to the scene. They should arrive just in time to take the thieves into custody. If she'd called the precinct herself, they would have ordered her to leave the area immediately and let them handle the arrest. That was simply unacceptable.

She rested her hand on the grip of her .45 and left the car. As she approached the building she could hear the muted barking of several dogs. The noise was welcome; it would help mask any sounds she made entering the building. Unfortunately it would also mask the sounds of her adversaries should they turn the tables on her.

The front door had probably once been glass, but was presently a metal frame with wooden boards where the glass had been, so there was no way for Rory to see what awaited her inside. She'd assumed she'd have to pick the lock, but when she tried the door, she was amazed to find it open. Someone was definitely feeling bulletproof today. She wasn't going to need her handy-dandy lock pick after all. With a deep, steadying breath and her right hand resting on the hilt of the .45, she slipped inside.

She found herself in a small reception area that was partially walled off from the rest of the building. The only furnishings were an old metal desk and a chair with its stuffing oozing out of a seam like custard from a doughnut. This first-class setup was most likely Debbie's domain. She didn't appear to be on the job that day.

Two male voices were coming from somewhere beyond the partition, but their words were garbled by the howling of their contraband. Rory waited a full minute to see if she could pick out any other voices. No, two seemed to be the full complement. All right, two to one weren't terrible odds when the element of surprise was factored in. These men had left the door unlocked, so they clearly had no idea they were about to be busted. No reason to have weapons in their hands.

As Rory stepped around the partition into the cavernous open space that made up the rest of the warehouse, she saw a half dozen dog crates arrayed against the back wall. Three of them were occupied. The two men had their backs to her. The deliveryman was looking on, while the other man knelt by an empty crate where he was working on the latch with a screwdriver. There was something about the man with the screwdriver, about the way he held himself, that immediately rang a bell in Rory's mind. But before she could put a name to him, the deliveryman looked up and saw her. He gave a little grunt of surprise that caused the other man to glance over his shoulder. In the dull glow of the single overhead light, Eddie Mays looked positively ghoulish.

"You haven't done much with the place," Rory said casually, her hand still resting on the hilt of the gun.

Eddie stood up. "What are you doing here? What do you want?"

"Well, to begin with I want to put an end to this dognapping ring of yours, and then I want to see you tried, convicted and sent to prison on felony charges, along with anyone else who's involved in this little enterprise."

"That's quite a wish list you've got," Eddie said pleasantly. "And you seem to be mistaking me for Santa Claus."

"Hey, hold on . . . dognapping ring? What are you talking about?" The deliveryman's voice was shaky, and he was backing away from Eddie as if to literally distance himself from whatever trouble the older man represented. "Oh my God, that's why you told me to be careful I wasn't being followed. You said you were worried about the dognappers finding this place, but you're the ones stealing the dogs!" He turned to Rory. "I thought this business was legit. I took it to make some extra cash. I didn't know the dogs were stolen. I've never been in trouble. Never even had a speeding ticket. I swear. I go to college over at Suffolk. My name's Keith Beal. Look, I can prove—"

"Stop your yapping," Eddie snapped at him. "You're worse than the dogs." He turned back to Rory, his mouth curved up in a malevolent smile. "How much? How much will it take to send you on your way? Come on, name your price. It'll just be between us three."

"Actually I prefer to leave it between you and the police," Rory replied. "But please feel free to make them the same offer." She watched Eddie's magnified eyes cloud over behind his thick lenses.

"Or maybe we should save them the trouble and take care of things before they get here," he said, moving toward her, the screwdriver tight in his fist.

"Stop right where you are and drop the screwdriver; otherwise I'm going to assume you're threatening me and I'll be forced to shoot you in self-defense."

Eddie paused briefly as if he were calculating his odds in such a skirmish. When he started toward her again, he was holding the screwdriver at shoulder height, poised to attack.

When he was six feet away, Rory drew her gun, cupped it in both hands and once again ordered him to stop.

"I don't think you got it in you," Eddie snickered, still coming at her. "What do you think of that?"

Rory knew if she let him get any closer, he'd have a good chance of lunging for the gun and wrestling it away from her. She aimed for his leg and squeezed off a round, slowly and evenly the way she'd been trained. The bullet missed its mark, but not by much, slamming into one of the cement walls and ricocheting off into another. The shot had the desired effect. Eddie stopped in his tracks.

She pulled a set of plastic cuffs out of the pocket where she'd stowed them early that morning and tossed them toward Keith. "If you want to impress me by cooperating, get those on him."

"Absolutely," Keith said, scrambling to retrieve the cuffs. "I'm cooperating. I'm definitely cooperating. You don't know my folks, but they're gonna kill me. They're gonna f—"

"Listen to you," Eddie snarled, venting his rage on Keith. "You sound like my grandmother."

"Both of you be quiet and stay put or you're going to wind up in a lot of pain," Rory reminded them, pleased by how steady and calm she sounded.

Eddie stood there glowering at her, while Keith fumbled with the cuffs until he managed to get them on him. Even the dogs were quiet. Rory figured she had another five minutes, maybe even less, before the cavalry arrived. No problem. But in the next moment she was startled by another voice, one that was so close to her that it made her jump. "Behind you," the voice whispered in her ear. Then more urgently, "Rory, behind you."

She swung around in time to see Joe Kovack coming at her, brandishing one of the large wrenches he used in his work. She trained her gun on him, backing away laterally so she could keep all the men in view. As soon as Rory's eyes met Joe's, she saw the fight go out of him. It was as if a fissure deep in his core had finally given way under too much pressure. His shoulders slumped and the wrench fell out of his hand, clattering to the cement floor.

"Coward," Eddie growled at him. "You had her. You were close enough to knock her out. You're a loser, Kovack. You've been a loser all along. I don't know why in hell I listened to you. 'Just let her think you're breaking into the house,' you said. 'That'll be enough to scare her,' you said. Well, look at her, Kovack. I nearly killed her damn dog too, yet here she is. She doesn't scare so easy, does she?"

"Oh, well, your way was much better, Mays," Joe said, his face flushing as anger rose in him, propping him up again. "If it was up to you, you would have killed her and hoped no one figured it out. You're a shark. All muscle, no brain."

Rory listened to the dialogue snap back and forth between the two men as if she were witnessing some bizarre piece of theater. It was clear that they'd never liked one another, and stress had caused that animosity to fester into something lethal. They didn't even seem to care that she was still standing there able to hear everything they said.

"Better a shark than a coward," Eddie sneered in disgust. "You didn't belong in this operation from the get-go."

"You know what? You're right. I don't know how I let Larry talk me—"

"Shut your damn trap," Eddie spit out, cutting him off.

"Why?" Joe's laugh was contemptuous. "You think your buddy Larry's going to protect us? They've got him on assault and murder. This here is penny-ante stuff in comparison. He'll roll on us the second he thinks it'll help his situation. You really thought you could keep this operation going without Larry to call the shots? Wake up, it's over. It's all over."

Rory's head was reeling. How could Joe be involved in this? Good, hardworking Joe who'd loved Tina since high school—had he really helped steal two of the dogs she doted on? Rory could barely stretch her mind around the idea. On the other hand, learning that Larry was the brains of the operation required no effort at all. She already knew he was a killer, a liar and a cheat. She wondered if anyone else was going to pop out of the woodwork before this day was over.

The dogs had started their howling again; seconds later Rory heard the wail of sirens approaching. As the police poured into the building, she recognized Detective Cirello, the sour old cop she'd met the day Brenda was killed. Since he appeared to be the ranking officer there, she went over to reintroduce herself and brief him on what had happened. She wasn't surprised to find that he hadn't mellowed any since their last encounter. She handed him her .45 and told him they'd find the missing bullet in the wall on the right.

Rory knew she'd have to follow him back to the precinct

to file a report, but she asked for his patience while she took care of one last matter. Assuming he'd deny the request, she turned away before he had a chance to respond and made her way to the back wall. She hunkered down in front of the three crates that held the dogs. They were barking and whining, confused by the sudden whirl of activity. She placed her hands against the bars so they could sniff her and know she was a friend.

"Hey, guys," she said to them in the bright but gentle tone Hobo seemed to love. "Everything's going to be fine. I promise. As soon as I can arrange it, you'll all be going home."

# Chapter 34

Hobo caught the ball, a high pop-up near the back fence, and did a triumphant trot around the yard before depositing it at Rory's feet. He plopped down beside it, panting heavily, his tongue lolling out of his mouth. Zeke levitated the ball and sent it arcing into the air again. The dog turned to watch it soar, but made no move to go after it. He looked back at Zeke and Rory with an expression that clearly said, "If you want that ball, you're going to have to get it yourselves. I'm done."

"I guess playtime is officially over," Rory said, laughing. They'd been outside for twenty minutes, and Zeke was still intact and functioning well, a new record for him. He'd likened the progress in his newfound ability to developing a muscle that had never been exercised before. He seemed mighty pleased about it too.

Rory still had mixed feelings about his progress, but since there was no way to force the genie back into the bottle, she knew she'd have to adapt to it. On the other hand, she wasn't at all ambivalent about the improving relationship between Zeke and Hobo, who were living together in something approaching harmony. She'd watched Zeke's distaste for the dog soften into acceptance and even subtle gratitude after he helped save Rory's life. For his part, Hobo seemed to have overcome some of his instinctive fear of the marshal since the poisoning incident. Rory could only assume that the dog had been aware enough to know that Zeke was instrumental in saving him.

The three of them trooped back into the warmth of the kitchen, Zeke eschewing the more direct path through the walls in favor of the mortal route. Rory worried that he was practicing the ways of the living with the intention of passing among them now that he could journey beyond the house. She didn't question him about it, though, since she wasn't ready to hear his response.

She shed her coat and gloves, her scarf and hat, draping them over the hooks she'd installed for that purpose in the laundry room. Hobo gave his coat a vigorous shake before ducking under the table, where he lay down with a sigh of pleasure. Having neither clothing to remove nor fur to shake, Zeke had immediately folded himself into his chair at the table, where he waited, noiselessly tapping his foot, while the mortals in the family settled in.

"How was that bunch you went to with Leah?" he asked, having clearly reached the end of his patience.

Rory filled the teakettle with water and set it on the stove to heat. She could hardly blame him for initiating the conversation. In fact, she'd expected him to start pumping her with questions the moment she'd returned.

"I think you mean 'brunch.'" She managed to keep a sober face, since laughing at his expense never ended well.

"Whatever you call it," he said with a dismissive wave of his hand. "Speakin' for myself, I can't see the benefit of combinin' two meals into one. I remember enjoyin' food enough to have three squares a day whenever the possibility presented itself."

Rory took a packet of cocoa mix from the pantry and poured the contents into a mug while she waited for him to circle back to the point.

"Brunch." His upper lip curled as if the word left a bad taste in his mouth. "It even sounds unnatural. No matter. I'm not interested in what you ate or where you ate it. I just want to hear the latest information from your detective friend."

The telephone rang before Rory could begin his briefing. Her "hello" was met with a rush of words that were nearly incomprehensible. Tina was in fine form.

"I'm so glad you're there—I had to stop by on our way home so you could see the fruits of your labor in person—come outside—come outside—I can't wait for you to meet George and Gracie!"

Rory set the phone down and told Zeke she'd be back in a minute, at which point he folded his arms, adopting a much-put-upon expression. "One minute, I swear." She headed for the front door without her coat, leaving it as collateral for the promise.

Tina's car was in the driveway with the window open and a little white, furry head on either side of hers like animated earmuffs. She introduced the pair to Rory, her voice choked with emotion. The return of the dogs was clearly helping to mitigate the shock and devastation she'd suffered over her husband's arrest for stealing them.

"You have no idea how much it means to have my babies back again."

Rory realized there was a time when that would have been true, but now that she had Hobo in her life, she understood completely. "It's wonderful how most of the people who were caught up in the scam were willing to return the stolen dogs without a court fight or some other nastiness," she said, scratching around the ears of the two Maltese.

"Dog people." Tina smiled. "It's just a pity they were out all that money. I felt so bad for the family that had George and Gracie that I gave them their money back out of my own—hey, I didn't realize you had company—I didn't mean to interrupt anything—I was just so excited and grateful. . . ."

"Company?" Rory repeated, taken by surprise.

"Well, if it's not company, then a thief broke into your house during the two minutes we've been talking." Tina laughed. "I could swear I saw someone at your living room window." She was looking past Rory at the house as if trying to confirm the sighting.

"Oh, you probably saw my aunt," Rory said, recovering quickly. "She drops by whenever she's in the neighborhood. I don't think of her as company."

"Well, I'll let you get back to your aunt—I've got to get these guys home anyway—thanks sooo much for your help. Backseat," she instructed the dogs, who withdrew from the window and hopped into the rear of the car by way of the center console.

When Rory returned to the kitchen, Zeke was in his chair looking as innocent as a schoolboy accused of shooting spitballs behind the teacher's back. But since the kettle she'd put up was whistling hysterically, she took a moment to pour the water into her mug and grab a spoon, before turning to him.

"Tina saw you," she said evenly. She was determined not to make too much of it, since they'd been doing so well together. With her hot cocoa in hand she sat down at the table. "You're going to have to be more careful."

"I was curious," Zeke replied without apology.

"The next time your curiosity gets the better of you, there's always the invisibility option."

"Fair enough," he allowed. "From what I could see, Tina seems to be copin' just fine."

"She's having her ups and downs. One day she's ready to divorce Joe and the next she's talking about marriage counseling down the road. Of course a lot depends on how his trial goes and what kind of time he might be facing. Anyway, she's coming to understand that she helped push him over the edge—a lesson that shouldn't be ignored," she added wryly.

"Speakin' of which, how much longer are you gonna make me wait for that update you've been promisin'?" Zeke asked, turning her insinuation to his advantage.

"I'm sorry—you have been patient." She took a quick sip of her cocoa. "Okay—according to the ME's report there was no physical evidence to support Larry's claim that he killed Brenda in self-defense—especially since the only prints on the knife were his. It's Leah's theory that Brenda wore rubber gloves when she washed the knife and left it on the drain board to dry. When Larry grabbed it, he assumed her prints would be on it too and that they would provide enough reasonable doubt to acquit him."

"I imagine that was one unhappy fella when Leah told him the only prints were his," Zeke said with a smile.

"Wait, there's more. When Larry realized he was being charged with murder as well as with a long list of other charges from the dognappings, he knew he wasn't going to walk away a free man anytime soon. Leah said that was when the floodgates burst open. Once Larry started talking, not even his lawyer could get him to shut up. He gave them a blow by blow of every one of his exploits, bragging as if they were accomplishments. He seemed particularly pleased to tell Leah that he'd had half a dozen mistresses during the course of his marriage."

"If he was as generous with them as Brenda claims he was with her, it's not hard to see how money would eventually become an issue. There's just so much you can hide from a spouse."

"Well, he did say the dognapping ring was his idea. No big surprise there. He may be a sociopath, but he's light-years ahead of the other two in the brains department."

"How did he know them anyway?"

"At the dog shows Marti was always dragging him to. Joe was there whenever Tina was showing one of her dogs, and Eddie haunted—oops, sorry—went to the shows to drum up business."

"Between the three of them they've gotta know where hundreds of dogs live."

"Exactly," Rory said. The cocoa had cooled enough for her to drink a couple of mouthfuls. "Joe serviced oil burners all over western Suffolk County. Eddie had a fairly extensive list of customers too. The men added to their files by canvassing dog parks in their spare time. And when they needed puppies, they stole them from pet stores or breeders, who made it easy for them by advertising their inventory."

Zeke shook his head. "So what was Joe's story?"

Rory shrugged. "It's complicated. Leah says he broke down sobbing as soon as they started questioning him. From what they could piece together, he'd been feeling like a kept man, if you know what that means."

Zeke nodded. "I get the drift."

"Tina managed all their finances, and since the bulk of the money came from her trust fund, Joe didn't think he had the right to argue about it. So whenever he needed or wanted anything, he had to ask her for the money. He was very clear about how generous Tina always was with him, but the arrangement seems to have whittled away at his self-respect over the years. He'd started to resent her for it. So when Dog's World got a buyer for a couple of Maltese, Larry suggested they take two of Tina's dogs. When Leah asked Joe why he agreed to it, he just shook his head. She thinks maybe it gave him back a sense of control. But later, when he saw how much Tina was suffering over the loss, he told Larry he wanted out. Larry threatened to spill it all to Tina if he left. So Joe was stuck. Leah said she almost felt bad for the guy."

"I'm willin' to bet that Eddie didn't do any sobbin' or confessin'," Zeke said.

"You're right—Eddie's definitely not the crying type. But he's also not as smart as he thinks he is. When he and Joe were arguing at the warehouse, he slipped and admitted to nearly killing Hobo."

"If you'd like, I can pay Eddie a little visit and scare him out of whatever wits he possesses," Zeke offered, the prospect making his eyes twinkle with mischief.

Rory was sorely tempted by the offer, but she knew it was bound to make her life more difficult. "We can't risk another episode of 'Wyatt Earp Returns,'" she said. "Especially since my name is linked with this case too."

"Folks'll just think you have yourself a secret weapon."

"You're only a 'secret' weapon if you remain a secret," Rory pointed out. She kept her tone light, but she could feel them sliding headlong toward the brink of the autonomy debate.

The divide between them on the issue was so deep that she wasn't sure they'd find a way to span it. She figured Zeke had come to the same conclusion, which was why he'd recently invested in good behavior.

"I'm not a child," he said bluntly, "and I don't need your permission to leave the house." And there it was, front and center.

"So that's the reason you've been trying to stay on my good side since you returned from your rehab or whatever it was?" Rory asked point-blank. "You thought you'd cajole me into your way of thinking?"

"I did spend some time mullin' over the situation while I was away."

"Is that why you've been working on your relationship with Hobo too?" She wanted the truth, even if it disappointed her.

"I take strong exception to that, Aurora," Zeke said, his face tightening like a fist. "I've developed a genuine affection for the mutt. And I'll have you know that I don't pretend to feelings I don't have, for animals or for people."

Rory was more relieved to hear him say that than she would have expected to be. "In that case I owe you an apology."

"Well, I suppose you do. But that ain't all that needs settlin' between us. I don't understand why you're so damned opposed to my leavin' my confinement here."

"I know you think you can pass for the living, but it won't work," Rory said, trying to sound as understanding and reasonable as she could. "You may have mastered the ability to appear intact, but there are a hundred ways reality can trip you up. What if someone sees you suddenly appear out of the ether—or disappear, for that matter? What if someone bumps into you and sends all your molecules flying? What if—"

"What if someone claims they've seen a UFO? The world doesn't end. No one locks them up and throws away the key."

"But if sightings of you always occur when I'm around— in no time at all I'll be the Medium and the Ghost Whisperer all rolled into one, the target of every photographer, journalist and anyone else who wants to see a ghost for himself. I'm a private investigator, Zeke. It would be pretty hard for me to conduct investigations with an entourage like that following me around." All right, that was a little heavy on the hyperbole, but she needed the marshal to consider the wider ramifications of following his bliss.

Zeke winked out of his chair and reappeared a second later near the sink, so overwrought that he'd apparently forgotten he'd been practicing to act like the living. "So why in tarnation have you been helpin' me practice? Was it just to shut me up while you kept hopin' I'd never get the hang of it?"

"That's not fair," Rory said, the accusation ruffling her feathers although there was more than a grain of truth to it.

"If you had your way, I'd stay cooped up in this house, except for the occasional sortie to rescue you." His expression was growing blacker by the moment.

"Don't go there," Rory warned him. "It may have been helpful to know that Joe was coming up behind me with that wrench, but I would have heard him myself in a matter of seconds. And we both know it was unlikely he would have used it on me anyway. So you've never actually rescued me. More to the point," she went on before he could rebut her claim, "you're not meant to be in this world anymore." That was cruel even if it was the truth, and she realized it just as the words left her mouth.

"You know damn well I'm not movin' on till I know who shot me," he snapped so sharply that he woke Hobo, who jumped up, banging his head on the underside of the table. He whimpered and nestled his head in Rory's lap for soothing.

"I've done my best to find the answer for you," she replied, stroking the dog's head, "but I've run through all my options here. If there's information to be found, it'll have to wait until I can look for it in Arizona."

Zeke's expression softened; the darkness lifted from his eyes. "You're plannin' to do that for me?"

"Yes, I'm just not sure exactly when," she said tersely. She'd been waiting for a good time to tell him about her plan. She'd wanted him to know it was a thank-you for helping to save Hobo. But the words had spilled out of her in the wrong way, at the wrong time, and she was annoyed with herself and with Zeke for causing that to happen.

If Zeke was put off by the testiness in her voice, he didn't show it. "That puts things in somewhat of a different light," he said after a moment's consideration. "Perhaps we shouldn't be talkin' in such absolute terms. I suppose we could take things a day at a time; let circumstances help us decide what's appropriate. I see no reason why two intelligent people can't come to some kind of accommodation that suits them both."

Rory was glad to hear him back down before she had to put her last chip into play. She didn't want to sell Mac's house, but the threat of it was her only leverage in their relationship. She knew one day she might have to follow through on it. But at least it wasn't today.

"When did you become such a philosopher?" she asked.

"You don't know the half of me, darlin'," he said, with the saddest smile Rory had ever seen.

Hobo lifted his head from the comfort of her lap. He padded over to where Zeke was standing, looked up at the marshal and whimpered as if in sympathy. Zeke shook his head and gave a little laugh. Then, with Hobo close behind, he walked back to his place at the table.

The three of them sat quietly for a while; it was Zeke who finally broke the silence. "Truth be told, Aurora, I'd miss you mightily if you left this place. Hell," he added with a wink, "I'd even miss the mutt."

Feeling charitable, Rory gave him a pass on calling her Aurora. "Speaking for myself and 'the mutt,' we'd miss you too," she said, knowing it was true. What she didn't know, however, was whether she and the rest of the world would ever be ready for a fully autonomous, traveling Zeke show.

THE NEWEST CHAPTER IN THE
*NEW YORK TIMES* BESTSELLING
BOOKTOWN MYSTERIES FROM

# LORNA BARRETT

# CHAPTER & HEARSE

Mystery bookstore owner Tricia Miles has been spending more time solving whodunits than reading them. Now a nearby gas explosion has injured Tricia's sister's boyfriend, Bob Kelly, the head of the Chamber of Commerce, and killed the owner of the town's history bookstore. Tricia's never been a fan of Bob, but when she reads that he's being tight-lipped about the "accident," it's time to take action.

M770T0910

# TOMB WITH A VIEW

**Cemeteries come alive for amateur sleuth
and reluctant medium Pepper Martin.**

Cleveland's Garden View Cemetery is hosting a James
A. Garfield commemoration. For Pepper Martin, this
means that she'll surely be hearing from the dead president
himself. And when she's assigned to help plan the
event with know-it-all volunteer and Garfield fanatic
Marjorie Klinker, she'll wish Marjorie were dead . . .
too bad someone beats Pepper to it.

DON'T MISS THE FIRST NOVEL IN
THE BOOKS BY THE BAY MYSTERIES FROM

# ELLERY ADAMS

# A Killer Plot

In the small coastal town of Oyster Bay, North Caro-
lina, you'll find plenty of characters, ne'er-do-wells,
and even a few celebs trying to duck the paparazzi.
But when murder joins this curious community,
writer Olivia Limoges and the Bayside Book Writ-
ers are determined to get the story before they meet
their own surprise ending.

penguin.com